To Denny

Best to you,

Rob Rahe

JESUS' MENTOR

ELIJAH
THE STORY OF TWO LIVES JOINED

A Historical Science Fiction Novel
By Robert Rasch

authorHOUSE®

AuthorHouse™
1663 Liberty Drive
Bloomington, IN 47403
www.authorhouse.com
Phone: 1 (800) 839-8640

© 2017 Robert Rasch. All rights reserved.
Special Thanks to Martin Davey for the cover image (UFO spaceship).
www.martindaveyillustration.co.uk

No part of this book may be reproduced, stored in a retrieval system, or transmitted by any means without the written permission of the author.

Published by AuthorHouse 02/28/2017

ISBN: 978-1-5246-7279-9 (sc)
ISBN: 978-1-5246-7278-2 (e)

Print information available on the last page.

Any people depicted in stock imagery provided by Thinkstock are models, and such images are being used for illustrative purposes only.
Certain stock imagery © Thinkstock.

This book is printed on acid-free paper.

Because of the dynamic nature of the Internet, any web addresses or links contained in this book may have changed since publication and may no longer be valid. The views expressed in this work are solely those of the author and do not necessarily reflect the views of the publisher, and the publisher hereby disclaims any responsibility for them.

Foreword

ELIJAH: HISTORICAL BACKGROUND
- The mentor of Jesus and the architect of the New Testament.
- Born: February 12, 2015 in the Hercules Dome, under the Polar Plateau, Antarctica.
- Miracle wonder worker during 852 BC to 860 BC.
- Known for his summer storms, hail, rain, thunder and dew.
- Fought to get rid of idolatry.
- He was taken in a whirlwind in a lighted fire vehicle into the heavens.
- Was the first profit to raise someone from the dead.
- He, who descends from the heavens, ascends back to the heavens.
- Author of the "Book of Elijah."

This story is based on information declassified from both the National Advisory Committee for Aeronautics *(NACA)* and the Vatican Archives. NACA was a U.S. federal agency founded on March 3, 1915, to undertake, promote and institutionalize aeronautical research. On October 1, 1958, the agency was dissolved and its assets and personnel were transferred to the newly created National Aeronautics and Space Administration *(NASA)*. The Vatican Archives cannot confirm the Book of Elijah, but does confirm that some of his works are in their possession.

This author's story is time released for the benefit and preparation of the human race so that they may gain an understanding to a broader view of their historic ancient ancestors and of the custodians, which till this day oversee this sector and galaxy in space.

****

There are certain people in life that rise beyond the norm at a perplexing and astonishing rate. There are some lives that are like no others. There is one life in particular that has had a resounding effect on others. A young boy, Elijah, will grow and mature to become a great motivator, thinker, inventor; all through innovation. By believing in his very own *probability theory* and with great discipline, he will pave a pathway that becomes paramount and will inspire him to strive for further knowledge. He will take action with a purpose and he will change the fabric of man's destiny to one that we embrace to this very day.

Religious factions would be greatly impacted by Elijah, and his teachings would resonate throughout the ages. His father was his mentor and instilled in him the virtues of humility and selflessness in such a poised cultured and systematic way, which can only be described as divinely inspired. Aligious, Elijah's father was "the architect of the Old Testament". Unknowingly, Elijah would become the creator of the New Testament. Elijah's life eventually reveals the secret prospective and in-betweens of Jesus' full existence; birth and through to His "Second Coming."

Elijah

"To live in harmony is to be truly living."

"Understanding relations is synonymous with distance."

"Worrying is just a poor way of praying."

"A gift is not a gift unless it is received."

A special thanks to my family and friends for sharing their research, as well as their advice.

The quotes and theories from this book have been taken from many different sources and are not intended to offend or sway any personal beliefs that are core to the reader.

Chapter One

CHILDHOOD

On a typically bright and temperate day in the city of Adelaide, a youth named Elijah was waiting for his father to pick him up from school. He casually strolled from the Atrium Erudition School to an area between the pyramid structures in anticipation of his father's arrival.

While waiting, he studied the precise angles of the pyramids' architecture and the uniquely chiseled stonework located near the flowing waters of the fountain. He wondered who could have created this place and why was it built that way?

All types of people hurried past him in all directions, as if they were being herded like sheep. The people appeared to Elijah as if all their movements were being controlled by the placement of the structures. He understood his father's reason for meeting in that place.

In his eyes, his father was great in so many ways. Aligious *(Eligious)* was in charge of overseeing the Earth's occupants and it was very well noted that he was respected amongst the people.

As he looked ahead, he sees his father is waiting for him. Eye contact is made and excitement consumes Elijah. He quickens his stride as he approaches his father with great admiration. He shakes his father's hand in the classic Mazone style, as it is the customary father to son handshake.

Aligious tells him that he has a very important meeting he must attend with the Elders in the Aitho Circle Towers. Initially Elijah is disappointed and hesitant to go. He then realizes the importance of this meeting to his father and agrees to join Aligious. Elijah understands that he has to sacrifice the planned sport and game time with his father.

Childhood

Aligious has a commanding presence, tall and broad with locks of silvery long hair. He shows great confidence but in a non-intimidating way. Elijah realized that he should not question his father about the meeting, especially because Aligious wants to use a Meta Mechin Gate machine, which is unusual for him because Elijah knows his father loves to travel places the conventional way, on foot.

Unable to control his curiosity any longer, Elijah asked his father why the conference was so important. Aligious sighed and looked up at the machine, not responding to Elijah's question. Aligious speaks aloud commands while staring into the machine. He dictates the coordinates of their destination into the location receptor. Aligious then looks down at Elijah and says, "One moment son, first let us go through." A loud sound emerges as if water is being crystallized. The noise continues to grow louder and louder and then suddenly it softens to a tolerable low hum. Seconds later, they have arrived at the Aitho Circle Towers and they exit the Meta Mechin Gate machine.

They approach the lobby of Aitho Circle Towers and Aligious turns to Elijah and says, "We will stay here in the lobby area while I wait for the eleven Elders to arrive. When they arrive I will have to go to the Conference Hall and you will have stay in this room because minors are not permitted entry into the Conference Hall." Elijah understood and responded with a question, "Father, I am curious as to why the Elders seem so united at times, but appear to be so different when talking about their own interests?" Aligious replied, "Well let me begin by confirming what you have heard are probably pieces of broken information that have you curious. The Council and I are responsible for influencing what happens on the Earth, mainly on the surface." He continues, "Son, it may seem confusing to you now, however, when you turn twenty one years of age you will be able to receive the *Synoptic Learn Ids* and then you will have an amazing amount of data and knowledge at your disposal. For now, certain information is restricted within the circle of youths." Aligious laughs heartily and winks at Elijah, "But, I will tell you an abbreviated version about the Elders and where they originated from while we are waiting." Elijah hears this and his eyes brighten with great interest as he swoops closer to his father. He fixes his silk garment and grabs the excess part of his leather braided belt in order to control it from flapping around while he is in motion. Aligious explains the complicated history as simply as possible. This is the conversation that will one day inspire Elijah to spawn creative ideas that will have a major influence in Earth's development.

Aligious begins to express, "We all create actions that move us forward, and in these actions we develop as individual existing entities and by using the positive essentials of love and understanding, we ignite our spirit. By experiencing many orbital cycles in towards the future, the species with their creative thoughts spur growth to a universal goal; that we all will eventually become one with the energy that we call life." Elijah listens further.

"A vast representation of this, is how far the Arcturians have come to be the most advanced and eloquent civilization in our galaxy. I have had a hard time grasping an understanding as to why some of the representatives of the Factions do not emulate the Arcturians, for their incredible abilities to transpose dimensionally with emotional spiritual energy, is quite the "raison d'être" *(reason for being)*. They are able to observe the pathways of death and observe the manifestation of birth. You see, they are of high frequency vibrational and translucent entities, which ingest energy from light, motion and create high levels of emotional accomplishments. Being grateful and thankful, for they the Arcturians have gifted and guided our collective galactic staff to agreements of peace and continuity amongst the Union of Worlds. In addition, they also protect the Earth by preventing any one Faction from dominating the geographic regions of the globe, thereby establishing a healthy balance."

Elijah is still and listens attentively, while placing his hand under his chin for support. Aligious moves closer and explains, "The places of origin amongst the factions lead us to an already understanding, that our native planets, size, location and atmospheric conditions determine the foundation of development. For entities that eventually become high structural intelligent beings, their pinnacle journey cannot mount without eons of evolution. Nonetheless, forward improvements to build upon and develop. This gives rise to a pathway that is predestined for almost all intellectual entities/species. This historical observation has produced proof that races of different worlds will be productive in a spiritual way, fulfilling a harmonious result in the order to move forward." Aligious takes a breath, then looks at Elijah with a serious stare and says in a steady tone, "Till one day, reaching and avoiding ones' demise and existing in an infinite timeless spherical energy, re-circulating paradise and becoming one, where from the frequency of which we all come."

A glowing Elijah immediately asks, "Can this frequency be seen?" Aligious looks away and is thinking of his upcoming meeting that is about to start, but then stares at the Meta Mechin and says to Elijah, while reaching out his hand and lifting Elijah forward, "Come with me son." Aligious walks toward the Meta and finally approaches the machines control panel, utters a code that lights up a triangulated spin of energy from the inside part of the machine. He does this in order to buy some time, thus to have a quick discussion with Elijah.

Aligious programs the machine hours earlier, so that he may attend the meeting on time. Aligious explains about the workings of the Meta Mechin, "Son, the longer we stay in *(this positioning)* once engaged, the further we will be back in time. Time is a very sensitive procedure and only certain selected individuals are permitted to use this part of the apparatus." "That's great Father, this is magnificent!"

Elijah begins to wonder and becomes concerned about his father's meeting. "Follow me Eli as I will take you to the Athenaeum. It is a wondrous building that will intrigue you architecturally, but also houses some of the best recorded historic visuals that will better explain the needful part to our conversation." Elijah with a big smile on his face races to Aligious' side and realizes his father will still be able to go to his important meeting, being a couple hours behind the appointment schedule.

Feeling his father's love for him, he realizes his father's sacrifice of the moment, to share in his curiosity.

Aligious begins to explain, "I have selected these time coordinates, because there is nobody attending the Athenaeum during this portion of the day. As they enter the Athenaeum, there are high trilateral pyramid vaulted ceilings with glass dot particles on the walls. Designed originally from overlapped specks of single crystal molecules and arranged in an odd geometric pattern, up-to the point where all four walls join together at the apex, to emulate a holographic studio. Towards the highest point of the pyramid, is the "Vertex Globe," an astrological apparatus simulator that has a translucent appearance. Aligious turns on the Vertex Globe and it immediately starts to produce swirls of plasma gas waves. An energized light suddenly becomes apparent at the apex of the inner peek of the pyramid. The walls are reflective grey, smooth with no seams, creating excitement in Elijah's expression.

Aligious commands the module with his voice and then unexpectedly an entire three dimensional layout of the galaxy appears; stars, planets, satellites, space stations, asteroids and with continuity clusters of orbits and wormholes connected together.

Elijah astonished, open mouth lets out a rising "ah" and with excitement says to his father, "All the solar systems of the sector seem to tie into one another in perfect harmony. How does everything become so organized from chaos?" Aligious explains, "Eli everything created in and of the Universe has an absolute supreme imprint of selected intelligence. For instance, the 3D Vertex simulation has a similar appearance to millions of neurons or arteries of the body or it may also appear like an image of the brain."

Aligious explains further, "The same way you cannot see the circuitry within your body, unless technology is applied, is the same way you're unable to see the vascular weaving of wormholes."

Aligious grunts. "Oh and unfortunately, even with our advanced technology, we can only measure the wormholes by restructuring an exact location. This is done by the detection of magnetic signatures, thus recreated for an approximate visual model." Elijah is intrigued and in awe, walking and spinning through the middle of the holographic galaxy, waving his hand through the mapped star system, having no effect on it, rather enjoying this stunning moving display. Elijah with his head held high, "Oh my, I love this, it is beyond imagination. Are these worm-holes in anyway the invisible connective bio frequencies?" "No and yes" Aligious answers, "Mainly, they are a means of travel between two points of time and location, connecting and linking all that you see here in the galaxy. Similar to the Meta Mechin, it's a doorway, a star-gate if you will, but of a natural one, unlike the Meta Mechin which is a mechanical device. I'll explain." Elijah quickly stops flowing through the holographic display and pays attention to Aligious. "The wormholes are the corridors that take someone or something from point A to B. Look closer, this beginning point over here is Earth and follow my finger through this particular vortex branch over to here, to our home planet. Basically, to start the (wormhole) transport process; let's say, to and from our planet to Earth, a phase transition takes place. Looking at this schematic display, the transition begins with the use of liquid crystal technology. While housed in a mica receptor container, a high intensity heated chemical reaction occurs."

"Over here is a sample of a small opening via entry point at the top of the cylinder, for a focused sharp lighted microwave beam to enter. In a direct delivery system called DDS, three microwave beams are delivered separately to each of the three focused mica containers targeted entrance way. The actual mica containers are in a cylindrical geometric shape, situated in a triangulated trefoil formation, spaced equidistant in their position. In this triangulated trefoil arrangement, the designated target at each of the end points of the triangle and remain at three separate connected points. A solid flora crystal contained at the center of each container is targeted with a microwave signal, thus heating up the liquid crystals surrounding the main solid crystal *(flora)*.

A narrow stream of energy is release, while the receptor outside the cylinder reflects the stream of energy back unto itself. This result clashes energy and an abrupt chemical reaction, causes the electrons to become magnetically disordered, stretching the electrons from the nuclei and thereby creating a metamorphosed plasma vortex field. The wormhole thus becomes open, and as a result, you must immediately enlarge the size of the opening, to encompass the entire ship." Elijah was surprised and gasped in astonishment. Aligious smiles and continues, "A combination of electrical magnetic energy becomes apparent, along with plasma erupting and fusing, creating the ability to immediately increase the size of the vortex around the vessel. This is done by two separate cylinders of lodestones, which are mounted parallel to the floor, facing one another *(with like magnetic poles)* with very little space between." Aligious gestures the measurement with his hands.

Aligious gets excited as he intensifies his assertions, feeling very intense at this climatic point of the conversation, Elijah's eyes widen up. Aligious continues, "While each of the lodestone cylinders are located at the orthocenter of the ship, they're situated on opposite-sides of each other and stand three feet high attached to the floor. The loadstone cylinders are pointed directly into the triangulated apparatus manufacturing waves of plasma, causing the opening of the wormhole to increase enough to envelop the entire ship. Once the controlled plasma enlarges, a diamagnetic reaction occurs, opening a proper rift in the spatial fabric *(lineage)* in space."

"Elijah, I had also said yes to your question as well. Simply, even though they are frequencies in wormholes, it is not the overall function of the anomaly. Frequencies are layered inter-dimensionally in every aspect of everything. There is the invisible connective signal and identifier for each particle within existence and were originally mistaken for "String Theory."

Both smiling, Elijah asks if the wormholes can somehow be seen and Aligious replies, "Not exactly, they are cloaked to us, but the fabrication of the wormholes that you see in front of you, are designed and simulated according to how the flux sensors absorb ions to pick up the wormhole signatures. Then they are reconstructed according to the sensor detector readings, as all wormholes are inter-dimensional and cloaked to our technology."

Aligious then slides his index finger down the bridge of his nose, points at his son then says confidently, "But nevertheless, a puzzle of doorways to intrigue your thoughts." Aligious snarls, then becomes serious and says, "Oh, to all that is dear, I would like to see a discovery that enables the full visual effect of seeing wormholes in its true form, hmm."

Aligious with a funny smug look, talking to himself announces, "Yes, that would be splendid." Elijah entertained by his father, laughs then asks another question, "Father, the Elders you are having the meeting with, are their planets in the vicinity of our world and this one?" Aligious responds, "The same way we travel easily to and from with the Meta Gate, it is also a connective simplicity between their worlds and ours. The 10 remaining Elders are mostly in the vicinity of the Big Dipper and or of Orion's Belt, which by the way, in an allegorical sense, has been hardwired into all human species of the Earth, whereas other constellations are unnoticed." Elijah looks interested, so Aligious carries the conversation further, "Other programs injected within human DNA for study, are the importance of gold, diamonds, oil and other commodities, even though they are in abundance on the Earth. Societies think they're rare, thereby setting the standard for the future, because these materials will be essential for space travel."

Childhood

A look of confusion set upon Elijah's face as he gripped his leather weaved belt. Aligious clarifies, "Adding to this program *(venue)* there are many different levels of other influential guidance agendas, geared towards behavioral operations. Such as, biological frequencies that stream down from the Moon to influence thoughts to certain portions of the Earth's population and imposes certain wills of the Elders *upon* mankind, in order to cultivate the species properly. This measure has been misused by certain Factions who have allowed the same technology used for ideological purposes and unfortunately, entertainment too." Elijah now appears disturbed but Aligious slows his speech and continues, "I can brief you at another time on this subject." Elijah quickly responds, "Sure, but please don't forget."

Elijah having a thought on his mind asks, "Father, where do the Elds giants come from?" Aligious amused with reverence, because he immediately understands that the children are often intrigued by the Elds. Aligious chuckles and responds, "The Elds are from a solar system of Anakin, some of them stand over 200 feet tall and are very helpful and caring in their nature, filled with serenity. On this Earth they no longer want to be involved, because of past discourses with humans. Orion was a famous popular Eld and along with many others, slain because the humans feared their size."

Elijah very concerned remains quiet and his father explains, "After the demise of Orion, the Elds disconnected from the council, even though they had assisted in the building of many ancient structures that are still existing to this very day; monolithic and megalithic structures thousands of years old. The Venetians were elected by the Elds as a delegate assigned to take their place within the Elder's table, sort of a liaison at this current juncture. As you know the Venetians are our neighbor on the eastern part of our homeland and are a well minded culture."

Elijah is confused about certain human behavior, evident by his expression, but then says, "Oh, yes of course", but a lingered thought stirs in his mind on how the humans chased away the Elds.

"Are you ready to head back to the Aitho Circle Building? We can always return here." Elijah responds, "Sure, would it be ok if I can speak into the command modular for our return back through the Meta?" Aligious blurts, "Yes you can, but first allow me to enter the time designation sequence and then get ready to speak away!"

As Elijah and Aligious make their way back to the Aitho building in the appointed time, Elijah then asks his father if he can retrieve and research some historical documents while his father is in the meeting, because he has ideas that are fresh in his mind. Aligious humbly agrees, and encourages Elijah to look at the Earth's historical findings from a macro overall prospective with a deep understanding, because there are many factions involved with many compromises throughout the millenniums.

As the meeting commences there is great need for clarity amongst the Elders. Disorganized static is apparent between the chairs of the council and a resolution at this juncture of the Earth's development should be reached. There is a barrier that is preventing planet Earth's assigned theoretical religious agenda and is falling short. It is heading towards a negative outcome.

Aligious a brilliant spokesman, stands up amidst the almost confrontational atmosphere and ascends to take control of the discussions. Giving order to the dishevelment, he then speaks directly to the Elders by proclaiming facts and expressing empathy towards the current juncture. Aligious states, "The juncture that has long ago peaked has reached a point of obvious counter productiveness." Aligious is standing tall with his right hand fisted along with his thumb up. "We are all clear that the religious undertone and guiding status amidst of all the twelve Factions are starting to become conflicting because of an increase of other types of agendas, to which we are responsible. We have met a climatic point of stifled growth. I ask you, isn't the whole purpose of our collective works, to eventually have a smooth integration of the human species amongst our own? All of us, throughout the millenniums have introduced excellent guidance. We provided rules of morals and foundations for all to excel throughout this planet and oh, let us not forget the science research governing agreements. Because of this and since all of us that are here, must recognize that we have been striving for perfection as per our life's quests and accomplishments." Aligious, gripping his leather belt, consequently delivers with a strong tone, while holding it puts his index finger pointing to the table, "Now! Now is the time to take a new measure, to conduct a plan that graduates this issue and allows for change and introduce a new methodology, so that we can reestablish once again growth, which is our priority."

Childhood

As Aligious lowers his voice almost to a whisper, he bends over while his two hands are laying flat and spread apart on the table, "Ankur, Enlil, Ziusudra, and Prometheus, have all integrated physically among their own seeded human factions. All taught great attributing factors to their human counterparts, thus governing responsibly in the geographical regions they controlled. We should not procrastinate, the time is here. Let us conclude this meeting and say that we all agree with one another. There should be immediate plans to segue the humans into our respective cultures now." Aligious clears his throat, as the council appears uncomfortable. Then he continues, "Understanding that most of us here feel that we are not ready for a complete integration," then lowering his voice to almost a whisper and says, "Then find a true and decisive way to create an overall shared religion that can bring the many to one, with all the factions and cultures of the Earth working together. While united, the people can become a partial or a full believer in what is wholesome and right, this is a win on all accounts. This can expedite our work with efficiency and increase the population for the integration process." Aligious slows his excitement, "Why not share with the humans what has taken us many years through scientific research to understand and pursue this motion responsibly. Our studies of probable futures are unacceptable to us all, correct?" Each of the councils bows their heads with approval as Aligious scans the members' faces while coming to an important point. "The pertinent time period to be selected is of the utmost importance for success," Aligious waits three seconds before continuing to capture their attention further as they appear to be agreeing. Aligious forwards another point, "But please, let us not forget to consider that we all understand that some of our constituents have fell upon the interest of science studies and are scattered away from the prime directive." Aligious glances over in view of the Zetas when making this point. "Earth is not a tryvlio piato *(Petri dish)* for extreme experiments, the integration will eventually happen, just like the documents have recorded with the PUA *(Planetary Union Alliance)*. We hereby, will have to be in unison on our future actions herein and working together as one. We will contemplate this dilemma that has plagued us for too long, for this great undertaking represents our initiatives and ideas. We all have come so far, over 210,000 earth years." Suddenly, Aligious halts his speech, as one of the Zetas/Grays blurts out, "Why have we not implemented the second choice of injecting a supreme religion, in your mention of millennia ago?" Aligious with a witty response says, "That's where we will probably go, the past!" Aligious has a subtle smile after his remark.

As the meeting is adjourned, certain delegates gather together, muddling as the Elders exit the conference hall. After a day passes, the council unanimously decides to go with Aligious' second proposal choice. The new innovative plan of one religion that pulls all the human factions of the earth together and that it should be implemented in an expeditious manner slightly in the past of a selected and specific time period." Aligious receiving this information is tussled in his thoughts, because at the close of the meeting it would be announced, that it will be Aligious' responsibility to carry out the plan.

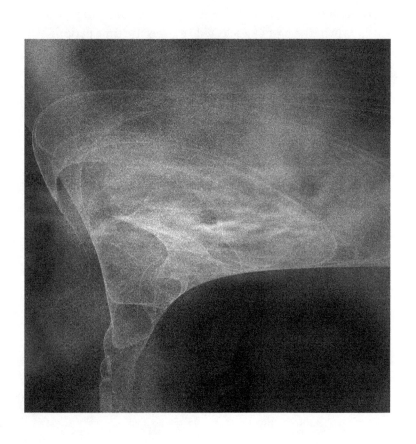

Chapter Two

ZOBZBALL

"Corner days" are recreational parts of a given week and very precious to Elijah. On these days Elijah especially loves to play a sport game called Zobzball with Aligious, and since Elijah's very first game, he has been unable to defeat his father but always up for the challenge. Elijah is now making his father work for the last few victories.

In the beginning of the first of the two corner days, Elijah and Aligious are heading for their game day ritual. Nearing the Olympiad Quadratus Arena, Elijah appreciates a breathtaking garden floral arrangement that is a recent new design. The horticulturist constructed the plants in a line on both sides of the light marbleized granite/andesite pathway. Elijah moves close to one of the colorful exotic flowers and stares hard into the center of the blossom. Then wondering about how tiny the pollen is. He begins to drift and dream about the smaller particles that make up the miniaturized invisible parts of the plant. Elijah is still contemplating, how there has to be different sub levels of natural architecture for a plant like this to exist.

"Ready and set to play Elijah?" Aligious puts his right hand on Elijah's shoulder to get his attention, but before his hand reaches Elijah, Aligious' wide sleeve slightly brushes up against Elijah's arm. Elijah while still in deep thought becomes startles and is distracted away from his fixation of the blossom. Aligious pulls back his hand, moves closer and says to Elijah in a whispered tone, "Appreciation of all makes a great scientist." Elijah replies, "Ready to engage sir." Elijah smitten with intent, smiles as they lead into the arena.

As they enter the Quadratus Arena, Elijah hails the commands into the modular, while both of them walk towards the equipment container to pick up the necessary pieces of attire. Elijah picks out his usual tag number three and a left and right hand racquet glove, which is part of the main equipment used to play the game of Zobzball. The hand racquets are oval oblong pieces of stranded netting equipment that is slightly bigger than a human hand. The racquet is flush mounted above the palm of the hand. The oval design is for low-ball floor shots, while the left hand side or thumb side of the racquet is extended higher above the hand. The opposite view applies to the left hand racquet.

All of a sudden the introduction of a crisp rhythm Zobzball anthem song begins, while simultaneously a holographic blue dot appears in the ceiling center simulating the looks of a Zobzball and then gradually grows larger, until it appears as its final 3D holographic structure of a huge score board. Elijah and Aligious look up and see both their names posted, past stats and anatomy readings of their bodies. The scoreboard has a trapezoid shape to it and bends and adjusts to follow the player whose eyes occasionally glance onto its direction of this massive hanging hologram. Elijah is excited, but delays the start of the game as he is scanning the area, contemplating a new strategy. Aligious backs up crouching like a sea crab and says to Elijah, "Your serve!" Aligious fully understanding that the person who is defeated first always begins as the server. Elijah looking back at his father snickering at his appearance of his set position, commands in a loud voice, "Zobz!" A Zobzball then drops out from the center of the scoreboard onto the service circle. The game begins.

With regard to the overall play rules of the game called Zobzball, Aligious and Elijah play in an unconventional way. There are usually many opponents when playing the game of Zobzball that are geographically at different locations. Just as long as an opponent has a Zobzball arena within their vicinity, they can join the unity and play.

Zobzball for Elijah and Aligious is personable, so they don't desire to play in the midst of others. Elijah is naturally attracted to Zobzball, because the game consists of many tesseracts and geometric shapes, such as pyramid structures, squares and triangles. The Zobz-court also has lots of spherical polygons, all attached to the six sides of this forty by forty foot surrounded inner stadium cube.

Normally in Zobzball, there are multiple players with an average tournament play with a total of seven players. The game begins by the selection of the lowest ranking player becoming the "server" *(player one)*. Thereafter, the other players are placed in an ascending order (assigned numbers) from the server on up to the last player *(player seven)*. *(The server having a slight advantage theoretically)* Player #1, as for this players turn will remain at a constant in an ascending order of play and so on for player #2, #3, ...

The next lowest ranking player will then become player #2, whose turn also keeps at a constant in the order of play. Once the Zobzball is served in the required service restricted boundary area, the full wide area of the court is now open for play, requiring the second player to strike the ball.

Should the ball hit the ground three times, without hitting any structures, objects, ceiling or walls, then the player is issued a point. Eleven points and you are eliminated for that round. When a player is eliminated for a round, he is required to wait in the holding area till the next round, while observing the remaining other players battle it out, in their attempt to resist elimination. A player waiting in the holding box can amuse himself by making comments through the scoreboard distracting the active players.

In order to win a title and for the game to be completely over, a player must win a total of any two full rounds amongst all current players, therefore, capturing a Zobzball Title. Till that moment, multiple games can partake, creating excitement and cheering.

Elijah quote: "Zobzball creates an extraordinary level of camaraderie, with excitement and anticipation, heightening a player's emotional status."

The longer the volley persists, the more ardent and intense Zobzball becomes. The playing field appearance of the inner sides of the "cube-like court" is surrounded by four solid walls. There is a chainlink fence surrounding the court and positioned (higher) above the solid six foot wall. The fence is designed to capture or reject a Zobzball. If the fence then captures a ball or the ball becomes wedged, the responsible player that hit the ball has then given all the other players a single point as a penalty. If the fence rejects the ball, then the ball is magnetically repelled across the playing field with an unknown destination, a very entertaining part of the game. All of the inner sides, walls, ceiling and floor of the cube have geometric shapes, sizes and lights up with neon colors. Consequently, when a Zobzball strikes any component/object in the arena, a different result occurs. There are sound effects during every bounce of the ball, including when a player strikes the ball. Also, if an object creates an unanticipated english speed bounce, it is difficult to anticipate or know the angle of acceleration, this is the biggest challenge of the game.

Hitting another player with the ball is permissible during an opponent's turn and counts as an object/component. In addition if the ball hits a player from another players serve or turn, that ball is considered live and is registered as that players hit or turn. Therefore the player that has been struck by the ball, cannot re-hit the ball unless the ball bounces off a player that is not their turn. This would be considered a (valid) successful turn.

This ultimately prevents players from crowding each other on the court and giving ample safe distance between each player. There are some anomalies in the matrix of the game, including those certain types of strategies that are used in order to outwit your opponent. One of those strategic elements became evident in Elijah's play. Elijah on this given day has currently changed an important facet in the strategy of his game. He has figured by sending the ball into opposite corners of the cube it will create a difficult deliverance for Aligious. The many variables that come out of this type of placement of the ball have now given Elijah a valid chance to win. With the current series of rounds tied at one a piece between the two players, the winner of the next round wins the Title and would be a lifetime first for Elijah. Eleven points is needed to attach onto your opponent in order to win the round (eleven and you're out). Also a player must acquire a victory by winning by a two point margin within a particular round. Sound effects rumble between points scored and elevated emotions become apparent.

At this moment there are only four points to go for either player to be the victor. A seven-seven score/tie in the final round. Aligious groans as he lands a shot high towards the corner ceiling. The ball with a glancing rebound floats near both players onto the center of the arena. Aligious is frozen in his stance while he anticipates Elijah's new strategic approach of sending the ball into the far corner of the court. However there is a sudden surprise as Elijah fakes his shot to the corner and then lightly hits and spins the ball right off Aligious' body unexpectedly, awarding a point to Elijah. A moan trumpets out of Aligious in frustration. Immediately after the point gained by Elijah, a rumbled sound effect and music erupts from the USSS (Ultra Sonic Sound Systems). There is heightened intensity as the Zobzball program reacts accordingly to the body's emotions, causing great excitement for the players.

Aligious is the server throughout this final round, since Elijah was the winner of the previous round. Determined in the service circle, Aligious serves the ball with a double fake and Elijah misses the ball completely, the score is tied again. Aligious' secret weapon is his wicked fast serves. He uses this speedy serve on Elijah two other additional times. Just one more point and Elijah will lose. Normally Elijah would be shaken at this point, but he is staying focused. He leans into Aligious hoping he would hit the ball to the opposite spot of the last previously mastered serves. He does! Elijah having no choice, dives alongside his father while face down and paddles the ball backwards, hitting the ball off the left ankle of Aligious, again a roll, gives another point to Elijah. *(A roll or three bounces on the floor without hitting anything is a point applied to the player who's turn it is about to be.)* Getting ready for the next serve, Elijah moves back and forth pivoting on the floor so Aligious does not have a bearing on him. Aligious drops the ball in the service circle to its required one bounce, before he strikes the ball. Elijah thinking a mistake will end his chances at finally capturing his first Zobzball Title.

Aligious tries to end it fast, by smashing a hard shot to the fenced in area and unfortunately for Aligious, the ball flows through the chain-linked fence out of bounds, making it a tie game. Laughing and sighing, Aligious runs to the service circle and immediately serves the ball, trying to catch Elijah off guard while he is not paying attention. Elijah, embraces the moment, enjoys the competition and the long exciting volley. Both players acknowledged the many turn of events, switching leads, along with some friendly banter. Now the required "winning by two points" has come to the pinnacle point. The score is Aligious 20 and Elijah -19. One more fault by Aligious and it would lead to Elijah's first ever title victory. As the two point overtime rule is in effect, the vital signs of the their anatomies and the score being received by the Zobzball computer scan, interprets and creates a never heard before amazing amplified sound effects with music, reinforcing this sudden death climatic moment.

The finale unfolds; Aligious squeezes his eyes closed and roars as he serves the ball, walloping the ball off his racquet. Elijah stretches his body and dives to reach for the ball. Misses it, and then falls as he feels the breeze of the ball so close, but because Aligious hit the ball extremely hard off the service mount, the ball stayed in play by hitting the tip of a miniature pyramid.

This gave Elijah a second chance to recapture his turn. Elijah immediately releases and disconnects his right hand racquet off his arm, in order to put the palm of his hand flat on the floor, while his body is faced down horizontally falling to the ground. While he grips the floor with his right hand for lift and supporting his body weight, Elijah springs up to launch his body back up to an immediate running position and darts across the arena.

Elijah is about to lose the volley, because the ball is about to take its third bounce on the floor. His face becomes contorted with an intense look as he concentrates. Quickly, he reattaches his racquet while his legs fumble. Tripping and falling towards the ball, Elijah reaches with a hyper-extended arm and sweeps the side of the racquet onto the surface of the floor, slapping a shot upward in the exact center of the fence portion within the Quadratus Arena. Amazingly, the ball wedged perfectly into the middle of the quadrant part of the chain-link fence, fortunately not going through.

Both players are frozen in their tall stature and wondering if the ball will stay wedged. There was an awkward silence as two seconds goes by; both their foreheads crinkle in expression at the same time, starring at the ball. It remains wedged and the final point terminates Aligious. Elijah and Aligious look at each other stunned realizing that Elijah has finally triumphed. Laughter immediately echoes and becomes blended with the victory music that fills the arena. Aligious' laugh comes to a stall and he announces, "You have grown and come so far, and look your name is now under the Title Trophy area on the scoreboard!" Elijah tries to hold a firm and proud stiff look, then folds and stutters a laugh, because he could not hold back the smiles.

Chapter Three

BOYHOOD

Erudition School concludes its cycle for Elijah, a strong student with an energetic ambition and quite willing to forge through the studies and interests of his father's accomplishments. Elijah is now about to journey onto the next phase of his life and is eagerly waiting.

Once a young Centurion man concludes his Corparalis School, it is customary to graduate onto the next phase of education. This is called Nonage; different levels of youth programs. Part of these programs includes an internship in order to become an expert in certain specialty areas. This phase of schooling is applied because of the importance of an individual's development of originality and a very high priority level in the Centurion customary belief system. This is simply the Centurion's way of helping the students develop naturally. After reaching a pinnacle point of maturity, under normal circumstances, the youths, through choice are permitted to be given a biological upload called the "DOVE." The DOVE is a pre-programmed data base, filled with universal knowledge of mathematics and history. This full knowledge is received through a machine apparatus named the "Philosophers Adaptive Stone." Together the connection accelerates an individual's chance to focus on innovation levels that yet have not been established in one's mind and balance away from a primitive type of rational. The process is offered when a person has reached the development phase of one's life where it is safe (Mainly, the age of twenty-one).

Most important for the Centurions, is that individuals can become strengthened in their own spirituality and many given choices as a result of the DOVE uploaded information. This is the reason as to why the Philosophers Adaptive Stone apparatus is used seasonably. The technology was made millennia ago, constructed and consisting of a quartz stone called the Prasiolite crystal. This crystal is noted for its piezoelectric properties.

The crystal enables the transfer of frequencies using pressure and heat into a radiant flow of photonic energy and absorption. Its storage ability of information is staggering. The transference is done by acquiring and focusing the frequency to the individual's encrypted psyche. By amplifying one's biological signature into the stone, it causes a chain reaction to complete the circuitry fields, thus transferring the imbedded synoptic wisdom to an image or impression with strong recall and recognition.

In order for this process to be permanent, there is a reverse process that overlaps instantaneously *(neurological stacking)* in a complete circle. This final part of the procedure expands and becomes magnetized with the generated information that interfuses, then transcends back from the crystal to the individual with an ultrasonic wave of pressure having a constant transformation of energy. All these condensed controlled energy amplifications become possible by the (tetragonal rosé) quartz crystal, *(liaison crystal)* hence the properties of recall, through memory absorption programming.

This shortcut is embraced by the Centurion race and other races to help develop one's ability to be enlightened. The Philosophers Adaptive Stone process is the third of the five chapters of enlightenment for the Centurions.

The first is Erudition Schooling, second is Novitiate (Nonage) Internship, the third is the Philosophers Adaptive Stone, otherwise known as PAS, the fourth is Ministry *(nimbus energy fully activated)* and the fifth is Enlightenment *(patina energy activated)*.

Pyramis Tenet; called for the format of these five categories, thus gathering the five chronological *(prioritized)* rituals for a purpose that is held dear amongst the various Factions. These five points/chapters are symbolically represented to be the equivalent and or compared to the total points in a four sided pyramid and or star. The apex portion of the pyramid represents the fifth point, "Enlightenment." The five points are derived in part of sacred geometry and embedded in many societies as the foundation of all life.

Jesus' Mentor

(Elijah's current agenda has not yet begun.)

Great days ahead, for the internship has been a long awaited event in Elijah's life. Some advisors had mention that Elijah should skip certain aspects of the Novitiate training segment, because he has already proven advanced achievements in his past youthful state.

At home in the Valley of Conflux, Elijah gets stoked about his first day of Novitiate Internship. He is focused and sets out his sheer "under garments" that clings to his body. The garments are made of numerous linked together hexagonal patterns. These undergarments are comprised of a collection of elements that react to one's body and temperature, activating microscopic metallic dust particles that are fused into the material. The fibers and particles release a residual energy that revitalizes the cellular tissues, while providing intermittent doses of nutrients to be replenished into a person's bloodstream.

This creates a regulated balance within the cells to slow age or decay. The garment protection system is activated by the heat and energy (fusion) that the body produces. This creates an impenetrable shield *(body armor)*, to prevent any harm to the person.

Elijah takes a deep breath as he gazes up at the ceiling while the reflective light connects to the warmth of energy throughout his body. He looks out through a transparent energy field below the lentil of the window, seeing an eclectic city as a whole, engulfed in greens with colorful exotic plants, flowing continuously on the landscaped hills, all the way through to the mouth of the two rivers (an inner Earth).

From across the room angled into the adjacent room, Elijah asks his father about the length of time that it took to make this dwelling *(home)*. Aligious getting his attire together raises the volume of his voice to answer and announces, "One day to build, but three Earth months to design and program." He continued, "I desired a customary design of my own making." Elijah lifts his voice and mumbles, "Hmm, I have seen many buildings in my travels, but I still don't understand the full procedure of completing a house."

Aligious walks closer to view Elijah from a distance and replies, "Well the building aspect is quite simple, it is more like entertainment. I actually listen to my favorite music when watching and enjoying the building procedure." Elijah utters an "Oh." Aligious looks back towards Elijah then articulates, "You see, while watching the house automatically build itself, you take great pleasure in finally observing all your creative planning and hard work unfold in plain sight. Ah, it is very satisfying.

You know we will be," Aligious hesitates then restates, "Sort of building during your internship." Elijah wonders about the unknown, but reassures his father that he is excited, even though he is really very nervous. Elijah finishes putting on his full attire and asks his father in a confused tone, "It only takes one day for the build?" His logical mind is having a hard time coming to grips with that thought. Elijah does not doubt it, but is having logical disbelief.

Aligious asks Elijah, "When you are situated, come outside the dwelling to look at the house from a distance, in order to describe the building procedure in its mechanical splendor."

As they exit the mid-room through the home, at first glance the interior design is so fitting in its perfect smooth thick fluted granite columns, with arced angular contours where the columns connect. The colored mosaic floral design ascends through to the curved ceilings, blended with ornate geometric crowned scribed stone molding placements. It is a beautified energetic magnum opus (masterpiece). It speaks to the onlooker, as to its spliced symmetric artwork and is astonishing that it has a forward appearance no matter what degree or location one stands in the room. A marvel or even a puzzle for the advanced observer, yet being viewed as antiquated as well. Fascinated as demonstrated in their movements, father and son pass through the dwelling as the artful structure welcomes their admiration and appears as if they are one with the building.

Once outside the two of them set forth into the distance from the dwelling. Leading his son to an elevated rest area for better viewing of their house, Aligious points across the horizon and explains, "There are many different building techniques amongst the various Factions that rest here; for now I will break down the components of our native home style constructing techniques."

Elijah stands while he juggles to observe the lands while giving his father full attention. Aligious talks on, "At the outer section of the Hercules City Dome there are quarry factories. They consist of various types of raw material located in sectional holding coops for use while programming the build applications. Throughout the ages, there have been assortments of geometric designs that produce certain variables of energies, which you have full knowledge of." Aligious suddenly turns and stares in a serious gesture towards Elijah, on anything related or connected to sources of divinity, he emphasizes once again.

As Elijah and Aligious are standing at a higher elevation, with a comfortable distance from their dwelling, they can see clearly both their home and the location of the distant quarry. Observing from the scenic overlook, Aligious explains and begins pointing into the direction of the quarry, with his loose sleeve flowing in a soft wind. *(The wind and atmospheric conditions that surrounds Aligious' home and his given territory, have been programmed accordingly to the residents liking by the Adelaide environmental master control systems)* With an authoritative fist point, Aligious says, "The building is born within the quarry, using a standard cutting stone procedure of thermal processing, in which a focused lighted beam is used to melt material in a localized area. A co-axial gas jet is then used to eject the molten material after the cut of a given stone, leaving a clean glass type edge. This process is coupled with residual light amplification housed in a container, used in junction to stem the cutting process."

Elijah questions the types of gases needed for the chemical reaction. Aligious squats low and motions a circle on the ground. "The gases are similar to that of the Earth's Sun or other stars. As you are aware, there is no fire on the surface of a Sun and it consists of approximately 33 elements. By the way, the phrase that "we are all made up of star dust" is actually true." Elijah quickly laughs and quickly says, "Yes but not all 33 elements?" Elijah smiling, then Aligious laughs relieved, "Correct good point," then continues in a downward revision. "The basic elements from the sun are what our bodies consist of, iron, carbon, hydrogen, oxygen, nitrogen and others." Aligious is sidetracked for some non apparent reason, while Elijah still eager to hear what he will say, Aligious then continues to lecture to one of his greatest listeners, "But in this case the machine apparatus is mostly using hydrogen and helium, elements that are interjected into the lighted concentrated beam. Once the carefully chosen stone is cut, it is then key toned with an ankh to figure the stones' center of gravity frequency for lifting. This is actually not a single tone resonating for the "Tractor Receptor" but receives and absorbs as a chord of sound frequencies.

the blocks signature and links it directly into the system for anti-gravity placement designation for transport." Elijah mouths a "Whoa!" Aligious nodding yes to Elijah in agreement, then getting up says, "Simultaneously, the magnetic shield encompasses the entire stone, and before you ask, the magnetic shield does need adjustments in order for the stone to be controlled properly. The apparatus that filters this procedure is called the" Field Generator." This machine scrambles and borrows a portion of the shield and charges static particles emitting them onto the structure *(stone)* or in this case a stone for a gravitational grab for momentum and lifting in its travels.

Amazingly, this result gives an elevating and weightlessness to the block of stone, no matter how large or heavy, it could be pushed along by a child's finger with ease as it suspends off the ground. Undoubtedly, the stone is then steered directly into a global positioning Worm Tram, but let's move on!" Aligious continues, "The many cut and loaded stones are instantly positioned one behind the other, appearing like a train of cars on a cloaked track. Suspended in this invisible field, the materials are all designated to travel to the exact safe GPU (Global Positioning Unit) locations that were preprogrammed."

Elijah restless, thinks silently to himself, "I would love to see the "one day building of a house" in action to have a clearer understanding?" Coincidentally his father next mentions to his son that he will soon witness a similar build, but in a slightly different capacity. Elijah while nodding his head says, "Excellent.

Aligious is amused and dotes over his son's witted grasp of things.

Then gives a sincere tap upon Elijah's shoulder, while holding a smile, thinking how alike he and his son are. Aligious then delivers a laugh with an excitable cry, "Come, let us travel to the Meta Mechin along near the river flow and start the long awaited first day." Elijah responding with a strict, "Affirmative sir," and is apparently excited. As they begin to walk, Aligious looks towards his son and says, "Oh and Elijah, I forgot an important tidbit; summing up our conversation about the completion of a dwelling. There is one important task that is done after the "one day build" that I didn't mention; that is the custom synchronization of all openings and passageways. The photonics energy grid fields, but when you see the building procedure in person, it would be best to explain it then ..."

Aligious stops as Elijah turns to listen, then Aligious grunts and says, "Let's walk and talk" then grunts again." Elijah responds, "Yes, yes," with a quick breath. Aligious starts to walk again; Aligious hesitates, looking up, then stops walking. He appears crossed in his thoughts, as their journey stumbles upon the rolling hills, bringing them near to the river bank that displays the view of the Meta Mechin. Elijah, reading his father's body language turns and waits.

Aligious proceeds to say, "I have to inform you that you and I are about to undertake a very exciting venture. But not to inform you too much, you will be slightly…" Aligious entertainingly snippy changes his voice, while rolling his eyes, then says, "Well I don't want you to become unnervingly shocked, because you are about to see your first…" Aligious becomes fluttered in his delivery, savoring the announcement of this exciting new experience for his son, with a bit of a tease. So he turns to Elijah with a serious display of concern, but also holding back his own excitement, he delivers a stare at his son, then finally speaks, "Once we are actualized at the Meta-Mechin gate, we will be taking a Tube Shuttle, entering then into an aeronautics facility beneath the earth to the geographical location called "Groom Lake" in the Northern Hemisphere of the Americas." Elijah's eyebrows lift with attention. Aligious explains, "There before you will be the appeal of grandeur within this mega facility, along with multiple subterranean levels, holding an assortment of all types of vessels used for different purposes. The vehicle which we will be traveling in *(flying)*, will be a "Bit-Cargo" submersible freighter."

Elijah, happy with excitement, cannot believe it, turns his head side to side and with a cracked voice says, "Truly? Can we get on?" Aligious nods his head yes as he is programming the Stargate (Meta Mechin). Aligious then spurts a firm, "Ready?" Then explains to Elijah how he is setting the sequences in the Meta Mechin Gate. Once a quick vibration sound occurs, they are instantly exiting out and into the Tube Shuttle Complex beneath Groom Lake, which appears to be 20th century technology design.

Aligious looks ahead as Elijah observes the different species that are amongst the underground base and questions himself on why the structure of the facility has a certain old style, contrary to how the vessels are so stunning in their advanced design and sizes.

The Tube Shuttle then leaves this corridor and pierces on through, at speeds of hundreds of miles per hour to a mega portion part of the facility. The Tube Shuttle decelerating, slowly pulling into an open hangar with immense size, as far as the eye can see. Aligious at this point, smiles and looks over at his son to witness the expression on his face. Elijah's chest expands, when a deep breath is forced upon him from the overwhelming vision of this dreamlike atmosphere.

Colorful lights surround while moving through the compound; working stations, shiny glass rock ceilings, ship platforms, holographic glass monitors and computer circuitry station areas, along with a vast sight of miles/kilometers of different vessels. Elijah asks his father a question while the Tube Shuttle drops off other passengers in transit. "How are the enormous tunnels constructed underground?"

As they approach the location area of Aligious' transport vehicle's *(hieroglyph indicated)* address station, Aligious perks up with a quick laugh and responds, "Well, there is an underground digging/burrowing machine "transformation" device that has the ability to expand in size and create a nuclear chemical reaction that omits high intensity frontal thermal heat that melts away stone and dirt. While the attached larger portion of the cylindrical machine moves forward, it uses arms with a high torque revolution, which spins angular diamond blades that cut and capture the molten liquid and distribute the excess material remains efficiently. This digging/burrowing process is done by pressing a certain amount of pressure to the wall sediment with a calculated rhythm of slow speed. This in turn gives the distribution of the liquefied material time to cool, to create a smooth new vitrifying glass surface that is left behind *(shiny rock surface)*. Amazingly, this whole facility is constructed by a (highly precise) stand alone mega machine, called the "Subterranean Nuclear Artificial Intelligence Lithium" thermodynamic boring machine, or otherwise known as simply the SNAIL or Mole, different design types." Elijah listens intently while looking at the vast facility.

Aligious suddenly shifts forward in his seat and appears as if they are at "their" portion of the facility, reaching and extending his neck while the shuttle comes to an abrupt turn. (A little light peers through the back of his garment) Elijah senses his father's movement, turns to look up as they turn the final corner, seeing a large and very live replica of the vessel that he has seen throughout the years in his childhood home. Emotion fills Elijah with excitement as he views the live vessel staring back at him, peacefully. Elijah then becomes quite content and feeling a bit proud, while giving a gracious glance to his father.

Elijah exclaims, "This is great!" Aligious embarks from the Tube Shuttle and begins explaining while walking around the vessel. He describes all of the different parts of the ship and how the vehicle works and the importance of its uses. The chief engineer and the mechanics are almost done with the vehicle, making sure it is ready for departure. Elijah notices a Zeta (Grey) and an Earth-human are working together, a first for Elijah. He remembers about the secrecy doctrine, thinking that the human was probably sworn to take an important oath. Elijah is curious and desires to interact with the human to ask questions. He wanted to find out if that person had conflicts about this systemic Earth operation.

Suddenly, Aligious raises his hand high and replies, "Oh! Before I explain any further about the ship and the mission, I would like to tell you about the exhausts and toxic fumes from the excavating of the Groom Lake facility, because it is related to my next point." Elijah becomes broken in his thoughts about the Earth-man, turns his attention back to Aligious and tells his father how impressive this experience is. But yes, please continue explaining about the exhausts." Elijah squeezes in his comment while looking attentive. Aligious walking to the back of the craft begins explaining, "The intriguing thing about the design of the bore machine," Aligious suddenly stops speaking and stares hard at Elijah. Elijah says, "What?" reacting defensively. Aligious replies, "When I said the intriguing thing about the design of the boring machine, you were thinking that I am the boring machine, weren't you?" Elijah's head leans back and says, "What?" "No!" Quickly shakes his head to match his answer. Aligious points at Elijah then says, "Ah," keeping his arm extended towards his son and continues to point… Again, Aligious taunts, "Ah, ha!" Elijah cracks a huge smile; he closes his eyes looking down to the floor trying to hold back his laughter with a snicker, but bursts into a vibrant laugh out loud. Elijah realizes that his father was joking with him the entire time. Before their funny moment subsides, Aligious repeats the same sentence with some more chortling (soft laughter), but eventually makes his statement.

Aligious says, "The intriguing thing about the design of the boring machine, is that most of the fumes are recycled back into the unit and converted to more energy by a process called flux photoresists, which is the recycling of the toxic fumes for energy. Even though this process recycles and runs repetitively, the toxic gases in small amounts must be safely steered out of the underground facility. The problem is rectified by the installation of a small module that is basically a miniature Meta Mechin (Star-Gate). However, it is used not for us to travel, but for the transfer of the toxic elements via a mini Meta cylinder installed on the back of the SNAIL machine. The exhaust system is linked far away from this location and is extended along the surface far away from any back-draft into the facility." Elijah is intrigued talking with his father about the mini Meta Mechin, on how you can use a type of Star-Gate as a transferee of gases.

Aligious now in the back of the vehicle is seated and points towards an area high above the rear of the ship. He speaks while heavy machinery is running close by, "Can you see those bars with blue lights leading down from the ceiling far apart from one another, having a similar design to the Meta Mechin?" Elijah replies, "Yes, they appear to be a larger version of the Meta Mechin Gate." Elijah smiles at Aligious and a smile is returned. Elijah then asks, "We are going to travel through that gate, are we not?" "Indeed," replies Aligious. "Indeed, this is a most interesting launch program because of two separate actions of reversed time." Aligious explains, "As we depart and release from the Meta Gate inside the facility, there will then be an aboveground connective receiving Meta Gate. This will be right outside above the facility in our first step of reversed time, where lake water will suddenly appear. So being many years back in time, we will be exiting out of the twin Meta Gate at the bottom of Groom Lake's water, which today is located on the surface view, hidden. Not to worry about the anomaly of passing through the depths of the water, because the ship has a residual field, that encompasses the entire outer portion of the vessel for protection. In essence the ship actually never touches the water as it passes vehemently amid the liquid of the lake, while traveling many kilometers to the surface. Well it appears the ship is ready for departure, come and follow."

Elijah strokes the alloy on the ship, sliding his hand along the curves of the vessel as he draws closer to the entrance of the vessel. Before entering, he begins to knock on the vehicle's frame to get the feel of the graphein anodic material from which the ship is made. Aligious announces to Elijah, "Here we go!" from inside the ship. Elijah then enters the ship between the glass angular doors. Located above to each side, is a linkage flow of riveting windows in a symmetrical pattern. The interior is plain and sleek; its shape has an octahedral (formed octagons) decor with transparent surface monitor control systems around the entire interior, as well as holographic projection dimensional readers. Overwhelmed with shock and excitement, Elijah falls back onto one of the two frontal seats near the control panel, in a state of wonder. He savors the moment.

Aligious moves to an observational position about the ship and begins to explain the operations of the vehicle. He overlooks the already programmed coordinates, taps the glass controls while he pivots in his chair. He then faces Elijah and articulates, "Undoubtedly you are aware of the efforts by the Unity of Councils in recent times. I have been in charge and in a position that has the capacity and purpose to oversee major important functions. Elijah, these functions must be finished exactly and according to specifications. Please understand the importance of certain procedures that are involved with temporal displacements or when time travels are involved. It is paramount to whoever is in charge, must follow strict and mathematical order to all procedures!" Elijah nervously nods once and replies with a resounding, "Yes," then nods once more with a serious staunch stare.

Aligious then changes his demeanor while putting his right hand and arm around part of his sons chair and verbalizes, "Eli, just to let you know, we are going to be traveling to Earth's satellite." Elijah quickly replies, "The Mene?" His mood immediately lightens while he demonstrates respect for his father. He now has a full understanding when his father strides along an authoritative instructional stance. Aligious utters, "Yes the *(Mene)* Moon, but the new Moon," Elijah in question, "New?" Aligious engages the security fields about the seats, then the protective field to the outer part of the ship, while explaining, "Well to start, let me cite a quote from a book I have read, called, "The Later Part of the Moon." *Paradox in a bemused way, it is our quest to travel eons into the past. We went back approximately 4.5 billion years ago to create the inception of the Moon's construct."*

Aligious cocks his right brow directed to Elijah, then looks ahead. Elijah reacts, looks forward and realizes that the ship is currently in motion, *(rising)* high up to the ceiling of the facility. A soothing hum fills the room. They are now hovering right in front of the Meta Transgate. Stunned, Elijah jerked back in silence, stifled and acknowledges the ships ability to move with slight noise, along with no motion shifting. This left him quiet and transfixed on the Transgate, staring and thinking upon traveling through the water and to be so far back in time.

Aligious says to Elijah, "Let's just enjoy the travel process and I will critique you thoroughly once we have arrived vis-a-vis at our destination. Are you ready to get on?" Elijah fidgeting with his posture delivers a sincere, "Yes sir." Instantly a bright azure horizontal light flashes across the Transgate and suddenly Elijah is breathless as he observes the ship in its positioned appearance. The ship is instantly on a forty degree angular ascent, propelling swiftly and silently through the ancient lake and its fresh waters. Now submerged in the water, Elijah crinkles his nose and is intrigued with the notion of being level and stabilized. Elijah is amazed as he slowly settles back in his chair with the sensation as if he was sitting at home.

The interior of the ship had no movement at all, even though the freighter vehicle was traveling very fast, while on an obscure trajectory angle. This day was becoming more interesting with every impressive experience for Elijah, with more to follow.

Aligious often glances over at Elijah, taking great joy in seeing his son filled with happiness. The water is undisturbed as they fly smoothly, not a single bubble, nor a wave, making Elijah more curious.

His attention is focused over to the historic fish that inhabit the lake. The ship was rapidly approaching toward the surface of the lake, but his curiosity was sparked. Before they reach the surface of the lake, Elijah decided he would like to study the prehistoric creatures, with the use of the REM *(Recoding Environmental Memory machine)* program that allows the user to record the complete surroundings outside the ship. A molecular read scanner that sends out pulses of hyper sped light, creating a nano-photon magnetic resonance. This absorbs the outer surroundings to a certain gamut spectrum, utilizing an optic transponder that emits frequency wavelengths, which are *(omnium-gatherum)* rebuilt by nano-photon "reminiscence particles" to replicate the environments signature. This technology eliminates any risks of recording in an unsafe condition and gives the user *(recordist)* miles of spherical recordings. Elijah is looking up and out of the window enjoying the motion effects within the sea. He suddenly sees a volume of light engulf the surface of their vehicle while the ship leaves the water into the sunlight.

On their ascending approach into the sky, Elijah looks back down at the lake, appreciating the reflections and glistened water that look like sprinkled diamonds dancing across the veneer of Groom Lake. The ship flies away while the lake becomes smaller in view, as their ascent from the water's surface leaves the taste of the remote past.

The ship whips itself into the proper longitude and latitude coordinates, self maneuvering by the pre-positioning system location that was previously programmed.

The accuracy of the precise vortexular location is of the upmost importance because of the severity of "rearward time" displacement that is involved. The selection process of this magnitude has to be formed in a two step procedure. The first being a minor time jump into the past, from a preselected time period. The second step includes a set up of a major destination chosen (vortex), because of the considerable leap back in time. This predetermined additional vortexular link results in a necessary step for safety and exactitude. As of now, Aligious and Elijah crossover to a particular time period billions of years in the past.

Chapter Four

THE MOON

Hovering high in the sky, waiting for the magnetic fields to move into alignment, all marks and functions are fully engaged. The two men are about to travel back in time approximately four and half billion years into a totally different astrological galactic alignment. They will exit the "fold" of the wormhole at an approximate distance *(location)* arriving between the Earth and its satellite facility base *(Moon)*.

Having already traveled through the first minor reversed time porthole, Aligious waits patiently for the mark to initiate an opening at the second *(huge)* vortex, to travel back" billions" into the remote past.

Aligious looks over and makes eye contact with Elijah, then starts to voice a countdown out loud. With a slur to his numbers, he cries out, "Engage!"

While Aligious and Elijah both quickly turn their heads forward, the vessel occupies volumes of dimensional space and hums. Elijah's hands grip the chair as his knuckles lift with tension, quickly; he takes a couple of deep breaths. Suddenly the vehicle enters the barrier of the wormhole. Time slowly becomes displaced as a silence fills the interior of the ship. Elijah experiences not only the silence but an extreme unfathomable soundless feeling, not hearing himself or able to move. He is being blinded, but with brightness! In addition, a strange feeling of a magnetic pulling sensation erupts all over the surface of his extremities *(body)*, causing paralysis and numbing his senses, yet experiencing a type of floating sensation.

Elijah, still able to have thoughts while in this dimensional anomaly, he is concerned about control and separation of his being. It felt as though he was becoming detached or lifting from his body. This weirdness was a noiseless vibratory sense of being, enveloped by a white energy void.

Suddenly, a wand of shuttered noise passes, followed by an apparent suction dense-pop sound, leaving the vessel still and peaceful in space. Finally arrived, Aligious checks the status and sees he has successfully arrived at the position systems destination, between the Moon and the Earth, hovering steady in space.

"Well well, we have arrived!" Aligious turns to Elijah speaking as soon as they reached their mark. Aligious used this familiar term often to his son, commonly in a moment of magnitude and excitement such as this. Elijah replies, "Will we do that again?" Staring straight and stiff, still in the moment of what he just experienced. Elijah settling down, he relaxes and corrects himself, "I meant, when we go back later on, will we be using the same method for our return?" Aligious laughs then replies, "Actually we will be residing here for a certain period of time in a subterranean technologically advanced city called Columbia, located on the far-side of the satellite or as the well known, infamous *Dark Side of the Moon*." Aligious gives his son a hardy, scary laugh while making note of this iconic phrase. He suddenly changes his demeanor and initiates a more serious conversation.

Aligious speaking about the project ahead says, "Eli, why don't you move about the ship, because we are going to stay docked at these coordinates for a short duration of time. Come and enjoy the complete view and ask away." Aligious smiles and anticipates the many questions that are to transpire. He becomes sidetracked thinking of how Elijah is so like himself, feeling solace knowing how the time goes by so fast, wanting to grab and lock onto this gratuitous moment. Elijah powering down his energy harness in order to stand up, explains to his father about his unique experience during the travel process. Elijah finds it difficult to keep a smooth flow to the conversation while he looks out the different windows, excited to see things in a unique perspective and is flabbergasted with what is around him.

Aligious retrieves data while in the midst of conversation and searches for the recording module that recorded the fish and the aquatic surroundings within the lake. These recordings are categorized in various analytical venues, giving an assortment of studies of life observed while they pass through the sea, using a highly technical advanced recording device called the "View Finder." This device collects audio and visual data in a reproducible format, yet not with conventional lenses or microphones, but with an internal field array called AMR. AMR *(Audiogenics Microphotometry Replicator)* is an instrument for measuring the amount of light transmitted or reflected, while absorbing vibratory friction for video reproduction. It collects waves of molecular signatures, then quantifies and assorts the scanned data array, measuring the relative densities of spectral lines on a recorded photonic and photographic format.

While waiting Aligious is setting up the collection of pooled information via monitors. He has one monitor showing a selected species of fish in a 3D view with multiple angular perspectives. Elijah is amazed when he notices the historic fish captured from the data base systems. He becomes fiddle-footed and takes the palm of his right hand and places it on his forehead. Energized in the moment, he leans forward slightly down in a tilted position and lifts his head back up with excitement, while sliding his hand with open fingers through his hair to the back of his head. Elijah sees his father with a smile from ear to ear.

Elijah gathers his composure while the ships windows reveal a backdrop view of the Universe, Galaxies and Earth's solar system. Elijah, suddenly notices an oddity about the Moon's surface (currently back in time billions of years). His eyebrows are crunched with curiosity, as he casts a desperate glance back and forth from the Moon to the Earth to the Sun. After the third time, Elijah frantically states, "Father, I understand why this younger Earth has these black and molten veins. It is due to its infant stage and of course the Sun is intact as it should be, but the Moon; it has a silvery type surface and appears to have geometric pentagonal patterns spaced apart in a controlled sectional design?"

Elijah about to mimic a phrase from an old popular tell-tube production because he is very happy and excited, but his confusion stymies his humor and decides he had better not. He realizes he is now an intern in a serious and most important project, so he reconsiders and decides to finish his question in a mature manner concerning this Moon anomaly. Aligious heads back to his seat and is about to sit and tells Elijah, "To best answer your question, it would be more suitable to travel into the planetary system of Mars. Being in the vicinity of Mars, will best explain the saga from start to finish. This historic story melds into an ending from one situation to the birth of another. So brace yourself, since we are about to charge up some astronomical speeds, no pun intended."

Aligious grunts a rough laugh while he powers up the control panel and observes Elijah setting his harness in place. Then reaching over, Aligious touches the control panel looking to Elijah, saying that he is going to slightly decelerate the motion safety field, so they can experience a genuine speed sensation. Elijah smiles and agrees in an upward tempo, but raises a concern of caution to himself because of his lack of experience with rapid space acceleration. Elijah converses with his father about the distance of over 33 million miles that will be traveled, with the use of only one vortex (wormhole) and the rest as Aligious states, "Will be on foot," meaning manual controls.

Before they reach the desired location, they start to enjoy the shooting, spinning and sharp aggressive turns swaying in space, having a great moment of solidarity (unity).

In the interim while enrooted, Aligious teaches Elijah certain interesting technological functions of the ship, such as hyperspace and cloaking capabilities. The journey would create a new fond memory by providing a shared experience between father and son.

While traveling through the asteroid belt, they engage the Bessel Tractor Beam, a device mechanism that locks onto matter in space, by means of magnetism photonics.

Rollicking, playing ducks and drakes, casting rocks and debris, they sharpen their skills and recapture the rocks with stealth maneuvers. Aligious begins to explain how the tractor beam works. Elijah is laughing as the ship turns and maneuvers, tossing debris. Aligious struggles to talk, as he fiddles in his seat because his attention is melded between steering the ship at high speeds in angled positions, while concentrating on timing the "grabs" of the asteroid rocks.

Still in action mode with a sporadic strained voice, Aligious explains, "The first action in using the tractor beam is to scan the object that you wish to tow. This is done to find out its center of gravity, similar to the ankh method." Aligious enjoying the thrill of the ride continues to navigate between the debris. "Next, send out a beam of light that surrounds the object, but limits the lighted distance, being parallel to just beyond the object."

He touches the screen and sets forth an aligned light around a targeted sizable rock-mass. Aligious times the event and releases all the instructions while in action to create an incredible high emotional state for his son. Aligious adds, "At this point you engage this command here." Aligious points to the purple icon amidst the clear screen and presses. This would be the final step in capturing your selective rock or object. Suddenly, from about the ship is a high intense reddish-orange narrow frequency, thus expanding into an adaptive radiation beam, which emits and pierces the foundation center of the enveloped light, traveling directly towards its target. Once the frequency engages *(reaches)* with the object, a vibratory signature of the object's center of gravity is instantaneously transposed and recycled at light speed, to propagate a controlled particle field, thus creating the gravitational controlled bond to and from the ship.

Leveling out the vessel, and then decelerating, Aligious smiles with a "Heh," and waits for some positive feedback from his son. Elijah shares with his father how thrilling this experience was and how he enjoyed it just as much as his competition when playing Zobzball.

Experiencing these wonderful challenges sparks a great appreciation towards his father in so many ways, giving Elijah the yearning to give back somehow.

Afterwards they reach their mark, coming to an abrupt halt after an exciting yet tedious journey. They become more serious now while they slowly fizzle out there laughter with a sigh and a breath. Aligious tells his son, "One moment" as he retrieves historical data related to the planet Mars and its surroundings and then moves forth to apply those records to different monitors.

Elijah is still enthused about the journey and goes on about the trek in a jovial way. Aligious waits for the close of Elijah's last sentence and begins his talk, "I have purposely situated us in an orbit around Mars at a calculated speed, so I can explain this saga to you, which will then give understanding to the oddity about Earth's Moon. Let me begin by telling you about the truth and inevitability of Earth's solar system.

The planets and moons that inhabit this solar system were deemed to be barren and fruitless, with no chance of any intelligent life. These findings were based upon the Time Flexion Team's analytical and proven results from the past, present and future. The Time Flexion Unit is a multi- faction based security team that monitors and secures all time temporal activity, in all of our sectors in the galaxy.

Their results coincide with the core beliefs amongst the Factions, to initiate and take action to supply life where there is none. Our species and other Factions through the millennia, after all advanced technology and evolution, feel and have come to the conclusion that the basis of our existence is about giving life."

Elijah interrupts, "Isn't there a conflict of a moral understanding that life is solely predicated by the Prime Creator, unto itself?" Aligious explains, "As our species developed, we experience the circle of life in a high spiritual realm of enlightenment, which confidently set forth the decisions to perpetuate (growth) life. The challenge amongst the factions, as well as ourselves, is not to abuse the gifts of life the Creator has bestowed upon us all, but to embellish it."

"Unfortunately, there has not been a clear understanding of unity between the Factions, past or present and if one is going to dabble *(play God)* in spawning new life, there should be an absolute in unification or oneness.

Which brings me to my next point; the term "many moons ago" derived from the saga I am about to tell you. Similar to Earth, there were two other previous terraforming attempts; "Genesis Projects," but unsuccessful to say the least. Terraforming is the deliberate attempt, by ways of technology to change the environment of a planet or moon in order to be habitable and support (Intelligent) life.

Explaining the order of terraforming that went on in this solar system was the first Genesis Project. It was short lived and practically ended before it could start." "What?!" Says a surprised Elijah, as Aligious continues, "Oh yes, way before my era in a manner of speaking, there was once a fifth planet within Earth's solar system, between Jupiter and Mars and is now referred to as "Evander," even though the planet does not exist anymore."

Aligious asks Elijah to look at a particular display monitor and says, "Sadly what you see here are the remnants of the fifth planet Evander and is now referred to as the Asteroid-Belt.

This concentrated region of interplanetary space holds a massive amount of debris, along with four abandoned moons, scattered in its original orbit around the Sun. Elijah looks puzzled and asks, "How did this happen?" "Well," Aligious answers, "After extensive planning for this huge undertaking, an unforeseen problem arose. Understanding that Evander's distance from the Sun was too far for the appropriate climate temperature, the leading scientists concluded to create five high density moons, one for each Faction involved. These moons would be placed in strategic orbital locations around the planet according to their size and center of gravity readings. The five moons' gravitational grab on the planets interior core would pull and release stored molten magma at a perfect rate to warm the planet's surface, to a hospitable temperature for life.

Each of the five Factions had built their own moon according to the specs that coincided with the unified project calculations. Each of the Factions installed an observation facility inside the moon they constructed and were responsible for."

"Since all Genesis Projects are done billions of years in the past, there is of course "the incubation period," during which the planet is given billions of years to evolve for life to spring up. In the planet Evander's case, the pulling of the core over a period of one billion years caused an unforeseen chemical reaction. An over abundance of Uraninite and other elements with valence electrons caused the planets core to become compressed to a smaller inner sphere. Layers of fusion simultaneously caused a chain reaction of radiation to an implosive state of obliteration to the fifth planet."

He continues, "Thankfully when the planet imploded, it was during the incubation period and nobody got hurt. Evander came to an abrupt end, causing an explosive bombardment of millions of meteorites that were launched out of its orbital zone, due to the implosion. Actually most of the crater impressions on Earth's moon were caused by this occurrence, along with two major impacts on Earth. Other planets and moons in the solar system are still getting pulverized from the projectile debris to this very day.

As so, the project was destroyed. For the five moons flow silently with the orbital scattered rock remnants, which marches with them as a reminder of what was?

Not long after, a decision was made by one of the Factions to destroy their constructed moon because of the failed project. This moon was called "Demeter," named after the goddess that presides over life till death, while baring fruit unto the lands. The other four moons reside amidst the asteroid belt, in the same orbit to the present day. Their names are, "Ceres,

Pallas, Vesta and Juno. Ceres, now the largest moon amongst the four was the twin satellite of the lost moon, Demeter."

Elijah shakes his head and rests back into his seat, then gets back up quickly and notices Aligious changes the information on the screen.

Elijah is mesmerized by the aerial views while in motion observing Mars' surface and in the present day future, seeing all the megalithic structures covered in thousands of years beneath the sand. Elijah walks up to his father and says, "The canyons are magnificent, I see cave openings throughout the landscape."

Aligious is ready and is about to tell Elijah about the second failed Genesis Project. Aligious indicates, "Here you can observe the planet Mars in its current time period from 4.5 billion years ago through the windows and on the monitors. For right now, Mars will be the window to your left." Aligious using his open forehand to present a particular screen, thus showing Elijah the next two monitors, informing what each screen will be displaying. Elijah eagerly follows and pays close attention to his father without a blink.

Aligious continues to explain, "This window is a smaller view of Mars, along with the planet Jupiter and Earth, in its current time period. The last monitor will display slide views from sixty six thousand years ago, along with other images that will appear before that time period as well."

Aligious hesitates and stares up at Elijah and says, "Mars was originally called POC4, not Mars, I'll explain; the last monitor to your right is the present day Mars." Aligious whispers "Elijah, listen closely." Aligious is very serious and is about to deliver a discussion on a tender topic. Elijah reacting to the moment is calm and acknowledges his father. Aligious says his sons name again, "Elijah, the Factions amongst the Council that I am in charge of currently," Aligious softens his eyes as he is sensitive on this subject matter, grinds further, "Consequentially in the past, the Factions/Council were not always unified, but nevertheless the groups of various Factions eventually connected to work together. Many of these unions strove towards massive undertakings, creating different types and locations of Genesis Projects throughout the galaxies. Thousands of Genesis Projects through time have been created across the millenniums. Life was created were there was none. Understandingly, there is a moral debate, but let's hold that aside, for as of now, I am going to give you the lineage and historic facts on our Genesis Sector, which is dear to our hearts. Please Elijah, like most information given to you, don't conclude or judge till you have heard the complete history. The difficulties and compromises are the puzzles to be overcome, that can lead to a divine cause." For some reason Aligious' eyes glaze over. Elijah thinks to himself that his father has mixed feelings about what he is going to say. On the one hand he is somewhat smiling because he is happy with a sense of pride. On the other hand, he appears to be somber and Elijah is not sure why. Aligious stands tall to begin the story in a lectionary fashion.

"To begin to answer your original question about the silvery look to the Moon, let me start, first and foremost to tell you the reason why the Moon that orbits the Earth has no name and all the other 172 moons do have names. First you must understand that all moons need to meet certain qualifications, of course meeting the criterion category of being an acceptable moon in this smaller than average solar system is curved to the calculations. All the moons that surround their given planet in this solar system are naturally formed moons by the Creator or the Factions and usually you will find in this system, more than one moon orbiting its planet. Our people, the Centurion Faction call what appears to be Earth's Moon a satellite and that is the term used when making reference to this particular moon, because Elijah, it is a manufactured object!" Elijah is visibly confused, as he stares at a monitor displaying the construction process of the Earth's Moon.

"At this moment in time you are observing the Wormvex portion of the operation. Let me show you on this holographic display. The Wormvex distributive functions create rotational balance points to the moon and transfers Earth's molten lava to the Moon's surface. The lava is disbursed through a sort of Meta Mechin stargate, called Wormvex. Its distributions morph into geometric sections over the skeleton of the Satellite (moon). The molten rock fusses above and below the metal caging in pentagonal sections and connected by a triangular metal network. This is done to balance out the weights and measures of the outer shell, all the way up to the two and half mile thick surface. This procedure will eventually take less than one, four thousandth of a percent of the Earth's surface and will be able to handle strong meteor impacts. It will be layered like a veneer of elements (meteorite proof) over a metal ribbed skeleton and inside the Moon will reside a marvel of sectional cities designed and built for different necessities and functions. Exits and entrances lay protected with huge openings that are accessible on the far side of the moon, allowing for spacecrafts having access and where space vehicles are maintained and fueled."

"The facility bases on the Moon are one of many stations that are inhabited by beings throughout this solar system. With regards to the facility bases, second to Earth is Mars, and strangely enough Mars has two remnant pieces of its broken moon. The smaller of Mars' two moons is used for storage and came from the center inner portion of Mars' original moon. The larger of the two remnant moons when disjoined provided a full functioning base, now antiquated and a post that was used as a vantage point for reconnaissance work and the monitoring of the planet PCO4/Mars." Elijah curious to what happened on Mars asks, "Father?" Aligious raises his left arm to motion wait, before Elijah can ask his question and says, "Eli, the explanation of Earth's moon, will segue into the second Genesis Project about Mars." Aligious quickly nods forward and then lifts both of his eyebrows up, to reassure that he will explain.

Aligious now reached the subject on why the Factions are present on Earth. He motions towards the planet to explain what Elijah might not fully understand. "In consideration of all the surface people on the planet, they have undergone DNA adjustments and have been tweaked for millennia in order to eventually become a part of the Unity of Planets. Before this can happen, many compromises were made within the Councils, not all agreeable by our people, but we as the Centurion race, felt it was extremely important to be a part of these Genesis Projects to limit the abuses. We monitor these experiments, yet our responsibilities are to introduce, as well as maintain certain moral behaviors and virtues in order to respect the sacredness of all things that are living.

Other different factions have proceeded with their own Genesis Projects to this region with or without our permission. Thankfully, our DNA was the dominate match, when chosen for the main species of planet Earth." Elijah asks, "Why were we chosen?" Aligious answers, "The selection process is figured by the density, size and distance (ratios) of the Earth and Moon to the Sun. This mathematical result gives credence to the best choice of dominate DNA available amongst the twelve factions (Genesis Project). The selection is made by choosing a rogue or limited solar system that has been around for over billions of years and does not have any significant intelligent life possibilities, as said before." Elijah says, "I understand," speaking in a tempo to encourage Aligious to proceed.

Aligious is glistening and is in need of some rest, but persists and carries on saying, "Learning from the other two Genesis Projects, the methodology has evolved to a precise collaboration and undertaking. To reiterate, as a given our scientists have learned by going back in time to the birth of a solar system and install a satellite or moons, as you say." Elijah smiles as Aligious continues "Provides the optimum production of life. In this case, the unique qualities of this particular Moon have sent this project into its own classic accomplishment. Twelve Factions working together, sharing technologies of advance systems to make one of the most sophisticated achievements the sector has ever seen."

Elijah asks about how Earth is teaming with life and why there is such an abundance of life when compared to most planets he has monitored. Aligious begins to tell Elijah about the reason how this was achieved by the Factions. He says, "Before we completed the Moon's infrastructure, the Factions designed plans of Earth's satellite according to the group's explicit research and development, with optimum potential for life. The Factions designed this satellite *(The only moon out of the other 172 existing moons in this solar system)* with perfect symmetry and with a flawless impeccable spherical shape. We also placed the Moon in a mathematically configured precise unique orbital zone at one four hundredth the distance, positioned between the Earth and the Sun.

We also created the moon to fit into 1/4 of the circumference of the Earth, along with intentionally making the Moon 1/400 of circumference of the Sun, from the perspective on Earth. These series of mathematical ratios regarding the relationship of the Earth, Sun and Moon are paramount to produce an exuberant amount of life."

Elijah is flawed with these statistics, and going to ask a question but chose rather to state, "I have heard of a literary published story called, "Eclipsed by the Moon" discussed at my Erudition School, on how popular the Earth's Moon is amongst the Factions." Aligious agrees with a short nod, and then adds, "Another marvel about Earth's Moon is the perfect 100% precise eclipse we designed! Also the orbit is a flawless perfect circular orbit, with pre-calculated parallax points, unlike all the other moons in the solar system, which are oblong or oval. Eli, the best feature and unique unto itself, is the uncanny ability to slightly rotate slowly at a fixed speed, to precisely and constantly face the Earth, allowing the inhabitants of Earth to only see one side. This unnatural occurrence is how the Factions maintain a surreptitious behind the scenes covert operations on the far-side *(dark side)* of the Moon. There are mining operations on the surface and glass pyramids to store toxic elements in order to maintain the operations throughout the project." Elijah sniffles and makes a "Hmmm" noise with an interested gesture, thinking about the massive planning and undertaking this entire project has delivered.

Aligious emphasizes, "Interesting enough, you will soon see the surface of the Moon receive Earth's natural molten crust adhered to the ribbed skeleton during its lava-like state *(the solidified state of the molten crust was timed according to its liquid to solid ratio, when the main elements were mined and filtered)*."

Elijah's eyes open with anticipation. Aligious piles on more information, "A percent of the Moon has a manufactured fiber dusts on its overall surface. This is actually a high condensed fuel source called Helium-3/6, for one ounce can power our dwelling for a lifetime, when combined using a Magnetic Lidar Duplicator. As I stated before, the soft dust on the surface of the Moon has been hit by small meteorites (remnants of Evander and or asteroid belt) over a period of four and half billion years.

Elijah voices, "I see this is why so many circular impressions throughout the Moon can be seen on the surface and odd, to be the only moon known with dust on its surface." Aligious tells Elijah, "Yes and in essence, this satellite is the representation of highly advanced technology, donated and combined with hard working volunteers in unison with species abroad. This camaraderie and unity is what we have brought to the Earth, representing different Factions and the variants of DNA that are the human species.

This becomes an established goal for all types and mixed species to come together and put aside individual conflictive beliefs. The United States of America was especially designed to emulate and simulate these principles, hence to its great success of accepting all religions and various cultures. This instituted a basis for the fundamental platform of the Foundation, to be the Unity of Planets."

Elijah wonders if the Factions are causing an irregular abundance of life to be spawned *(correlating deeper thoughts towards the creator's probability design)*. Aligious mentions to Elijah, he is now going to begin telling him about the tragedy on POC4/Mars. "Mars initially was the second choice out of the three total Genesis projects, because of its orbital location, its smaller size and being an easier construct of the planet. Its design only needed one moon/satellite. Nonetheless not all the Factions were involved, which from the very beginning caused controversy."

Aligious carries on, "The moon around Mars was made with raw materials, with only a handful of underground bases. Mars' moon construct was actually made to emulate a moon around Saturn, called Enceladus, same texture and topography, but smaller. In Greek history, Enceladus was a giant person and the offspring of Gaia, who was the deity of "the great mother of all," the Mother Goddess. She was the creator and giver of birth to all, a heavenly goddess. Whereas, the meaning of Gaia is "Land or Earth" and became the fitting name for *(POC4/Mars')* the moon. This designated name (Gaia) was the unanimous decision at the time, not knowing that the destruction of Gaia (Mars' moon), would ironically pave the way for the new Genesis undertaking, and *that* was to be called "Earth" *(the meaning of Gaia)*. Though Gaia, authentic and *was* a celestial work of art, it regrettably lacked the functional characteristics, slightly enough to cause problems.

This allowed only portions of the planet to flourish with acceptable life and water, but leaving the rest of the planet in a non productive yield *(non-fertile)*. These issues with different Factions involved and not involved in the project, caused and created further controversy. Three different Faction Leaders became upset that their respective species DNA had not been chosen. One Faction complained they were not considered to assist with the raw material and excluded from the base facility development on this Genesis Project."

"The territories of this solar system are a part of a large sector that all Factions were and are entitled according to provisions." Aligious looks at Elijah and says, "Long story for another time." He continues, "So unfortunately, this led to a violent war sixty six thousand plus years ago, on and completely around POC4/Mars.

The devastation was an onslaught, with the pouring out of bombardments, spreading nuclear and electromagnetic annihilation over a large portion of the planet. Consequently, there was an ample quantity of life transferred, saved, or destroyed, sending the planet practically back to its previous original lifeless state. Gaia (Mars' moon) was then destroyed with a single explosion, leaving the remnants of two pieces that did not perish from the planets gravitational grasp.

The people that lived on the surface were ignorant and innocent of these doings and there were many. For the impending battle there came a high ranking Centurion, who risked his life and the lives of his crew for the many hybrid beings abandoned on this planet. His name was "Mars." He fought to protect the innocent, who inhabited the planet's surface from the adversarial Factions who wanted to terminate and exterminate POC4/Mars. Fortunately Mars was triumphant with winning the battle and saved most of the population, but was unfortunate to save the environment of the planet. For Mars' future was sealed, blatantly because before one of the enemies had retreated they obliterated the fabricated moon, *(Gaia)* thus halting the replenishment of life."

Aligious was speaking faster with conviction, "Currently, special operations are still maintained on POC4 although, the colonies have been long deserted from this climatic watershed in time. The occurrence personified the name "Mars" to take the place of the appellative acronym POC4.

The remnants from the destruction are two broken pieces from the original assembled moon, presently called, Phobos and Deimos. Phobos is the larger of the two unnatural satellites and means to "feel fear" as it stares out towards the red planet. Phobos was the son of Ares and Aphrodite. Deimos, the smaller of the two moons, is the twin brother of Phobos and whose name means "dread and terror." Ares who raced into battle to save Gaia *(moon)* accompanied by his two sons, Phobos and Deimos, failed to protect the moon because of his two sons panic stricken behavior, thus leaving the moon vulnerable and leading to its destruction. The names of the moons were a reminder for all to protect life at any costs.

Reconstruction and renovation on Phobos was done on its interior, having one of the bases still intact inside, but is now used for different purposes. Any attempt to save cites or moving things forward, proved to be futile, because Mars started slowly losing its atmosphere and with a weak ionosphere to keep the moisture intact. The populations started dwindling and it was decided to transfer the remaining people over the millennia, if they so chose, to go to Earth and begin anew. In essence these people would be delivered to a specific geographical location through Star-gates on Earth once the definitive new Genesis Project was built and finished.

The war had paved the way for the Unification of Planets to be found, and now a fair and equal twelve part Faction alliance. The new Genesis Project would now be based on DNA from the various factions, along with certain territorial locations for hybrid development on the ripened Earth."

Elijah asks Aligious, "What procedure was taken to understand the type of life that planet Earth wielded and did the planet spawn intelligent life naturally?" Aligious has the ship orbit Mars during their discussions, giving visual confirmations and adding further incite to a series of historic actions that will assist and conduct their operations with better understanding when working together.

Aligious continues, "The process is as follows, the development of the planet Earth in its natural state over billions of years led to an under abundance of life (simple forms), and not intelligible communicative beings. The scientists then extrapolated over 99% of various primates' DNA that are indigenous to the planet. They chose primates, being the closest relatives to our DNA, *(Centurion)* but also injected into the original design of the human genome, a secondary signature of DNA with a certain type of sectional strands. These strands were added to a small sprinkled mixture of bird, insect and a variety of other types of DNA for adaptive qualities, called *"Primate Select".*

The Primate Select, which includes the major mammal primate DNA along with other minor variations, is a sequence that is already adjusted to the original DNA *(indigenous blend)* to allow for proper breathing of the gaseous atmosphere and gravitational environment bequeathed to this planet. While in this secondary procedure, an additional minor alteration to the DNA is needed for blending and balancing during the implementation of two hundred and thirty three genes. *(Primate Select, Centurion and Faction Minor = Human Genome)* The human genome is made up of billions nucleotides, and ten of the 233 genes, were translucent by design, and they are the woven important strands that latch together with the Primate Select DNA."

"These ten *(Centurion/Faction)* tangible genes activate and connect through proteins that incur with neurological enzymes, which fuse to the mitochondrial portion of the strand, thus producing psychological reasoning and communication abilities. On Earth each Faction among the twelve were given twelve variants of their personal DNA, leaving a total of 144 chosen genomic variants, furthering the chances of success and securing abilities of a particular hybrid *(practically indigenous)*. Secondly, every Faction was given an allotted sectional proportion of the Earth, whereas designated solely for the particular Faction. If at any time a Faction was not satisfied with geographical localities, then they were allowed to either move or alter the weather to the climate of their subsequent location."

Elijah frozen in his stature offers questions about his concern for the people, having special given knowledge in order for them to survive without suffering. Aligious explains, "Various languages and writing capabilities for communications were given, appointing a non indigenous leader or hybrid of their *(Faction heads)* own choice, in connection to the area to be governed. The "Heads" would also teach different mathematical skills to be used for stone building constructs, up-to the appropriate level of their primitive capabilities.

The final leg of the process, and the most necessary was the installation of religions. Many of the religions were carefully selected and quite similar to a particular Faction's primitive *(indigenous natural)* historic religions from their home planets. This kept morals in order, except oddly enough, on the Earth, where the new human indigenous species in many cases used religion to wage war because of the non like faction DNA. The Elders did not see this measure becoming so severe.

Adding to another unfortunate occurrence, something that has been ongoing, is that certain hybrid Earth Faction leaders have botched up some religious programs. Many of the teachers used technology to impress the humans, so as to be worshipped, which was unacceptable. Another unacceptable practice was the Zetas approach to a fastidious way to do excessive experimentation for the cause of their-own scientific probability obsession. They believe scientific knowledge gives dominance. The Zetas thrived for control, but granted in the realm of things, there were some adjustments that had to be implemented in the DNA. Nevertheless, the Zetas went beyond the scope of work; citing abductions and hybrid experiments between animals and humans. In addition, the Zetas forwarded staunch agreements with human heads of state in exchange for technology and to further studies on their influential frequencies that are sent down to Earth from their Moon station, to target certain areas of the planet."

Elijah is concerned why the people do not challenge or question anything. Aligious looks at him rigidly and then his look softens with relief as shown in his eyes. "Elijah, the people on earth are quite intelligent, so it is hard for me to understand how a species does not question the facts. They accept things at face value. They never question the most obvious oddities; like why they no longer have fur on their bodies in a short evolutionary time period. Most mammals have an abundance of fur, resulting in a conflict of why they need clothes to prevent themselves from freezing to death. Ironically the humans that are from the coldest climates have the least amount of hair. The shedding of fur is an evolutionary process that is aligned with any indigenous species on their planet, but normally that takes millions of years, yet it doesn't even raise an eyebrow to the human race."

"They do not question why other indigenous animals do not have hundreds of health problems *(diseases)* like the way humans do, along with dozens of abnormalities at birth. As infant babies need immediate assistance and can't walk for almost two years. Never questioning why the need to have their tonsils, appendix, teeth or hair physically removed. Why must they take baths or perform circumcisions for that matter." Aligious takes a breath and says, "Well, let's go back to the Moon at a faster pace, what do you say!" Elijah responds with a positive gesture of agreement, smiling away.

Elijah: "Nevertheless, I know there is an underlying human seriousness that we must recognize." Aligious gives a light gasp with a short laugh while listening; he understands that Elijah is sensitive to this subject. Elijah continues, "Father, I now see that my energies would best be served by studying the languages, writings and religions. Hopefully to speed up the qualities of this "agenda" process, so not to see any more people suffer or to be herded like cattle in the name of science."

Aligious is amused and tells Elijah, "You're starting to sound like me, ha ha. Why don't you take the helm (steer) and let's make our way back to the Earth's Moon." Elijah acknowledges his father's request. His expression lights up and gathers himself to embark with control of the ship at his fingertips, then asks his father if he can use the manual steering during their travels. Aligious agrees and they set off to return back to the Moon, where the construction process is talking place.

When they arrive, Elijah is mesmerized by the artificial atmosphere that is surrounding the outer perimeter of the Moon, and the AI *(Artificial Intelligence)* used for gravity so workers can accomplish tasks in an easier manner.

Many months go by with Elijah and his father living in the Columbian city, getting into a rhythmic enjoyable lifestyle. They are productive with the expedition of the Lunar Project.

In the midst of the project, Aligious surprises Elijah one day with the thrill of being able to oversee a certain portion of the pre-automated residential building process within the city. Amongst the Planning Commission there were many lot parcels drawn with substantial sizes. The land had a beautiful sculptured topography landscape, where assortments of houses were going to be constructed.

Elijah was eager to start on these twenty-one residential dwellings. When he looked at the site plans, he took note on twenty of the pre-programmed AI codes, for one did not appear to be completed. Somewhat concerned, Elijah looks for his father to inquire why the architectural layout was incomplete. Aligious, was out managing the surface building of the Moon under the artificial atmospheric field dome. He was double checking the energy emissions area, finishing up for the day when he sees Elijah approaching. Elijah whisks towards Aligious and smiles. Aligious noticing the monitor display in his sons right hand and is aware what the question is going to be. Aligious still smiling, says, "Am I running late or are you early?" Elijah utters a, "Hello good Sir, no I believe we are both on time and I figured we would walk down to the Tube Shuttle together." Aligious declares, "So you not here about the one missing dwelling on the Housing Development Plans?" As they board the Tube Shuttle to sit down. Elijah looks fast at his father stunned then quickly anticipates there will be a twist coming, so Elijah laughs once, then let's out an "Ahhhh!" Aligious reaches into his pocket while grabbing the mobile display pad from Elijah then talks while both of them are enjoying the moment.

"Here is the one you are missing." Aligious presses a small magnetic chip against the screen, which just happens to be the process code for the dwelling of the missing spot on the display pad. Aligious quickly looks at his son and indicates, "I purposely left this dwelling out on the survey so I could tell you personally that the code for this dwelling is the original ordinal program of the home you grew up in." Elijah is taken back and lost for words, and then Aligious suddenly spouts, "Wait before you say anything, I have allotted an "editing vertex" for each section of the program, so you can make custom changes in each or all of the settings." Elijah's heart filled with warmth as he feels his skin tingle from the fresh air and responds with a, "Thank you. I will thoroughly enjoy this! In fact this is the first thing I am going to do when I get to my quarters, but no worries about the changes, I already know what they are and there only 3. I'm sure you will like them."

Elijah still looking at the code on the display pad as his father pats him on the back and is about to get up to disembark from the Tube Shuttle. Aligious walks with Elijah and states, "Okay that sounds good, but don't forget, I'm going to be living in there after you finish your internship. In the meantime get her done. " Elijah feeling blessed says, "Thanks again," while he looks up at his father with joy.

The Satellite Project is almost finished, with great assistance from Elijah and his influence on the project, to create innovations that improved the project's production of the build.

Aligious was proud and grateful when the internship was finished for his son. Aligious was filled with great honor, because of the high levels achieved by Elijah, punctuated by the memorable moment of his son's graduation. Elijah knows he has pleased his Father and is joyful as he gathers some of his belongings. He is going to have to leave his Father behind to finish the Moon construct. Very grateful, but understanding it's his time to move forth and travel alone to the space station within the quadrants of his father's home planet.

CHAPTER FIVE

HISTORIC DATA MACHINE

The rite of passage is upon Elijah. He is about to receive an amazing amount of knowledge internally by a machine that uses artificial intelligence. This advanced technology is intrinsically based in biogenetical principals. The apparatus' downloads and uploads are in a simultaneous boomerang trade off. The neurological overlap becomes memories that adhere to the mind and therefore, easily accessible for the individual.

The results of the procedure have been very successful because a wealth of information is attained without any involvement of altering one's own developed or established personality.

The apparatus is called the "Philosophers Adaptive Stone" and is the act of "neuronal feedback insertion" of historic documents; quantum mathematics and an accumulation of all universal planetary historic data in the sector. This information is an assortment from the Faction's past histories, current cultures, languages, actions and writings.

What is withdrawn from the historic documents is any portion of history that the user/receiver is connected to or from. The historic information that is relative to someone's future will not be included in the transfer. This precaution constitutes that history will not be affected, nor the time continuum. Nonetheless, the program will be figured accordingly and not installed until the user has reached maturity and qualifies.

Since Elijah had one of the most significant outcomes in the time continuum (history), extra care will be taken. Does his father already know that Elijah created and set a moral path for families to advance in all facets of our society?

The Time Flexion Security is assigned to monitor the life of Elijah. His position in time is at the highest level of security and is tracked through the inter-dimensional monitoring system, which uses transponders that are variable and constantly readjusting. The time security is precise in its deliveries, implementing high speeds of frequencies that are released at a constant. If anything appears non-synced in the time continuum, the system alert detection becomes instantly noted days before the occurrence to deal with the non authorized jump.

The universal mathematical data upload and the low intensity historic data fusion are the main programs inserted. Afterwards, both procedures will require medic monitoring for an approximate thirty day period. During this segment there are slight adjustments therapeutically, with tests that involve physical and mental monitoring, during and after the medicinal process. These actions are only performed on adults and are customary to be applicable during the twenty first year of life, unlike the nimbus, which arrives naturally during the thirtieth birth year (some brighter than others). The beginning stage of the nimbus needs to be transfigured (assistance from other Centurions) before being fully active.

The nimbus has been mistaken as "wings" after the fifth century and before that era; the human interpretation was a "halo." It was customary for the Centurions, when mingling with society to hide their light. In fact there was a fashion introduced early in mans development just for the purpose of hiding the nimbus light. Ironically, as the future unfolded and startling to say the least, it is still amongst the fashion in the same geographical region where it originated. The Centurion nimbus has healing power abilities, but needs to be mentally accessed by the individual, but can be draining if overused. Yet in addition, there are certain super powerful capabilities that can be accomplished when a Centurion couples the nimbus/halo energy with an array of different technologies.

Impressively the most profound feature of the Centurion race is that upon the body's demise, after the age of thirty, *(with all extremities intact)* a metamorphosis takes place upon death. The anatomy retreats into a type of hibernation *(altered state)* once the nimbus *(halo)* dims after death. Then within a forty hour period of time, the nimbus while almost completely lightless (unlit), reemerges in an altered state, where subatomic particles implode within the cells, suchlike a supernova star that spurs energy. This photonics process ignites molecular fusion that transforms cells governing the body into a vat of cellular chemical reactors.

After the quantum of bio-electromagnetic radiation is settled, the body begins to heal in an altered state. Interestingly enough, the body itself is then no longer the governing part that controls the physical functions of the anatomy, but the new residual energy that overlaps the body's cells from within. The entity *(Centurion)* transforms by a blend of spiritual energy that presides over the new resurrected body, controlled by and called the "patina." The patina is the spiritualized energy that has dominance over the body's temple in a translucent state. At this point, the individual cells of the body are in more of a double dimensional holographic energy field/status that has a divine overtone.

For the energy at this juncture *(patina),* has been with Aligious for over three centuries, which is the average life span of a Centurion patina (life). This long life span accrues up until "Quietus," which is the absorption of the energy into the dynamic realm (death), whereas the aura of the body can no longer adhere to the old imprint of the body's structure, dimming then evanescing (spirit transfer). This is the dematerializing, fourth and final stage of a Centurions physical life. The first stage is called "Springtime," *(nonage).* The second stage is named "Zodiac Nimbi" which is the halo of light energies that becomes controlled by the physical body. Upon physical death the nimbus changes or metamorphosis to the "patinas" *(third stage)* and has the reverse effect, whereas the patina controls the physical extremities instead of the body controlling it, this would be the tri-stage. It is unusual from birth to death among most cultures, to have an understanding of the immense time that the universe has existed. Even a species such as the Centurions, who have been around for unimaginable length of time, cannot possibly understand where humanity is headed.

Elijah is waiting in a prep area while staring into the main room and is relaxed as he clears his mind. He is administered a series of unit strides (medicine) distributed by a process called, "chemical mechanisms" that allows quantification monoaminergic as a means of balance in the fusion procedure. This chemical procedure is coupled with the bijection of bio-electronic sharing, where all the informational data transferred is done by a high density data micro-compressor to enable a large amount of data blending with safety and viability. In addition, protective inhibitors are used in conjunction with the aromatic carbon bands in relation to certain efficiency levels to keep a condensed focused area.

This is done to prevent info-overlapping according to the functionality of the neurotransmission when the reaction is traversed. The rapid neuron-reception and transmitters are directly modulated in a safe trade off towards the neuronic systems in relation with the brain and body. The neuro-modulation becomes an even distribution through to the neurotransmitters, by bio-electronics and chemical means, which include norepinephrine, serotonin, dopamine, and melatonin adjustments.

Elijah walks into a ziggurat stone shaped structure and notices the stone interior to have a smooth quartz crystal surface, gleaming out from a fifty one by fifty one foot pyramid, followed by a marriage of angled vaulted walls, measuring fifty one degrees, coupled with a four sided wall/ceiling towards the apex. While Elijah looks for any seems in this energetic four sided room, he realizes the huge structure is carved from one enormous stone. Elijah then gulps as he sees a circular platform on which he is supposed to stand, knowing he will lose consciousness. There are field barriers that will keep him in a residual standing position for the procedure, so the performance will be at its optimum capacity. He walks slowly noticing blue and green lighted reactors connected to some sort of cylindrical canisters, housing tall thin obelisk crystals. Some are at different sizes lined in a parallel formation.

Now approaching the center of the room, he looks down to see the wireless mechanical transponders. There are four recessed wireless transponders smooth to the floor's surface. All of them are equidistant at fourteen feet three inches from each of the *bisectional triangulated* segments, from which the floor line passes through the midpoint of the given quadrate (square) area.

While he is about to be engaged to the Philosophers Stone, he is receiving instructions from the numerous professionals who are among the coverage staff at hand. Various members of the staff finish explaining the process and brief Elijah on how to breathe during the procedure. They reassure and remind him, that the area of the mind that is being utilized during this procedure is only 1% of your entire capacity.

Elijah smiles, then nods and steps completely onto the cylindrical platform as the staff operators move away within a range of twenty feet.

Elijah is still waiting and before he connects, there is a sudden spherical force field dome that encompasses him. Running high levels of pressurized oxygen that is in abundance inside the field, the four floor transponders are engaging and lying in a connective frequency at a fifty one degree angle directed towards different parts of Elijah's cranium. Each of the four transponders are pursuing a task: the first is reading and traversing messages to the appropriators, which is an instantaneous selection of stimulations. This is to be implemented in order to balance the bio-chemical reactants and keep the process of information on a safe forward path. The second transponder is the integration of an altered dreamscape state, which is woven towards and directed beneath the cerebral hemispheres. This produces and stimulates neurotransmitters while increasing the blood vessel flow, having an unprecedented effect, which gives pathway directional results of the transition.

Transponder number three fuses the neuron receptors to the information coming from the historical and mathematic crystals. When the procedure is completed, the multitude of information is "fresh" for recall at anytime. When you access this information, the individual is aware that you are retrieving it from the Philosophers Stone, separate from your own experiences.

The fourth frequency is the main systems monitoring drive. It receives data on every aspect of the procedure from the three other transponders and then deciphers the data for safety monitoring. This instantaneously transmits commands to complete a circuit of syntax absorption to become embedded in the memory permanently for the user.

The arduous (exhausting) procedure is finished and Elijah is drowsy, docile and in a meditative state. The team then monitors, adjusts nutrients and through attentive means, reassures Elijah's recovery and allows him to rest.

After the third day Elijah starts to feel clear and contemplates all the new information. He is beside himself with the knowledge of hundreds of lifetimes. Strangely enough, Elijah's first thought was of a regenerative bath, where flowers, herbs and oils are amidst the bath waters with low voltage magnetic massage pulses that are evenly distributed between the water molecules, stimulating the epidermis (skins) tissue for an absorbent result.

Elijah realizes this is one of the contributing factors and reasons for the Centurions ability to live for a few centuries. Elijah thinks, "Maybe that's why we are called Centurions." Then he immediately draws a blank thought and gets chipper, understanding that his previous thought had no merit. Elijah smiles as he looks up with a gazed expression, turns his body to the right in a circular slow motion, with his hands and palms open face up, sees things now as though every "sight to thought" process is transparent and he is grateful.

Elijah makes an observation and comes to a conclusion that ties everything together. He switches thoughts immediately, wonders about the barriers that have held the human race from accelerating beyond their capabilities. His thoughts tussled in a search for answers to help the people of Earth.

Ignorant on how to put all of this into action, he spurs a thought and comes to the realization that the humans were given religions and diligently worship, but overall did not understand what they were worshiping. They are doing what they were told by their parents, peers and leaders.

Every day that passes, more conclusions are reached, enhancing his already outstanding intellect and great personality. This collaboration is then setting the stage towards the best plan possible in preserving morals and insights without trickeries of technologies in order to pass along information essentially for thousands of years.

The answer was through religion, considering the aptitude levels of mankind, this was the only solution. The question must be asked, how do you decipher the best exact time to implement and teach this religion? Understanding, it would be in a non technological era, sometime in the remote past.

Elijah, after considerable contemplation over a period of time, *(the exact length of time is excluded from the records)* sets out to one day start his own ministry and eventually "over-time" this ministry through his love and actions, spark a religion that would both accelerate and bring mankind together as one.

CHAPTER SIX

THE MANHOOD

The "Manhood" section of chapter six was originally in the Book of Elijah, but only as a title, whereas the texts were omitted, withdrawn or lost.

Chapter Seven

EIGHT YEAR MINISTRY

Time is fleeing and Elijah is currently busy preparing for his teachings and building a foundation for his ministry, while learning a vivid way to walk with righteousness, grace, sharing forgiveness and words that will breathe a divine result.

Elijah understands about the people who are burdened with sin and the rigidness of Earth's challenges that are seemingly very severe, lending to the evidence of human inability to evolve over a long period of time if left alone.

As a given, the Centurions are confident that the "will" of the people will eventually come to a manageable level within themselves, to cope and understand what they are truly capable of.

This work in progress is classified under a genome study titled Stranded Identification Nucleases *(SIN)*. This became a highly successful campaign to influence most Earth societies by installing beliefs with the connection between Satan/Lucifer and sin *(SIN Personified)*. The SIN program was originally a genetic program to advance the human species, by inserting certain genetic codes and diseases for a more progressive evolution. Later on, the SIN program morphed from a physiological program to a psychological conditioning campaign based on fear, in order for mankind to behave better.

Halting these particular advancements of sequencing, gave way to a doctrine implemented in the thirteen hundreds. Even though, this program was terminated hundreds of years ago, it still has a strong hold on certain societies. Part of the new doctrine stated that the Zetas and related Factions can no longer exterminate major colonies abroad, using force, posing floods, earthquakes, epidemics, nuclear attacks or any other aggressive actions. Also, alien or hybrid leaders and or emperors were not permitted to engage, live or rule in public view, owing to this dogma *(1333)*.

The abandonment of the Faction's controlled colonies was necessary because the technological assistance from the Factions became daunting to the natural evolutionary process.

This purposely planned abandonment helped the survivors to spread throughout the land, keeping what they learned from the superior architects (Factions) and begin anew. Geographically scattered, a new blend of DNA was created and the melding with different cultures became apparent and sprung up nuances among societies.

Now man was free to go about the lands, not under totalitarian influence but this was short-lived. The societies were not moving in an acceptable direction, because the guidelines of change and moral standards became compromised. It was decided to then bring back certain revolting choices because of the immense volume of problems *(DNA Infractions)*.

The Zetas (Grays) had directed plagues to geographic areas of choice in the past; in addition they were involved with selective survival adjustment breeding and or completely remove an entire society because of concern for compromising the overall plan. The Zetas and other Factions felt this was the way to tame and limit cantankerous populations abroad, while controlling the DNA adjustments. This inevitably led to the demise of hundreds of millions of people on Earth but soon after, there was a new agreement limiting the Zetas to a ten year window of inducing diseases and monitoring/studying. This added to a better methodology and techniques to boost DNA advancements, with the cure to follow.

Elijah trying hard to understand the Zetas analytics when coming to science and the human genome, for Elijah is bitter on many accounts. One in particular is the various diseases installed directly into the original design of the human DNA and at any point in an individual's life, the Zetas can activate *(or just by stress)* any one of these numerous diseases for analytical studies. This was designed, because the Zetas explained that since mankind was not indigenous to the Earth, their DNA strands had to propagate accordingly, such as the natural selection of all the other indigenous populations throughout the worlds sectors.

Elijah learning that when any individual becomes infected, a case study is opened and activated, using a bio-frequency monitoring system, called Chrono-Vision *(Chrono-Vision has the ability to view (possess) every aspect of an individual person, animal, fish or insect)*. The Zetas utilize this technology to observe how the individual behaves, along with the reactions and levels of choices chosen by ones' self and or in a group or family setting, this is called the "Fellowship of Family Pack Study" *(family behavior and reactions)*.

There is also important data that details how the body reacts and fights the disease, while monitoring the will to survive, and coupled with results from medications. The results are factored into eventually adjusting and strengthening the DNA and are used to advance the evolutionary track for mankind.

Overstepping in certain instances the Zetas have employed a time temporal diversion, an unauthorized device that takes data results from the future. They use the device to eliminate people abroad whose offspring are not conducive to the required standards of the new world. In effect they use the personal Bio-Frequencies on innocent individuals and target them for elimination by activating diseases.

Elijah processes this information and contemplates what will be the best approach for major improvements, after considering all for what is to come.

Mission

Elijah has to choose a time period for his mission in which the results would have the most productiveness and would therefore be worthy of a religious movement. This was of the utmost importance to Elijah. He wondered if he could possibly use the probability program as assistance in this matter, but instead decided to turn to his superiors for guidance.

A compromise with his superiors was quite a challenge, but they agreed on Elijah being placed in the 9th century BC, to help boost mankind. Being in the post King Solomon Era at a time when the kingdoms were divided, with one kingdom to the south and one to the north. In the north was the Kingdom of Israel, which was ruled by Omri *(the first King to be mentioned in the Bible)*. Omri built temples in the representation of the Canaanite god. In the south was the Kingdom of Judah, whose leaders concentrated on and who stayed in the tradition of Moses' teachings, as worshiped in Jerusalem.

Omri had a son Ahab who eventually became the ruler of the Northern Territory. Ahab married the daughter of the King of Sidon in Phoenicia, who worshiped the foreign god called Baal. Ahab, looking to accelerate idol worship, implores his wife to convince the masses of people to the greatness of the god Baal. Ahab and his wife, entice the tribes from outside their country to join them on a quest of economic and spiritual bliss.

Elijah aware of these deceptive practices is appalled and furious, because one of his own has broken the prime directive of avoiding human interactions in this capacity. Elijah concluded that Ahab's ratchet narcissism had deluded himself into believing he was a Baal. As a Baal, he put himself before the people and portrayed himself as a god in order to receive worship from his people. In truth, Ahab exploited their ignorance. Elijah knows exactly what to do and confidently addresses Ahab and the people and tells them, "There will be years of drought upon this land, for the people of the land need to be reconciled."

Once this has commenced, Elijah leaves the land and meets with his superiors, who advise him to take care of the innocent and to ensure they will not be affected by the modified weather in selected locations.

Elijah sets forth from the city and is provided a Manna device by his superiors, to produce food from simplistic elements that will aid and assist the needy. Elijah gives it to a lady whose village is lacking food, she then shares it with many of her people, but at the same moment the woman's son dies suddenly. Her suspicion grows because of the timing death of her son, along with the odd Manna machine appearing at the same moment. She questions Elijah, that he is responsible.

Elijah converses with the elders and a decision is made, to tell Elijah to do what he feels is right, and that he no longer needs to consult with them. Elijah is then granted carte blanche because of his trustworthiness, positive traits and his decision making abilities.

Elijah returns to the lady and explains very little, but then kneels down alongside the woman's son; he slowly pushes away the hair from the son's forehead. Elijah's hand lies flat over the child's eyes, while the mother is on her knees repenting her sins, quivering as her voice scratches with hesitation and effort to pray. Elijah concentrates to increase the nimbus energy that emanates through his spirit. He then transfers a dynamic aura of veracity around the boy, causing the boy's own spirit to be retrieved, swayed in a magnetize direction back to the body and further joining to an already healed body.

The child is revived, *(this was the first known, of the raising of the dead by a prophet)* and the mother is hysterically thanking Elijah, "Whatever can I do, whatever can I do for you?" She cries. Elijah responds in making it clear that, "All the people should worship Yahweh, which is the one and only God, not an idol, rather the creator of heaven and of these worlds. Today you have seen and believed, but since the Creator cannot be seen, your faith will be your sight and your heart will build your love for him and each other, this will be done!" Elijah reassures her with a warm smile as he departs.

Elijah moves on to various regions and spreads the teachings of the "one God" and is highly successful bringing together the troubled tribes. By being innovative, Elijah shared some techniques that developed special skills within numerous tribes, but only certain techniques were given onto a particular tribe, so that each of the tribes had to share and trade with the other tribe villages.

After three years of drought and turmoil, Elijah announces his return to revisit Ahab and his Kingdom. Upon arrival, Elijah finds that there are many good faith people that adhered to what he spoke of three years prior, "The belief in one God." Yet, there was no change in the heart of Ahab and his ways. Elijah realizes he is going to continue to be stubborn and without contrition. Trying something new, Elijah attempts to challenge Ahab in a display of action and wit, but to no avail because Ahab refuses.

When Elijah announces that the three year drought is over, he then comes to the conclusion that he has captured the old devoted believers and does not need to sway Ahab.

Elijah reassured and convinced the people, of what was the resurrected platform of Moses. The majority of tribes and followers overcame the worship of Baal and devoted themselves to believe in one God, "Yahweh."

Chapter Eight

THE QUIETUS

As Elijah travels on foot alongside the river Jordan, heading to his next and last mission with only 30 days remaining. The silence surrounds him and his thoughts are in motion, appreciating the beauty of the river. Walking relaxed, he is at a distance from his destination. Suddenly, Elijah's body is drawn to see a sheen reflection in the sky, a vehicle of some sort. Quickly, his view turns from above to diagonally down across the horizon. Appearing in the distance is a man coming towards Elijah.

As the man gets closer, Elijah recognizes that it is Elisha, his replacement a month early. Elijah confused, tears out a warm boisterous nervous welcome. Elisha looks uneasy. Elijah can tell that there is something wrong, because Elisha's face is stern and concerned. Elijah then moves closer in the direction of Elisha, mutters, "What is wrong?" After his nervous greeting, then asks again, "What's wrong," but in a downward slur. Elisha answers, "Elijah, your father has just been found not well, drifting in his vessel in an odd area in space, out of our region. Aligious was discovered by a stranger that is not of this sector. This is all I could gather because of the difficulty in the time positioning sensors, I am sorry."

Elijah gazes down while he listens, head tilted and recites an old prayer in his mind, keeping silent while Elisha continues to speak, "I have brought the only ship that I could access immediately, so you can get to your father as soon as you can. I will stay here and take care of the rest of your works and they have been wonderful works Elijah." Elijah's throat constricts and barely gets out a, "Thank you," then turns to the river Jordan and realizes that the small chauffeured hover shuttle ship cannot pick him up on the sandy area.

Patiently, the ship hovers high waiting for his command. Elijah then unties part of his garment around his neck and rolls up his mantle cloth and uses it to hold a "magnetic field disburser." He wraps it in a cloth because of the heat and high temperatures that are reached when using the apparatus.

Elijah raises his now tightened wrapped mantle and thrusts downward quickly, striking the surface of the river. Immediately the water divides, parting the river as a bustle of energy, sounding similar to a swarm of flying locusts. Energy surrounds Elijah, followed by the lifting of the river waters, to form sides of liquid curved walls on either portion of the river and establishing a firm area for the ship to land. The water defying the laws of gravity spurts up no higher than a man. Clearing this large graveled area, the dam of liquid water is holding, but resisting the southern flow of the river. The men have to move fast, because an accumulation of raised water levels.

Elijah has to hurry and signals the Hover ship to the cleared pickup point. The ship hovers while bright lights in a triangulated pattern erupt, spewing out an orange and red glare. A whirlwind circumventing the immediate area creates sprays of mist from the liquid curved walls. A beam of light is about to surround Elijah, as he quickly tosses his rolled up mantle with the disburser to Elisha who is moving back towards the bank, watching the river close back up. Elisha looking across at Elijah, while he is ascending into the vessel, makes eye contact and motions a serious stern stare to Elijah in a manner of prayer.

Back a few days ago.

A space time continuum alarm is generated days before to the Time Flexion Security Team. The security team is on alert and in place to respond to any time disturbance. The Reckon Cipher locate calculation settles in position at systems 1444.5 Moon alt, mark 12.2015 by -3.303, the Moon's orbital area. Awaits and anticipates someone or something to appear in this approximate location.

A flash of energy suddenly appears on the security teams monitor. They initiate an immediate pursuit, knowing that all their counter plans are in place. The Flexion Security Team is now on an intercept course of action approaching a foreign vessel; pyramidical in its appearance and noting that it is a non familiar ship.

The security team quickly begins to cross reference all possible vehicles in the data base, yet unable to find a match. Consequently, after scanning the visitor's ship, the team detects two life readings, one a Centurion and the other unknown. The security team lowers their alert level and attempts to hail the detected ship, but before they do, the foreign vessel sends a request to communicate. Surprised, but quick to react, the team security leader responds and curtails the recipient with a standard greeting message. Fascinated, how the foreign entity quickly answers in the native Centurion language, using metaphors of a vernacular quality. Nonetheless, the message was to the point and understood, "Aligious is not well and found unconscious, adrift in his vessel very far from his observatory mark."

The security team is well aware, after the scan, that Aligious bears the final stages of his three hundred seventy six year old life, signifying the closing of the unpredictable natural life cycle of a Centurions lifespan or patinas, which was now becoming irregular and episodic.

This bedimmed somber natural phenomenon, is the clustering process of micro vibratory pulses that weaken the generative magnetism field that surrounds the individual, while naturally transposing throughout the body of a Centurion.

While the patina (Spirit Energy of a Centurion) loses the gravitational grasp on the body, the lighted energy is being repelled away from the body, slowly dissolving into the expiry vortices. This final stage of a Centurion's life is known as the "Quietus," an activated transition, because of the patinas inability to cling on to the physical body of this world/life.

Aligious unfortunately, is in the last stages of the Quietus, unable to talk because the stages within the Quietus are based on a forty hour transformation. During the first twenty hours of the forty hour window, the person is conscious and able to communicate, however they become limited in their functions as the spirit is gathering energies above the body for its final transformation/departure.

This Centurion all knowing process is the unequivocal understanding that the spirit itself is from a slice of divine energy, eons ago from the beginning design of the Universe. A privately formed spirit is dimensionless *(invisible)* in any universal reality. The spirit itself never leaves the realm in which it was originally created from *(a host to matter)*. Even though the temple of the body is merely able to hold and accommodate the visiting spiritual entity *temporarily*, it is exclusive to the length of the lease on life; coinciding that the body is of working order.

Until the deterioration and breakdown of the anatomy or patinas while alive, the soul has the ability to collect "Spiritualistic Nutritives," *intellectual energy*. The positive nutritive energy accumulates from only the good works one produces during life, giving the spirit stored nutritives, *(fuel)* and automatically quantifies the amount of choices to be reached in the afterlife.

Bear in mind that the body/temple which was formed and gathered from millions of years of molecular material, *(stardust)* needs a host in order to exist in a final dimension. This renewal/recycled process, give the gift of the conscious mind and the spirit's ability to establish its own choices with free will.

The intellectual energy is established by overcoming adversities and making the correct choices. The more positive outcomes from your choices you have or obstacles you overcome, is the nutritive reward *(Choices Define Existence)*. This reasoning is why the lion devours the lamb. Without this negative or the underlined positive, you would not be you, and or have a free will to do what you do here or how many times you try in this life or the next. The utmost importance from within the proverbial old soul is to lift and guide your temple/body with your spirit. Within a lifecycle, the spirit borrows your body/material/matter and therefore, *you must return it.)*

The next twenty hours of the Quietus, the mind/body is non cognitive, while the separation process from the spirit will have already begun. For Elijah, there remains only a small window of opportunity to see his father, who meant everything to him. Elijah is rushing and must see this sacred transitioning of his father, but it is becoming more evident that Elijah will have little or no time left because the very last hours of Aligious' life is at hand. Elijah focused and en route while information is racing about his mind. He understands, in emergency situations such as this, that there is no allowance for time overlap travels. It is not permitted under any circumstances to scud time, even for a high ranking member of the elite Council, such as Aligious.

Yesterday:

The security team is now engineering a connective field transfer between the foreign ship and their own. The information from the security team's findings is immediately being channeled through to the time period where Elijah is stationed. Elijah will soon learn who the stranger was that rescued his father.

Soon after, Elijah receives a portion of data, stating that the stranger is from the Andromeda Galaxy. This galaxy is an immeasurable distance from this sector in space, even though it is our closest neighboring galaxy.

Nevertheless, the benevolent entity (person) stated that they have been using a cloaked monitoring system on our sector for all of the Genesis Projects performed. For a millennium this species has been observing this sector through a subspace *(frequency linked)* program called View Finder. Their View Finder monitoring stations receive alarm signals when an unusual occurrence appears out of the norm and immediately triggers a detection ping. Which, fortunately for Aligious, his vessel was detected drifting, then located and was brought to the attention of their species alert detectors.

Knowingly, the entities were aware how important Aligious was to our inhabiting sector. Therefore, the foreign male species called Archan, and he alone had made the decision to "break" the prime directive of his world, *(not to interfere with species on personal matters)* hence the rescue of Aligious in the adrift ship.

This species was never seen before by the Centurions. The Centurions were quite astonished at the species many attributes, mainly their way of communicating. They used a lighted sound vibration that had a spiral delivery system. Another intriguing characteristic was that their anatomy had textured skin and appeared shiny, as the look of white light shimmering on their body's surface.

The initial information on this species was overwhelming. However, at this time the team is in the midst of the exchange, levitating the body moving slowly through interstellar space in an energy field connecting the two ships. The field array in space is very bright and has two yellowish parallel beams with a helix coil, circulating and spinning an angular field of lighted magnetic energy. This let the separate parties to safely open hatches to release and trap the proper concentration of air to be delivered into the tube like energy-field chamber.

Aligious is now transferred safely into the security team vessel, and the team disengages the levitation retrieval signal, as the outer energy-fields power down. The security team vessel proceeds to the far-side of the Moon, to the city of Columbia. They are met by a decorated dispatch team to take Aligious to the comfort of his own dwelling, where he and Elijah lived. The group enters into Aligious' home using a levitating gurney to bring his body to the center part of the dwelling for the most energetic positioning, facing his body east to west, with his elbows pointing north and south.

Aligious is lying still as his light becomes brighter above his body's surface and dimmer from within. His hands are one on top of each other, right over left and his head is slightly elevated. Aligious is alone as the group exits the home, surrounded by all the momentous objects that he and his son have collected through the years.

Words had transpired throughout the sector that the last hour had begun for Aligious. Multitudes of people are outside the dwelling. Amongst the crowd are the heads of state and sectors, patiently waiting besides the dwelling to support Elijah during this private Quietus.

Elijah in flight, is about to reach his base transfer point, eager as he stares at the ship that he is going to be taking. From a distance Elijah contemplates his next move, even though his ship has not landed yet. He addresses the pilot to hold a safe distance to the landing area, a few measures above the floor.

Elijah jumps out of the hover craft, hustles over to his waiting "single man" transport vehicle, ready to launch. He quickly approaches the diamond shaped forward time travel distribute ship and enters. Elijah is familiar with this style ship and understands its amazing high speed capabilities. Elijah offers a thank you to the men that prepared the ship to the proper coordinates. He then proceeds with take off and brings the ship out of Mount Horeb, taking a curved path to the marked entrance of the wormhole about twelve miles in distance from his starting point.

Coming to his mark, he engages and is now feeling the result of time warp, still in all he is feeling the pulling effect and feels tingles throughout his body. His thoughts settle as he becomes melancholy. Picturing his father in the final stages of a Centurion's life and having the same repetitive mirrored helpless image thought occurrence. He frantically lets his emotions flood his thinking. Defenseless, he sees an image of his father being absorbed into the abyss. While his thoughts continue to run wild, his eyes mount pressure, resisting tears of sorrow.

Elijah pushes onward with his overwhelming sorrowful feelings. A sudden pop occurs and Elijah is only a short distance from Earth's young satellite. He then takes a deep breath and is flushed right back into reality, his heart and eyes focused on his destination. Thereupon, Elijah takes the manual controls of the ship and speeds up to an extreme rate of speed and because of the hypersonic acceleration, he has to arc a connective path in order to enter the opening on the far-side of the Moon. He turns the ship sharp into the entrance, but the ship is going too fast, so Elijah slams the field engines in reverse, flushed for two seconds. This makes the ship fall sideways in a drift. He immediately pops the vehicle back into forward acceleration, forcing the ship to whip ahead into a stable safe level of control. Despite this high risk maneuver, Elijah successfully arrives in an instant. Once inside he spins the craft 180 degrees and slingshots to his old dwelling, inasmuch alerted to the fact that crowds of people are amongst his dwelling grounds.

Elijah carefully approaches safely once closer to the landing site. He comes to a quiet halt above the area and then lowers the vehicle to the side of the dwelling. Elijah looks out the windows of the vessel as he shuts down the vehicle and is taken back as he notices the droves of people lining the grounds, even some heads of states from different sectors. He is flabbergasted by the number of people gathered to pay their respects.

Elijah has settled the ship as close to the house as possible and exits the vehicle. He passes a portion of the crowd as he approaches the front entryway. Decorated heads of Factions salute and give respectful gestures to him, along with associates and other people praying in a sorrowful state.

After receiving careful pats on his shoulders, he fell to numbness. Following a breath of silence, he enters the dwelling somber and solo, focused on his father as he approaches. His eyes are shiny with blurred vision as he slows his motion and moves closer to his father.

Paralyzed as he sees the light particles hover and slowly recollect above his father's still body. The full completion in the gathering of spiritualistic light is approaching. Elijah looks up and inwardly smiles as he glances at a rock that he and his father had laughed about because it looked like a monkey.

His feelings quickly reversed and his airways become restricted to a choked sob. Elijah then looks down at his father while sliding and turning his hand upright underneath his father's overlapped hands. He bends his fingers to grasp the right hand of Aligious, holding it tight.

While Elijah has one knee to the floor, he tilts his head down as a deluge of emotions flow through his head, as pressure builds up from behind his eye sockets. He then pulls his father's arm towards his chest and strains his grip, as he embellishes and presses his father's hand against his heart. Holding on for dear life, rocking back and forth, Elijah murmurs then chunters, wishes for time to stop. Elijah knows that these are the last moments. His voice is rattled and musters out these broken words, "I want, will be, like you, you are everything. Promise to keep you close, all to my heart, will promise to give, all because of you. I'll make you proud with love."

Elijah feeling helpless, ruffled, goes blank and stares at nothing while in shock. As the dazed look fades, he looks and peers right into Aligious' eyes and releases a stuttered cry with a nervous short laugh. He then takes his left hand and settles his fingertips on his father's right shoulder, pats once and then grips firmly and tells him, "Choose paradise Father, I will miss you and hold you here." Elijah motions his faint fist tapping against his heart, then says his last words to his father and repeats, "Please choose paradise!"

Elijah is moved by the suddenness of the glorious radiance gleaming about Aligious. Elijah distraught becomes stunned and feels his chest and stomach retract as all the pores of his body open. He becomes fixated and mesmerized in the acceptance that his father's spiritual aura was about to be completed. Elijah rises from his knelt position and stands hunched over the sparkling light, realizes that this is now where his father is, and no longer within his body. Elijah stretches while still leaning over the luminescence of spiritual light and tries to reach out to flutter his hand in the glistening energy, but is afraid.

As the energy is starting to slowly deplete into the vortices, Elijah becomes filled with love and brings himself cautiously closer, about to touch the light that hovers above his father. He carefully starts to pet the field of glittered particles as a moist smile enters his expression, saying good bye to his father. As the third teardrop from Elijah disappears into the dissolving remaining light, then so does his father. Thus, the "Quietus" is over.

Whilst the spirit is being called to the afterlife, it is known amongst the Centurions as the "Revivification Passing."

Chapter Nine

MINISTRY CONCLUSION

Elijah stated in his ministry and concluded that the work of Moses and other profits have been somewhat undone. The Elders were in agreement and extremely frustrated, but Elijah's ministration did steer this sector back on track for now. It is well known, the world would need thousands of Elijah/s to keep a sustainable order. Elijah thinking that there must be a better way. Then prays, "Oh dear God, what can be done to keep the people on track without them straying away?" Elijah's ministry was from 852 BC to 860 BC (Old Testament) one year beyond his required stay within the territory. Now in present day, there are various religions that recognize this great prophet for his teachings and his monumental accomplishments. Elijah was a band of action, with numerous miracles of weather, multiplying food, countless healing of the sick and strengthening the family unit.

Elijah's list of outstanding miracles:

Shutting the heavens and stopping the rain for three years (1 Kings 17:1)
Oil multiplied, the grain increased daily, the widow woman (1 Kings 17:2)
Widow's son raised from the dead (1 Kings 17:22, 23)
Fire from heaven on the soaked altar (1 Kings 18:38)
Rain returns (1 Kings 18:45)
Fire brought down on the 51 soldiers (2 Kings 1:10)
Fire brought down of the second 51 soldiers (2 Kings 1:12)
The parting of the river Jordan (2 Kings 2:8)

Ministry Conclusion

Elijah's life is noted in history (Old Testament only) as the "Wonder Worker" during his ministry. He is noted as one of the greatest prophets that ever lived, but as the future unfolds, Elijah becomes one of the most influential people in the history of humanity!

It has been said that Aligious was the architect of the "Old Testament" and from the Dead Sea scrolls, fragments point to Elijah being responsible for the "New Testament." His relationship to Jesus/Yeshua as a mentor goes far beyond from the original writings.

The fragments from "The Book of Elijah," have been omitted from the New Testament (withheld), understandably, but as the future unfolds, it reveals the connection between the Old and New Testaments are one and the same!

"They as a species have learned that the deficiency or neutrality sense of behavior in ones' life, fuels no energy to the spirits' passage. The conscious actions, thoughts and decisions that have a positive result is the heart & betterment of a wide array of all things in the spirit's choice. He, who has the will to thrust that spirit, yet not unto an aesthetic distance, but with the discretionary love and divinity, is to elevate choices for ones' sequential destiny."

Elijah

Chapter Ten

CAVE INNOVATION

Aligious' death upsets Elijah greatly and so he leaves to go back to the distant past onward to Judah, where he embarks on a journey of spiritual cleansing, thus traveling the desert for forty days. This pilgrimage was something that Elijah was not required to do, unlike many other prophets who were required. The Elders chose Elijah not because his father was Aligious, but for the mere fact that Elijah was gifted. The Elders wanted Elijah to start his ministry as soon as he completed the school for Prophesiers, as he did with an excellent outcome.

Following his father's demise, his thoughts strained on his conscience. So without notifying anyone, Elijah journeyed to a specific time period only known to him, to start a pilgrimage in the rocky barren Judaean Desert. After three days missing, the Elders had tracked his whereabouts, yet not alerting Elijah of their presence. While monitoring him during the morning of the thirtieth day, the guardians had to intercede and place bread with water beside him for every morning until the fortieth day was completed. This was the practice for all Prophets/Seers during the journey of divine spiritual cleansing *(desert)* pilgrimages.

Elijah is finishing his final days of his journey of spiritual cleansing. Still in need of answers, his mind starts to drift and begins to think about how the Elders were so concerned with his well being and how they searched to find him in order to supply him with nourishment. Thinking of this, he has a flashback to when he and his father were walking along a huge cluster of gardens set up in trifoliate pattern. He proceeded to ask his father's permission to pick and take one of the flowers to bring home, because they were all so vibrant and so many. His father said, "If you take just one flower from the garden, would the next person who lays their eyes upon them, would they see the same beautiful floral arrangement that gave you such joy? Elijah, this moment reminds me of a story my father told me. He asked me if I tended to a large flock of sheep and one of the herd was lost, would I search for the one, even though you have so many? Then he proceeded to say, "There will be more joy over one sinner who repents, than many righteous people who need no repentance." Elijah shakes his head with gratitude in his heart, recalling the words he had spoken to his father during the Quietus, giving him the extra energy needed to complete the forty days.

At the end of the pilgrimage, his destination is just two days away. He should be within the vicinity and able to steer his way to the grotto entrance located at the site of Mount Horeb. On this mount is a cave near the summit, where Moses received the Ten Commandments over millennia ago. Within this summit is the entrance to an old facility where his father had worked and shared some of his experiences with Elijah a long time ago. Undoubtedly, getting to Mount Horeb becomes a near death experience for Elijah. He has now been without proper food, water and technology and is becoming dangerously dehydrated for close to six weeks, with still reoccurring thoughts of Aligious.

Fortunately, during his ministry as well as this journey, he was monitored and again looked after by the Elders. In this instance, even after the 40 days were up, Elijah was still supplied with small nutritional rations of food when he awoke, this after his long arid land pilgrimage. The strain was so severe that Elijah felt like he was going to die, but did not lose his faith.

Elijah's father's death continues to weigh heavy on his heart; he then was precipitated into a state of conflict, of mind, body and soul. The aftermath of his journey lingers within him, as he seeks his destination of refuge. Elijah meanders his way to the old genetics facility base called "Sinai" in Mount Horeb. He was very familiar with the facility, but by and large an abandoned vast emptiness of space at this time, with the exception of a small segment of the complex that is used as a monitoring station.

Elijah being very familiar with the grounds within the mountain walls, looks up from a distance to see the cave/tursina of Moses and is now at the foothill of Mount Horeb *(Jabel)* standing still.

His emotions are running high. Suddenly, his left leg collapses as his knee lands to the sand, creating a pounding sound as the light sand grains whisk about his leg while he grasps his emotions.

Elijah releases a grunt of exhaustion. He then places his right elbow crossed onto his top thigh, leaning on his bent perpendicular right leg. He then captures his head with his hand as it swept forward in its decent. His face rested hidden in the palm of his hand as he prays, "Father, who is heaven, ask God if I can receive the goodness of *(His)* Glory and the Greatness of *(His)* Graces, thy will it, please!"

Elijah intense in admiration has conflicting thoughts staring at the sand, still with no movement. He feels a tear roll pass his cheek towards the right side of his chin, with more to follow. Elijah sees a transparent drop, unfocused and cloudy as it wisps towards the sand, hearing the soft tear tap the land as it becomes absorbed. As the tearstained grains of sand receive a cascade of sorrow, his dampened face facilitates a diffused expression. Suddenly, with his head down, a vibrancy of sunlight reappears from behind a cloud, casting a shimmering appeal to the wet specks of sand, looking like lighted crystals and reminding Elijah of his father's Quietus.

Nonetheless, still melancholy and indecisive, he unexpectedly recalls and hears Aligious saying, "Worrying is just a poor way of praying." Elijah pauses and becomes filled with a strong feeling of nostalgia. Then remembers what his father mentioned when he was younger, "You can throw all your sins into the depths of the sea and God will forgive you, and to show His love for you. He will put up a "No fishing sign!" Aligious then restated this saying when Elijah was older, stating, "God forgives all our sins, except for one, if you do not repent, you cannot have forgiveness, unless you are sorry for your sins." Elijah spurts a quick and short chortle murmur, while he clears a restricted knot from his throat.

At this time Elijah rises to stand while closing his eyelids as he looks in the direction of the sun. Motionless, he wipes away the liquid that surrounds his irritated eyes.

Elijah enters the cave through an old air duct he used to play in when he was a child, insofar to remember a sliding technique that he hasn't done in many years. Pursuing slowly he will now be entering the chamber that will lead him to his old quarters. In the branches of corridors Elijah is passing different rooms and notices a haven of technological parts and materials. He becomes furthermore intrigued and stops to look into some of the laboratory rooms which spans to an endless view.

Elijah enters into a vast area with huge high ceilings. It is a hanger used for lodging assorted vessels, yet he only sees maybe two operable ships, the rest is barren or with missing pieces. Finally, Elijah reaches his long ago stateroom, which is located at the rear of the facility with easy access to the surface. Upon opening the door he sees that everything is more or less intact, as it was left all those years ago. Elijah spent many years in this location before his ministry began.

The room inspired a happy thought but then immediately his face reverts to a drawn look that suddenly comes upon him. He reminisces about the past and now that his father is gone, he is inundated with sad feelings of loneliness.

Elijah experiences bouts of depression, which lasts for a duration of time, followed by agony, lack of ambition and enthusiasm with no motivation. Suddenly, gravitated in one moment of time, a proposition enters into his deep thoughts, sparked by a single drop of water causing ripples in a basin. He thinks about his devote promises to his father and the fact that he vowed to keep them dear.

Elijah's thoughts crossed on the idea that the present religious movement was lacking effectiveness because of the many avenues of inconsistencies. He realizes that it will no longer be adequate to use holographic imagery or magically draw on buildings to impress and sway man. Even resorting to weather controlling tactics to win over the hearts of many humans as a fear or power tactic was no longer an option. These methods are no longer accepted to be effective. Elijah prays, "I will persevere to find the answers and I am to be here in Your presence oh God, so that I may do Your will."

Elijah adapts quickly into a daily routine. At sunrise he walks to the cuisine counter which reads and scans your individual anamorphic anatomy and automatically prepares foods to ingest according to the incremental adjustments that are needed to bring your body up to perform at an optimum focused level. This efficient dieting was what Elijah was lacking ever since his father's Quietus.

Also, in this eatery there is a hyperbaric preserver processor that synthesizes organic material by multiplying the molecules of the nutrients for practically an endless production of nutritional material. While in consumption mode, Elijah has to be doing something in addition to just eating, he must multitask. He is always working in a utilitarian style. He loves to rummage through the compound gathering any material that is interesting to him and brings it back to the largest most advanced laboratory.

Strict with fastidious organization skills, he lines up items and categorizes each and every individual part of his collection. Elijah concludes this is essential for innovation, aside from obtaining a legitimate amount of exercise in order to keep sharp and non lethargic. Elijah often finds himself for hours taking apart and searching for certain key significant components in and on the abandoned crafts. He believes in having an assorted collection for an easy, *everything at your fingertips*, type of preparation for great probable selection.

All and all, Elijah puts aside the time to take daily strolls over to the secondary leg of the complex to interact with the monitoring staff, even though he has a brutal regiment work schedule and long arduous days.

Historical Data

Months have passed and Elijah is now reviewing the historic data on the various religions of the Factions, wondering about the effects that were positive. Elijah is very comfortable in his semi octagon layout of holographic and crystalline monitors, running research programs interjecting certain algorithms and overlapping keywords, searching for definitive results. He is a one man enterprise who doesn't believe in chairs but would rather have all the equipment propped up at shoulder height.

Elijah's spirits are the highest they have been in a while and now that he is focused, he is becoming super efficient as he rapidly flows through an unprecedented amount of historic information. He is fascinated with certain eras in time. Though, he pauses his research when he comes across the DNA *(Deoxyribonucleic acid)* data, which is connected to the coincidence term," Distributors National Alliance." This was the alliance and agreement amongst the twelve Factions, for an individual Faction to distribute their own DNA throughout the geographical land which they accepted. From these agreements came the introduction to a special blend of DNA, *(Y-MRCA)* the inception of Adam. Y-MRCA *(DNA)* was agreed upon to become the foundation of the Human-Kind Species to inhabit Earth.

This "Planetary Union" agreement, settled and chose the Centurion class of DNA as the best basis for humankind, because it had the closest results or match, for the atmospheric conditions coupled with the size and density of the Earth's gravitational compression. Therefore, the majority of the "mixed DNA" was applied as the foundation for Centurion/Human DNA on Earth.

The secondary portion of the genome would be distributed and modified amongst the individual twelve Factions, along with twelve variants within each single faction, leaving 144 total DNA sequences to be mixed and distributed to specific geographical locations around the globe. The Factions, representing 12 variations of DNA, would have the ability to choose one of the many primate blends among the lands of the Earth. The DNA would be used as a basis of up to 99% of that primates DNA.

According to the chosen animals indigenous qualities of DNA, the new species *(humans)* will benefit from the harmonious adaptabilities formed along eons ago by the already established and evolved DNA from these Earth primitive creatures.

(Note: there are an extremely high percentage of primates DNA blended with a sub-level/ low percentage of other indigenous species, such as marsupial, insects and aquatic creatures)

Consequently, multiple DNA transfers induces the birth of the new Human species, which lays credence for the "reasoning" of present day mankind's misconception and misleading assumption of the origination theory of being of African descent. This notion steers mankind into a confusing mutation theory which has slight merit, but that is not the case.

Elijah scrolls further and comes upon a list of results that are inherent towards the Faction choices of DNA with their geographical locations, exclusive to the Earth:

Centurion	Primate	Faction	Location
FOXP2	27GTTGG	ZETA	ASIA
FOXP2	6OBPP/GWGG	ELDS	AFRICA
FOXP2	TCSO68	ANILIANS	INDIA
FOXP2.	6MSCS4	CETIANS	S. EUROPE
FOXP2	RZCPK14	ARCHURIANS	N. EUROPE
FOXP2	TGG45	PELEIDIANS	PN. ISLANDS
FOXP2	7CBCF29	SIRAINS	BALTIC'S
FOXP2	LBTLC5.	RENDIANS	C. AMERICA
FOXP2	IPMMP29	MINTAKAS	N. AMERICA
FOXP2	4RKK	NAZCANS	S. AMERICA
FOXP2	LBTLC831	ANNUNAKI	MIDDLE EAST
FOXP2	29PBP	CENTURIONS	AUSTRALIAN

Related information is displayed on Elijah's left monitor, which explains the basic seeding process for the basis of planet Earth, along with the current statistics on miscegenation (mix) and biodiversity arrangement of cultures.

Elijah's conceptual thought is that it is going to be a very difficult to bring all the different cultures and ethnic hearts of many to join in one religious multilateral effort with a unison outcome.

More assembled data is combined into two views, concluding measures that are taken from the extreme past. Elijah is engrossed in the release and deposit of prehistoric animals, mostly for the sowing of North America. These deposits also included some reptilian creatures from the Rendian's home planet. Most came from Earths indigenous species, from the preexisting Earth, before the Moon was created/constructed.

When the Moon was constructed in the very remote past, these wonderful creatures would have died out and be forever lost because of the creation of the *new* Moon. The release and deposits of most dinosaurs were done millions of years ago mostly in North America. Only handfuls of dinosaurs would be released around the globe. This was done primarily not to cause logical disconcerts in the future for man to question their global existence.

It was necessary to spread myths throughout societies about their development. It is a fallacy that the bones from these overall large animals are the reason for the current day natural oil or energy materials. The dinosaurs would thrive and live for millions of years on planet Earth. Then very surprisingly the Council agreed to exterminate these large creatures by the use of antimatter initialized fusion. This happen sixty-four million years in the past as evidence provided in the Earth's rock sediment *(Xenon)*.

These nuclear propulsion pulse detonations spread throughout an enormously wide area, leaving radioactive deposits. The evidence left behind in the sediment is called, *transuranic actinides*. These deposits can be measured decisively even till this current day. The remnants and historic documents not only indicate that there were exterminations applicable to animal control, but in addition many cities and unacceptable societies, were also extinguished during the Earths' development. Other methods for the removal of past civilizations were the ice-age, floods and plagues.

The positive results from this new agenda and actions, introduced not only the much needed DNA upgrade adjustment, but provided new moral and religious foundations *(e.g. Book of Genesis)*.

Elijah sneers at a note that was attached to the historic documents, claiming that the people among these tragedies did not die in vain. It stated that they were contributory to the event and is still a part of the natural history of Earth that helped mankind develop into what they are today. Yet Elijah couldn't help think that the people should have been relocated, to live out the remaining part of their lives, instead of enduring these unacceptable fierce deaths. Furthering his thoughts on these blatant decisions of human replacement, he sighs wondering about the biological results. Accordingly, once the species has blossomed to an acceptable satisfactory interval, the DNA is extracted then enhanced. Following the re-release, this hopefully after a multitude of modifications over the millennia, will allow the evolutionary last milestone to come to fruition.

Elijah is about to retire for the night as he finishes organizing his collections of certain historical documents that are pertinent in developing a clear precise goal and in formulating a plan.

Elijah is in deep thought, due to the fact that the generic approach to religions resulted in multiple systemic behaviors that have led to controversy, along with an adversarial role, such as revolts and the separation of human societies.

Walking to his flat (room), he develops a sense of how the Architect of these worlds created an infinite amount of marvels and fractional portions of everything, by using creative energies that are in each and everything. He ponders that it stands to reason why we all are attracted to prayer in various ways in order to be connected to this Creative Force. He contemplates, "Wouldn't it be wonderful to take the conditioning of faith with prayer and enable a physical as well as conscious continuity with the Creator." Elijah thoughts overlap, "By emulating that conscience thought into an undeniable supplicant thread and being indivisible from the origin of the Creative Force, yet visible or type of awareness at a constant.

Elijah arriving into his quarters winding down his routines, voices out-loud a line of questions; "How do I make that connection? How can I equate the best and greatest outcome? I need to visualize," Elijah stops mid sentence and becomes quiet and falls back into his chair, turns slightly while staring up. Remembering a moment from his childhood, when his father brought him to a building completion ceremony of an Erudition dwelling. He visualizes a communion ritual with his father and colleagues sharing bread, drinking wine and pouring dabs of that wine on the inscribed cornerstone, thus remembering the speech clearly.

> *"To the bread that nourishes our bodies, to the particles of all who has lived and of the wine that replenishes our heartening souls. As to afar nobler harmonious life. Onward, to creating equality and gratitude, of which is to come. Live as one with-all!"*

Elijah

Innovation

Relaxed in a leaned backward position, Elijah is reminiscing and figuring that certain things cannot be seen, while looking at the aged ceiling. He recalls that the unseen can be measured and detected by field sensors found in assimilation programs for anomalies; such as wormholes, magnetic fields and other invisible manifestations. Elijah gets excited, stands up while clinching his fist, "Yes!" readily connects with one of his father's quotes, "That certain things can't be seen, but can be visualized." This was a phrase heard on more than one occasion by Elijah and first spoken by Aligious at the building ceremony. Elijah realizes that through his deciphering ability, is the key to his success to create a divine connection. "To see what can't be seen." The true form of reality, aside from any measurements or assimilation programs, is to recognize something new that doesn't exist.

It was the start of a new day and Elijah enters his laboratory eager to run his own probability programs. He begins by looking at the archives that surround him and then delves in. He concentrates on the quantum physics algorithms while simultaneously running data searches for special animal eye lenses that come from blind creatures. Elijah's eyes focus on a portion of the monitor listing numerous Troglodytes, along with explanations to show that the cave dwelling creatures nervous systems are so unique.

Also displayed in a different category is a single final search result out of all the tens of thousands of planetary permissible life entities that exist throughout the sector and the final result was the "flatworm." He then takes the important data from these creatures that are millions of years old and combines the selective Troglodytes information into a new elevated propagated data stream. He turns to another console, bringing up information on microbiology, nanotechnology and subatomic particle studies simultaneously to cross reference, while having the fundamentals of quantum physics displayed.

He is wondering about conglomerates of disorder regarding matter and suddenly he hesitates, because of a memorable thought that breaks his concentration. He hears an old voice in his head saying, "The answer is usually simplicity for conflicting problems. When things are too hard to cope with, or a problem arises, the resolution was almost all the time *simple.*

Elijah smiles and feels less anxious as he looks over the basics for the spatial fabric that makes up space and time. He studies the equation E=MC2+S, then meditates in a deep thought, starring and studying the formula. *(E)*, meaning the energy that equals mass *(M)*, multiplied by the speed of light squared *(C2)*, plus the motion or stir/spiral *(S)*, that someone or something has to engage consciously, even if one is to assume that the speed of light is the action of motion shift/stir. Elijah thinks rapidly in his mind, "Would this only be one accord? The assumption that light is at a constant, when actually in our reality there is an inconstancy of every single thing. As for the equation itself, should I subtract the stir/spiral *(S)* from the equation or not. Nevertheless, I have to form a link between subatomic particles in an actual organized spiral distortion, in order to perfect the knowledge of bio-frequencies and the modalities of vorticular dynamics as it relates to the quantum meshwork for spatial anomalies." Elijah'sNote:E=MC2+S=R-recycle?

> *"Everything invented has been reinvented 99.9%*
> *of the time, but necessary for all times."*
> *Aligious*

Convex Spectacles

Elijah is now focused on making a visual apparatus to see what cannot be seen. According to his findings and through a customary program, he is going to search for the best probability result. He is attempting to create a non-invasive bio-electric frequency signal that is a couple of inches above the bridge, on a pair of goggle like spectacles. Elijah strongly feels the apparatus could be the key to the connectivity of the almighty creative force or even possibly God, *(Allah, Elohim, Yahweh, Jehovah)*. This hopefully can be done by simulating the milliwatt frequencies of the flatworm's nervous systems signals and modifying eye lenses from key cave creatures. Elijah is digitally decoding the pulses for electro-magnetic emissions from and to the brain, while capturing the fluctuation and cycles of a hertz pattern *(equal to one cycle per second)*.

Next, it would require the identification of a person's own custom bioelectric field signature with minor adjustments made to match the neuronal activity of that particular brain. That would then allow the aligning fluctuation patterns of the magnetic flux lines to form a constricted direction and allow a constant signal. This would then give a clear view to be sustained through the field lenses, and optics, in order to witness the dimensionless darkened matter or other anomalies.

Elijah is now eagerly contemplating as he leans on the high-top table. His left elbow rests against the table and his torso bends forward as he settles his head comfortably in his left hand. The palm of his hand is pressed up against his forehead and his thumb and index fingers are on either side of his temples. While massaging his temples, he tries to relax and allows his thoughts to flow through a meditative mindset.

He then focuses his thoughts on the pineal gland, which is also known as the conarium. He recollects that the pineal gland is a small gland known for its hormone secretion, located in the dorsal, upper vertebrate. It is at the center bottom of the thalamus hemispheres portion of the brain. This grey pinkish organ duct, that looks like an Alpinia/Ginger tropical flower and is about the size of a pine nut, *(1/4 of an inch)* located laterally and positioned in the thalamic body, assisting the production of spinal fluid.

Elijah is trying to visualize this photoreceptive gland, so-called third parietal eye or an inner "Third Eye Wave" as called by scientists hundreds of millennia ago. It possesses divine importance and has powerful abilities. It has been identified as an invisible God-tether (link) that is a beacon transponder located at the pineal center of the brain.

This central activation location emits a detected measured signal that travels to a magnetically intelligent records field. Called by many Factions, the "Hall of Records", which is a timeless inter-dimensional connection of all that is, was and will be. It connects all the lives one has chosen, all that you are, all that you do and records your every moment. It accounts for every breeze that flows unto your body, along with every living entity that has ever lived or been accounted for since the beginning of creation.

Encrypted in the "Records Field" is believed to have a direct connection to the Creator, or a biological frequency that cannot be seen, only measured and felt. Elijah is aimlessly trying to gather thoughts while looking through the figures and facts. He attempts to blend in anything that appears to be related to the connective frequency.

Elijah ponders the thought that the energy within the spectacle's bridge source emitter could be directed to the pineal gland and then linked to layered sheets of sensory-related receptors, similar to that of the flatworm. The sensory input from the user's eyes can be combined with the modified sensory systems including the thought center, the limbic or hypothalamus emotional systems, as well as the auditory cortex for sound absorption.

Elijah drags information from multiple displays in a smooth rhythmic fashion, tries to move quickly to keep up with his train of thoughts. He mulls over the fact that intermittently transmitting and decoding the resonance frequency to the thalamus, acts as a relay station. This will send the oscillated information to be received and delivered to the optic tectum area of the brain. This paired structure is the major component that must work as one with the lens field in order to produce the image.

Elijah has figured that a miniature variable wireless auto-adjust knob, would be the key component in viewing the assorted array of the inter-dimensional phenomenon. Now the focusing could be done manually. A wireless connection to each categorized program of the bioelectric signature has to be aligned, in order to tap into a type of an anomalous anomaly for each individual to visualize.

Elijah moves towards the middle of two pillars that are huge and support an arc of stone at the highest point of the grotto. For what seemed like hours he was standing and pacing while deep in thought. Then suddenly he has an overwhelming thought from the past, when he used the food multiplier synthesizer, to multiply grains for bread during his ministry.

His thoughts are elevated, then he speaks out loud in a low under-breath tone, "Hmm, by using a miniature multi-synthesizer in sync with the natural basis of interaction between the lenses molecules, while keeping a basin feeder full of the chemical mixtures that are compatible with the lenses, similar to the food multiplier. This should keep the circuit field running."

Elijah heads back to his working zone and starts immediately and grabs hold of some Troglodyte natural molecular tubes and starts to dissect the molecules in order to extract the proper balance that is needed for delivery to the lenses. Following this he will consequently send a program command to have the apparatus rearrange the molecules to their original form, so they are redelivered and disbursed into the optic fields.

Elijah is now plugged into the central computer where all of the anomaly magnetic signatures are located. He connects the transponders that will signal the pineal gland and relay systems. All brain functions were tested and the lenses are ready for activation.

Suddenly a subatomic particle error occurs as Elijah squints at the screen. He sees that the acceleration of the electrons is being dragged behind because the subatomic particles are being affected by a magnetic field disturbance.

Elijah puzzled, searches then checks, assumes it is field particle decay. While running diagnostics, a data resolution comes up and reads, "Use filters to remove the narrowband interference by injecting a low frequency sine wave in each segment of the projection, with a vibratory wave filter of plasma."

Elijah smiles and thinks to himself, "How ironic, sending sound in rhythms, just like music!" He then recognizes the 432 Hz natural harmonic overtones that he is now using in the filtration application and is deep rooted in the bifurcation makeup of the Universe. How his father told him, that there is not only God particles, but God's music, a symphony orchestrated by the 432 Hz and is the universal harmonic tuning of all things. The spiraling *(the stir)* portion of relativity is the 432 Hz vibratory motion *(recycling)* that emulates and resonates in DNA, matter, liquids, time, wormholes, magnetism, brain functionality and are the preset ratios that create and gives functional credence to the solar systems.

Elijah remembers when his father spoke of 432 Hz and its importance to music, how it enhances and heightens your conscious minds awareness, as well as its uses in its tremendous healing powers. He also mentioned that the ancient sacred structures throughout the Earth were also built with this fine tuning with the solar spectrum, using archeoastronomy for the correlation between colored lighting and solstices/ equinoxes with relation to site localities.

Elijah goes back to work, fussing with some issues with trial and error and becomes mystified that only one particular sound seems to work. Nevertheless, this fine tuning set the precedence to finally test the Convex Spectacles, which was the name given later on, by someone other than Elijah.

Longtime waiting, Elijah powers up the glasses, nervousness fills his being with anticipation. He is excited and sets a pre-list of anomalies in which he is eager to view. He places the glasses over his eyes and turns on the appropriate engagement triggers. Simultaneously, he chooses to see the signatures of oxygen atoms, *(via the program)* midst the air in the laboratory as a test. When a sudden loss of balance came upon him, he began to feel light headed; Elijah then disburses the glasses temporarily and moves close to a vertical jack-stud on an open wall for support.

Now knowing why this happened, he takes a safety precaution and decides to tie a wire from a metallic hanger strut that is slightly lower than the ceiling level, to the spectacle glasses. Elijah chose to do this, because if he were to lose his balance completely, the wire would then pull the glasses from his head, just in case to avoid any mishaps.

Ready to go again, Elijah has preset the transitional slide injection *(potion)* and sets up *(intermittent)* views for approximately 30 seconds, from one anomaly signature to another in an assorted view mode. He combines the anomalies with custom identification dimensional intensities with various categories. The visual categories are molecules, wormholes, vortex fields, atoms, subatomic particles, bio-electric frequencies, and more. These views range in levels of amplification depending on the anomaly being observed, which are then magnified for viewing consideration. Thus, bringing out the anomaly and seeing subatomic particles or strands that make up a particular inter-dimensional anomaly *(example: wormhole)* or just to observe a variation of spatial distances for analogy.

The glasses are ready to wear and Elijah leans into them with his left hand as the handler, putting them on and positions them in place. He pauses briefly and asks for a blessing. As he begins to open his eyes, he begins to spin slowly spanning the area and quickly he notices a blur. He then uses the cylindrical manual adjuster with his thumb and index finger on the right metal ocular frame, to slightly tweak and fine tune the flow of energy. Finally, the unbelievable truth! A strong cheer of, "Yeah!"(Flutters from Elijah's mouth). Focusing on the clear contrast, he realizes the room is filled with O2 (diatomic oxygen atoms). A barrage of oxygen molecules melded together, appearing spherical in a pinkish red thickened skin, with a holographic appearance.

Jesus' Mentor

The program running was in the process of overlapping further additional anomalies that came into sight, propagating and fine tuning a complete display after just a few minutes. All of the anomalies began to appear one by one in its harmonious true state.

Elijah is in a complete invigorated state of rapture, as he grabs sight to a symphony of networking anomalies. Through this exhilarating experience, Elijah is feeling inundated with God's presence. His heart becomes overjoyed and thumping with excitement, when a thought of sharing this moment with his father transforms to a surreal humble prayer that engulfs his presence.

As if time had slowed down, his hand reaches out in appreciation with admiration and he sweeps his hand in motion through the now seen reality of patterns. Again, reminiscing of a moment as a child when he danced in the middle of a holographic galaxy dis*play* with his father. He recalls enjoying the show of different colors of clusters, while experiencing the variety of molecules swaying at the command of his hand. Elijah becomes curious, but understands that he will have plenty of time to relish in this opulent landscape of displays.

Setting aside his personal wants, he marches towards his goals. He takes a quick breath and figures it would be prudent to receive a biological scan evaluation to make sure that his vital signs have not been affected by wearing the spectacles. At this moment he removes the glasses and starts back to his work, focusing on one particular anomaly.

Elijah begins work on programming a key component. He then focuses immediately on increasing the magnifications on this part of an anomaly, *(x/millions)* by using the wireless Nano-Magnetic Frequency Scanner *(NMFS)*. This is a simple method using particles of photons to absorb and scan the object you wish to magnify by an absorption rate that signals back and forth on a loop. This received information along the imagery particle interpreters, are at twice the magnification rate of an object. This propagation rate develops almost at the speed of light, duplicating twofold per millisecond, until the focus view results coincide with the programmer's original command.

Elijah peers into one branch of a miniature wormhole, to discern and observe a never before seen type of subatomic particles mixture, called "Vestige Particles" *(the inter-dimensional subatomic particles of a wormhole)*.

These (VP's) subatomic bits, which have a cloaked dimensional fabric with layers, resonate as if their alive and up to this point in time, measured through only magnetic detectors.

Astoundingly, Elijah is witnessing VP subatomic bits in their true state of motion. He describes the VP subatomic type particles as having similar properties of a normal atom but opposite features in other regards. The atom of a wormhole is called a v-atom/vatom, a vortexular atom. Elijah is fascinated by the spherical reflective membrane, it appears to be a sought of translucent mercury field. Amused, he notices a similarity to a regular atom, which also has 99.9% of hollow space within. As its bits or particles, fill less than .01% of the holographic sphere.

Elijah looking up in a daze was remembering and humbled by a phrase that echoes within him since childhood, "Everything invented has been reinvented 99.9% of the time, but necessary for all times." Elijah smirks and mutters a laugh and shakes his head with a smile.

Optional Read: Elijah focuses back to the VP's subatomic bits and notices another oddity; the effect on the sub particles' rules of engagement, specifically in the matter of the SSOR, "Slip Stitch Orbital Revolutions." Elijah starts to compare data while he transfers all of his visual discoveries to a display unit. He further reads. The SSOR is the process path between smaller particles of an electron within an atom. These families of particles always rotate and orbit in a high speed capacity. The pathways of the subatomic bits, orbit around a specific electron while partially leaving the under-skin and outer membrane of an atom. This happens in union with the electrons, as they are orbiting around the nucleus.

This gives rise to a magnetized field according to the particles polar speed, resulting in the atoms' given density. Yet, while in the motion of orbiting and revolving, the subatomic particles create quasi magnetic densities due to a hyper speed weave (SSOR). This slip stitch weave holds onto an atoms existence and locks itself in this reality (third dimension).

Furthering the "Slip Stitch Orbital Revolution," SSOR simply comprises with other groups of subatomic particles that orbit. In detail; one is positive, one negative and thus creates a special spiral weave forming and sewn onto the inter-dimensional spatial fabric with orbits and revolutions close to light speed (moving particles appear to be at a constant because of the almost light travel speed).

The power fusion and rapid spinning particle speed from the interior of an atom, takes place because of the inter-dimensional fabric, transparently filtering through an atom at light speed. The light speed inter-dimensional (syncytial) energy funnels within the spatial fabric, causing the atom's particles to be energized, in order to skip (spin and rotate) off the fabric at almost light speed.

The fabric in turn causes the proton decay in all atoms and cells. Therefore, the fabric itself creates "time," so that the proton decay can exist and eventual lead to become recycled!

The subatomic stitch particles quintessentially balance the atom in our (3D) dimension (world): for example; 37.5% of copper (Cu) subatomic particles leave our reality, while weaving and orbiting in and out at a preset pattern. Thus, the other 62.5% of its orbit stays within our reality (This percentage varies according to the particular type of atom and is based upon the atomic weight/mass/density). This discovery became known as the "Creator's Handshake" and is the basic foundation and premises of all that is, your reality held in place.

The final classification of an atoms existence is an inter-dimensional frequency directed at the nucleus of every atom (or cell). This is called the "Inter-Dimensional Transfusion" frequencies or also called "Transponder Identification Datum" (TID's or TID frequencies).

These inter-dimensional induction frequency coils, travel from an incubated source and traverses back into the interior of the nucleus of all atoms/cells and are launched from a pool of informational identifiable assorted energy, bestowed by the Creator. These wireless tethered frequencies are receiving and transmitting at a constant, to signal what types of atoms are to exist, for example: the hydrogen atom. One hydrogen atom has its own TID signal directed at the nucleus; it gives directions for the completion (identification) of that particular Hydrogen atom.

In conclusion, the inter-dimensional TID frequencies are layered, whereas each group of individual "like" atoms, have their own signature lines of inter-dimensional frequencies and do not overlap or can be seen together with any other "unlike" atom TID frequencies.

In 2038, the TID identifier frequency will become the new "String Theory," labeled as frequencies/strings (not particles) and the String Theory's vibratory particle theories of the past will become a piece of the SSOR's design. The God particle will no longer be a particle but a frequency.

Nonetheless, if these TID signals and the make-up of the SSOR can be manipulated, through the separation of spatial fabric, then the user of these technologies will be able to travel through time, walk through walls and transform a vehicle into another object.

Note: once the atoms are altered, the probability void will be filled by aligning distortion. This will be done by either the Creator or us, to propagate in fulfilling every probability.

Elijah makes adjustments to the spectacles and eagerly puts them back on. He becomes stunned, as he notices his reflection in the glass window of his laboratory and realizes that there are auras, fields and biological frequencies emerging from his body. He has a flurry of excitement that encourages him to run. He looks to exit the cave base to see the whereabouts, of what direction his "now seen" own biological frequency is pointed.

Realizing he is carrying sensitive equipment to the surface, Elijah slows his pace to be careful as he approaches the surface. When he emerges, he ironically is at the same point where the tabular stones were quarried for Moses. Elijah looks up and smiles.

Setting up his equipment quickly, on a natural stone bench near the summit, he sets the Convex Spectacles into place. He then looks up and is quite interested to follow an amber colored string of light, emanating from his forehead. It seems to be pointed towards the sky in a slight horizontal incline. Elijah is not sure where the thin light originates to or from, and is unable to track the long length of the frequency. He is at first disappointed and then becomes distracted, as dusk is upon him.

Unable to pursue his main objective today, he switches his focus to the attention of the other anomalies in their entirety. Elijah enjoys the elaborate view of the enigmas while they are blossoming into focus. He is amazed as he gazes into the heavens while witnessing a thick mesh of woven fabric, in a framework of geometric tesseracts. It's hypnotic and mesmerizing, watching the infrastructure of the fabric wave about, funneling through the cosmos at speed of light.

Elijah understands the illusion of the expanding universe and is now intrigued with new visional aspects/pieces of the galaxies. He relaxes to observe more of the moving of spherical vacuous action and reaction of the spatial fabric. He is mystified as he witnesses the never ending widespread layers upon layers of fabric that are absorbed from the nucleus of our universe.

Elijah observes the flux field within the fabric. The layers are in a equidistant design pattern that expands outward, then curls and is brought back into the nucleus center of the Galaxy, *(spiraling black hole)* creating many types of gravitational flux fields with an enormous pull.

This action of extracting and detracting is caused by a powerful mega Source, causing vortexular motion within the center of the Galaxy. Elijah is thinking that this phenomenon is connected to a frequency of something or someone, observing a parallel barrier that is in a shadowed state, emulating our Universe's patterns.

Cave Innovation

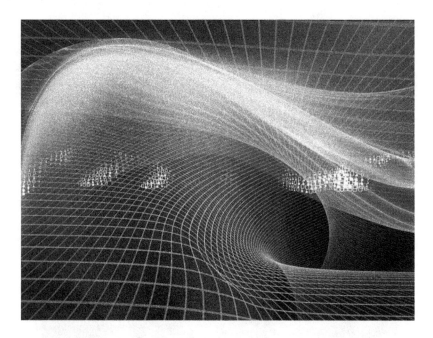

Elijah brings up again, related data to what he is witnessing and reads, "The process of vortexular alternating energy is necessary because it generates the spatial fabrics precise motion at light-speed, enabling for our reality to have an important ingredient called *time*. The overlapping dimensional fabric travels and is produced at instant light speed which is constant and coincides with the expandability of the galaxies, stars and planets. This gives the impression that the individual solar systems are traveling at high rates of speed, when actually they are moving gingerly in a magnetic resonance, biting off the spatial fabrics invisible magnetomotive force, lending to certain planets that have been captured in its orbit.

As planets begin to finally settle within their solar system the friction between the spatial fabrics combined with the planets massive density, will incite a pivoting process that assists with the development of the magnetic repellant. The planets own gravitational wave density will resist the pull from a larger object, locked *(scalar)*, while giving its own *(polynomial ring)* elliptical orbiting *(vector)* speed and rotation *(tensor)*. This process will secure the magnetic resonance of an object in space, because of the spinning, orbiting and pulling in a constant enveloping dimensional fabric field.

Elijah is dozing while looking at the display monitor, because he had no rest, due to the excitement. He starts to close his eyes and begins to consider how wondrous these atypical anomalies are, punctuated with smirk of relief. Elijah lies still, relaxing in a dreamscape recalling a childhood lullaby that has been passed down from generation to generation. He is drowsy as he thinks of the words of the tune; "Time is to light, sound is to matter, air is to breathe, love is *too* flatter, so be that all you can be and sleep, da deat!"

Elijah shakes his head and laughs as he snaps out of his twilight nap, then overlaps two positive thoughts, from past to present, of childhood memories to the current great success of accomplishments. He was feeling joy as he savors the moment. He twitches and tries to snap back into work mode, but is unsuccessful. His final thought descents with the anomalies in the lullaby; time, light and sound, how they connect to the Universe along with the works of the Creator, as he inevitably falls asleep.

"To pave the way for a final and single purpose, reason and result; for each of us to have our own individual conscious mind, full of choice with billions of years worth of establishment. A phenomenon that is taking place, to the cause and effect in all our lives!"

Elijah

Elijah is filled with gratitude, realizes the visions he is encountering and is laying credence with respect to the effectiveness of seeing the once invisible biological frequencies. He appreciates being able to measure parts of the anomalies and locate them within the rapid fabric speed of a systematic circuitry of wormholes.

He looks about as he has programmed the glasses to see all of the anomalies together in unison, noticing and making a comparison that everything he sees is relative and similar to other aspects of our lives. Such as the wormholes, spatial fabric and bio-frequencies are clustered together and appear to look exact in comparison to the circulatory system of a body and even the brain's functionality display, with regard to diagram of neurons.

Cave Innovation

In another most bizarre aspect of his findings is the selectional display portion of the inner dimensional array of anomalies. If miniaturized to a scaled down view, astonishingly, it looks like a replica of an electronic circuit board and in a similar observation, emulating a small urban city from an aerial view.

Elijah studies the tiny scaled down displays; all lined up and is amused. He expresses a side smile, then stares and thinks, "You would not be able to tell the difference on all the display monitors, they look identical." His mouth opens as the imagery becomes profound in his thoughts and continues along the same line of thinking. "Energy that powers our towns and low voltage that passes through circuit boards, is quite ironically similar to the source fueling the alternating fabric that stems from the heart of the Creator's central reactor.

Elijah rests, and a new day awakens as a lingering dreamscape plays his conscious thoughts on how important the Convex Spectacles are and that only a handful of trusted colleagues would have permission to have access to the technology.

Elijah then modifies the format of the spectacles and uses its technology on other components of his equipment. He sets up a new station to work, in an area where he has exposure to the sky, yet sheltered in a cavern room for computer operations. This area of the facility was used for ventilation and communication stations in the past. These carved openings in the mountain, are made to look natural and ideal for Elijah to do testing, because of the indoor outdoor access.

Elijah is now programming and standing at one of the monitors, designing and sending a frequency positioning sensor probe inward to the biological frequency that emanates from his own being/pineal gland in order to find the thin lighted frequency's destination.

Elijah understands that most of the Centurion Race has the ability to access this bio-dimensional destination with a meditative subconscious state.

This bio-dimensional destination place is referred to as the Hall of Records or Compendium Space (Akashic records). It is an inner dimensional epicenter loci that connects an individual's spirit energy signature in real time, every breath, all that one feels or does. The recording manifest from the hub of records is at a constant and because it imprints with dimensional bioluminescence within the spherical receptor, it can be tracked by its lighted inter-dimensional signature.

This area is tethered with an inter-dimensional bio frequency modulation to an individual's spirit. The spirit cannot exist without this constant connection. The connection's core function is to feed the soul/spirit with bioenergetic transformation information, while the spirit transmits residually.

Giving the results of "Biocentrism," the spirits essential intrinsic characteristics, the Hall of Records is paramount for your spirits total existence and does so in a spherical timeless void, without time. A major purpose of the Hall of Records is to have access to your past and future existences; from when you were sliced from the original spiritual chasm multi-billions of years ago or where your spirit will be billions of years to come.

There are a variety of entities that have access to the Compendium Space Records during the course of their conscious life. The access engages when the individual being/entity, uses their spiritual energy to connect through the subconscious and conscious mind in a meditative state. This is done by tightening one's grip to meld with their mind while separating mind from soul, while being in a secure relaxed state.

Most beings that travel through the lighted frequency to the Hall of Records have difficulty, because of the resistance of frequencies natural characteristics is to favor the receiving portion of the transmissions circuit. This impedes the entities ability to traverse back with the coherence of information, making the clarity not to be precise.

One might access the records to see what mistakes they have made in their past travels, so to improve their mark for divinity, as well as making sure there are no obstructions being caused by an outside force or entity.

Spectra

Elijah "physically" tracking his own frequency location through positioning technology and seems as though the frequency is connected to a sub-inner dimensional spherical hub. This energetic hub is resonating from the center of the universe in the same location of the megalithic black hole, yet setting in its own dimension. Either of them can be seen at the same time, unless programmed to do so by Elijah.

Elijah's heightened interest of physically witnessing these two phenomenal anomalies is a gift and his spirit becomes filled with gratuitous energy. Overwhelmed in seeing what no one has ever seen before, the spherical Hall of Records and now sets his vision upon an enormous outer spherical field skin of energy, called Spectra. Elijah changes to a state of euphoria by the amazing wonder of Spectra's size. He looks across to the massive energy field surrounding the Hall of Records and notices the Hall of Records is miniature to Spectra. Elijah realizing, the Hall of Records is purely a component of a massive network.

Spectra, is the all of all, which is the complete timeless reality of the Universe, from the beginning to its end. Spectra is absorbing, recording and deciphering every cell, atom or molecule, every grain of sand, stone or planet, every living thing, past present and future, every second of every moment logged and accessible. It is the prime component that produces a smooth filter in our Universe to secure the full functionality of the probability program, which is instilled to produce our conscious existence of having free will.

The probability matrix program is called "Binomial Distribution," which interjects intervals of selective outcomes and growths in order to create every possible outcome with limits, in order for "You" to return glorified in a divine state as an individual entity. Within the "Binomial Distribution," is the celestial embodiment that is the productive portion of the program called, "Bifurcation Production," which is the dynamic systems, that makes changes to the structure of everything, to its perimeter values so no two things can be created equal.

This qualitative geometric component of production is steered by the Binomial Distributer *(probability program)* with limits and makes adjustments concerning itself with forward priority progression towards everything and taking precedence over individual entities, while creating a canvas of life. This program in its entirety is not just for the physical reality, but is governed in outcomes for all.

Elijah is amazed and excited. Now, one thing is his ultimate priority and that is to find out where the Hall of Records and or Spectra are being routed to. He feels it may be connected directly to the Creator through another bio-electric frequency.

Elijah starts to gear up and collect certain belongings to bring along with the vital equipment he is going to take on a vessel, to the centre part of the Universe. He plans to investigate the biological records and the makeup of this tremendous anomaly. He travels swiftly and within hours he is passing through numerous wormholes.

He finally arrives in the vicinity of the Spectra field and quickly adjusts his equipment to set up. Elijah is attempting to magnify and observe the inner makings of the Hall of Records. He connects his new mobile view sensor, which is compatible to the Convex Glasses and is mounted on the outside of the vessel, synched to the ships mainframe computer.

Standing tall, at a fixed location in space near the mega vortex funnel, he now views and focuses in-on the Hall of Records through the outer spherical field skin of Spectra. He sees hubs of dimples in the trillions along with webbed frequencies, bright and white with a tint of blue, shooting out in every direction, but magnetically clustered. It appears to look like millions of fiberglass optics *(fiber-optics)* in a residual static cluttered bunch. Elijah is startled as he notices that some of the dimpled imprints are empty of the souls that are connected to the Record Hall and are most likely living their lives.

Astonishingly, there were a small percentage of the hubs that had spirit energy in some sort of limbo or in a storage capacity. He looks directly at one hub of spiritual energy and contemplates if this entity is waiting for another soul or if it is waiting for a specific time period to reengage, or simply trying to gain purification in a sort of anti-time *(purgatory)*.

Elijah takes a closer look and discerns that all the dimples of the hubs were the carved birthplaces of all the spirit energies since the beginning of creation. He was pleased to see many of the spirit energies in this vibrant state, but realizes that only a few in comparisons have reached the purification status. Elijah stares and wonders if his father has reached this state, given the fact that he was a special person.

The searching continues as Elijah magnifies the Hall of Records on his Convex System. He is following the reception of the lighted frequencies into the hubs of records that comes from spirits and whom are in the transition of living a life.

Suddenly, he becomes stiff and fully enchanted with these high density accumulative blue tinted strands that are statically spread outwards towards the inner portion of the much larger Spectra Sphere. These stands are emanating from the millions upon millions of assorted hubs and are the relay transmission frequencies from the entities spirit hub. Elijah sees the frequencies relayed and absorbed into the skin field of Spectra's enormous network. Feeling overwhelmed, he tries to break it down to a simplistic observation.

He has now tracked, surmised and understood that the pineal gland sends a lighted frequency signal from an entity or person. Elijah is amazed that the bio-frequency travels and traverses to their personal spirit hub instantly, across the entire Universe. Then the frequency is filtered and relayed to the main inner field of Spectra.

"Where does is it go from here?" Elijah asked himself, as he tinkers with the equipment, making the necessary adjustments while trying to figuring out where the frequencies are headed. Elijah is honing in on the visual telemetry that views a light green translucent enmesh entanglement pattern. It appears strait and tubular collecting magnetic sound and light particles and is unlike any anomaly he would ever evaluate. Its characteristics are unfamiliar and adjustments have to be made because of the rapid speeds. Elijah is trying to fathom the amount of information coming from the entire Universe and is being funneled then circulated in this transference frequency tunnel/tube.

The readings are coming back to Elijah and he is trying to decipher the uncountable particles within the connective tube structure. They appear to be a type of subatomic sound and plasma light particles that possess a tachyon *(traveling faster than light speed)* quality, racing in and out of view. Each particle is behaving as if it has a negative and positive charge going to and from somewhere else, but in real time when measured what is visible.

Another fascinating occurrence is that the subatomic plasma light particles are representing a sort of entanglement with the sound particles traveling in groups, as if it is thinking while infinite amount information is dispatching and sorting messages.

Elijah realizes that no two particles are alike and learns that the information being received is instantly evaluated and filtered with specifications of a presumptive probability, then layered back out overlapping the bifurcation program *(which is an auto-growth motion program)*. It is then sent back, coded to signal automatic adjustments to enhance the creative probability process, which is to create every probability without duplication, but with limitations where the probability distortion doesn't equal the stage of purity or until purity.

Optional Read: Elijah scrolls through his new findings and evaluations that pertains to the spatial fabric, biological frequencies, wormholes, and subatomic particle behavior and learns that the key to functional growth and creating a platform that stems from everything, is relativity spinning into unlike parts. He then searches to figure where the source emanates from and does this fuel the Bifurcation and Probability Programs? He figures that the probability portion of the program is a command, overlapped within the physical bifurcate matrix program (Binomial Distribution). Therefore delving deeper into the bifurcate complexities without prejudice.

Elijah decides to record the methodical summation order for the circuitry of life, immediately after experiencing these anomalies, as follows:

> *The Creator/Deity is responsible for the creation of all the cosmos. The Creator is a single God, after quantifying quantum analysis and logic assertions with the removal of all possibilities, resulting in Monotheism. "Axiomatic systems" can be deemed true in an absolute!*

> *The inverse of these analyses is to create a growth program that selects what to move ahead and what not to, while making no two things alike, but compatible in a metaphysical sense.*

> *Where the Deity plugs in, is the beginning of the "How." There is a reactor for power, a building program for structure and command instructional program, posing to the eventual "why."*

The Creator's globular reactor does more than power the circumventing of the inter-dimensional spherical spatial fabric at the speed of light, (constructed of tesseracts) it also is overlapped with the program commands and building instructions that circulate and filter in unison with the power source.

The Probability Program aspect is a command that creates everything that is possible with limits within the final dimension (our reality) without duplicates. By using a physiological/physical bio-coded growth sequence called "Bifurcation Program," which is the building mechanism in massive proportions with distributed instructions (Binomial Distribution) from subatomic inter- dimensional signal particles. These mobile signal particles receive their original information from the Probability Resultant and are the liaison between the two programs (Binomial Distribution and Bifurcation).

If the Probability Resultant establishes a need for a new species of maple trees in a particular adaptive location and has not existed, it will then circulate the creative signal with the attributes and internal structure of this selection, filling the necessary void. The tree itself then begins from a seedling with its already signaled characteristics. Its matter is programmed and arranged by subatomic particles and within the subatomic particle signature are MSB's, Mitochondria Signal Branches which metamorphoses a species type to emerge in a sequence of steps, such as developing the bark of the tree or a leaf. Eventually through time the tree will evolve and its signals will change to improve its survival according to the environment, but if deemed necessary in the befitting probable cause. Its purpose might no longer be needed and has fulfilled its important placement for propelling the probability data, through the Bifurcation growth program. These occurrences are also determined by the "Probability Resultant."

Elijah leaves the computer station and walks towards the window of the ship, turns off all the lights in the ship, his arms crossed as he stands still watching the many stars in space. Silence is apparent with a slight hum as his vessel is moving at a slow speed. Jammed with loneliness, he doesn't know whether to plead or pray, to ask God for direction.

Elijah approaches the monitors and continues some inquiries about other Faction interpretations on this subject, trying to find that something different.

He reads, *"The initiation of frequency signals stands to exist by merging with the dimensional spherical fabric mesh flowing at the light speed through the subatomic particles, thus creating a magnetic orbit and rotation to the subatomic transponder particles (receiving and transmitting) to enhance the signal, to strengthen the temporary health of the protons."* Elijah skips this already researched part and reads further, *"If a plant has been selected by the probability sequence and the signals are about to steer the biological makeup, then the bifurcation process begins. In order to produce an elected portion of the tree, there are invariant molecular sets in a system that connect and are related, so that these are distinguishable parts of the species is this particular maple tree. Although by bifurcating the growth process and molecules with being family alike, none are to be exactly the same. Action of the (logistics) bifurcate mapping is 1+1=2+1=3+2=5+...is an implemented growth sequence so no two things are created exact. This pattern can be quantified in everything and breaking down to a simple growth or improvement preset algorithm between 62.5% to 68.75%. This graphical mark fluctuates, but leans in a more forward progression to keep everything in the Universe growing and improving in order to create all probabilities with a platform for all to exist and to eventually become divine in the purest state as an individual entity or entities. This (bifurcation) pattern is found in behavior, physical movements, breathing, heartbeat, economic cycles, sleeping, day to night, and it all can be measured to the exact sequence."* Elijah feeling compelled to select certain information from the readings and to save it, the same way he collects mechanical material or parts.

Elijah trying to connect his thoughts with his goal, *"Now the bark of the tree can be created in a unique pattern found only to that one unique tree, amongst a forest of the similar species of trees. The signals know how to borrow from the existing elements in the given environment to fortify and complete the bifurcation process. The program utilizes integral patterns of vector fields creating and building dynamical systems, by engaging in slight adjustments and changes made to the parameter values, leaving nature here at the final dimension, our existence."* Elijah gathers his sixth and final note on this subject.

> *This is Quantum chaos and distortion, but with an aligned organized pattern. Why the lion eats the lamb and the growth of the people/spirit recycle until purity sets in. All made possible for you to exist, to have consciousness and spiritual individualism.*

Elijah realizes and sees a slight similarity to the Faction's agenda; with God's love of having all entities join together and to be connected by God in a purified state. Understanding that man cannot be a part of the Factions because of the destructive impurities they bestow on each other and handing humans highly advance technology would then threatened the continuity of others throughout the sector.

Elijah stymied, but feels as if he is close to complete his goal. Seeking the solution of finding the connecting factor, hoping to get a further understanding or see even more parts of creation.

Elijah scans and accumulates all the data involved in the tubular message connector. Drumming up his final evaluations, he takes off to track the light green *(frequency)* informational tube, emanating from Spectra. He accelerates his vessel, warping into one wormhole after another to eventually travel to an appropriate position to launch nano-probes, in order to see where the tube designates.

Elijah retires and regenerates to become fresh in a new day that awaits him, along with the data that is hopefully promising. Nevertheless the results are displayed, but unfortunately the probes tracked the message tube exiting our Universe in an alternating dimension. The stoppage was towards the barrier reef *(outer-sphere)* of our Universe, adding some complications to the cause.

Elijah's perseverance is incredibly rewarding when he locates the end area of the barrier and is able to travel to its location. Until this point, scientists were unable to decipher the Universe's outer skin of the barrier, because of its circumvention inter-dimensional motion.

Understanding the illusion of the barrier is a representation of shadowing the entrance of one doorway, then exiting the same doorway, just to find yourself back at the original entrance again. This paradox is furthered by the vastness of the Universe and its rapid movement and unable to tell where the barrier begins or ends, until now.

Fortunately, Elijah's probes had given the exact location of the egress marks of the tube. Knowing it is impossible to travel past this point, because not only does the Universe halt here, but it is a dimensionless/void.

Elijah focused in his attempt to be able to see through the barrier after using the data that was deciphered from the tubular structure and without making major alterations to the convex (spectacle's) manifold. Elijah has finally reached a location where he feels the Creator's Spirit presence is at hand, even though it is afar. Filled with fear and swiped with shock, Elijah is without movement. He holds steady at the precise point of the rift and tracks the tubular frequency where it emanates from.

Elijah watches through the ships mobile convex lenses, as the appearance of the tube changes leaving out of our Universe, then enters the abyss/void. He is restricted behind the barrier, waiting for the lenses to detect an energy signature, by magnifying a variety of points and casts further into the void of darkness. He sees only the lonely lighted frequency extend, that derived an immeasurable distance from Spectra.

He further magnifies, and then suddenly expels a rout of breath. Elijah's eyes open completely, feeling suspended as he discharges his entire sight on an infinite endless soft brightness. This brightness is without color, yet appears to be luminescence and flowering in every direction. His body becomes lighter as his heart and mind becomes crossed bursting with euphoria. He lies stiff and still in his posture. Time has fleeted and he touches his lips to make sure he is still alive, while his thoughts are regrouped surviving the beautifying experience.

How was he able to get this far? Additionally, he witnesses the majesty of the Almighty, in an accumulative pattern of other informational tubes circulating and disappearing into this brightness. Elijah quickly understands, "It appears there are other individual informational tubes that are coming inward formed from other Universes, as ours are one of many."

"Is this God or an extension of His Hallowed Spirit?" Elijah is now feeling such a strong presence of love and effortless in controlling his own fulfillment, challenging his worthiness to a level of questioning.

So he asks himself, "Do I have the permissibility or the right in this quest of connecting to this heavenly force or trying to engage in a type of communication?" Elijah mind ways heavy that the Faction leaders will illuminate any humans that don't meet the criteria of the "New Age."

Grappling with the thought, "Would it be alright for the purpose of love, in the quest for helping others or to be given the graces to come this far? For my quest is clear, to give and save the burgeoning accelerated populations of the Earth from unnecessary suffering and provide assistance for many to peek within their existence."

After making his final analysis of the informational tube, Elijah realizes he has to find a substance that has the similar characteristics in relation to the functions of the informational tube, but on a minor scale. Considering that this inner-dimensional anomaly passes through our world and into an abyss territory, before it is fused about the magnificent brightness of what can be described as a type of God-*like* alive energy.

Collected and focused onward towards Earth with a vast distance ahead, Elijah contemplates a full developed initial plan.

He configures a program that is set with a certain criterion and systematically chooses the best probable result after cross referencing billions of data bases. Having adversities will give certain challenges, yet Elijah is hopeful that he can combine this program at a constant, in unison with the divine energy of what Elijah calls, "God's Right Hand."

After a long journey, Elijah has made a stop or temporary deviation on the far-side of the moon, to visit some friends while his ship was receiving maintenance.

He visits his dwelling where he and his father resided during his internship. Another important visit on this layover was to be introduced to Aligious' successor, the new head of the Council, an old colleague of his fathers, who had helped as the acting liaison with the Elds.

Elijah confides with the new head of the Council, in need of support, for Elijah explains that the human race has/had too many conflicts in the way of unity amongst most religions of the Earth. He continues to tell some of the stories and thoughts from discussions with his father on this subject and how he was prepped and groomed as a young man for his ministry.

When Elijah eventually told the head of the council his proposal, it was marked with excitement, because of a long awaited possibility of resolving conflicts amongst the Earth's religious issues. "This new idea will have full support of the Council," says the Centurion leader, as a confident secret handshake closes their discussion. Elijah heads to his ship and the next destination is the laboratory at Mount Horeb.

Moldavite Crystal

Back in his laboratory, smitten with confidence, Elijah stretches his neck with his hands and fingers from both hands interlocked behind the lower portion of his head, then pulling and bending to feel exuberant. He is ready to jumpstart the work ahead of him in an endearing way.

Elijah joins the ships database to the network in the laboratory. He tries to search for a similar match or molecular makeup of the lighted green informational frequency tube connected from Spectra.

The database results match (coincidently) a *green* rock called Moldavite. The Moldavite crystal stone is of the Tektite classification, consisting of natural portions of silicon dioxide and much smaller amounts of metallic oxides morphed into an amorphous formation. Tektite is a derivative of a Greek word meaning molten, as to the original formations of the crystal stone that were born by interplanetary and meteorically high impact debris collisions billions of years ago.

Moldavite turns blackish-brownish towards the outer layers of the rock when an intensified amount of heat is applied, but the centre part of the stone remains a glassy clear translucent green crystal.

Search results for locations indicate the radiant rare stone is only found near the Moldau River, in which the rocks name derives from and located in a country on Earth, called Czechoslovakia. After these readings, Elijah's excitement grows when he uncovers that the stone is well noted for its ability to send and receive intense frequencies and store an endless amount of data and information.

Elijah now parked in the facility of Mount Horeb, realizes he is only a short distance from his current location, to the River Moldau. He churns with excitement gathering some geological instruments and transport gear, carting them to his ship. While approaching the vehicle, he gazes up at the ship's trapezoid windows, creating a frown of approval towards the vessel. Then, thinks of his father in a respectable emotional bond.

Arriving in Czechoslovakia above the River Moldau, he hovers in midair in order to have an aerial view for surveying the topography along the river. He is being careful, because in the surrounding location is a very high dense population of people. Elijah does not want to draw attention, because of the ethical directive.

Elijah plugs in the criterion requirements into the main computer with a connection to the scanning equipment, running an overlapping probability program to select the best possible Tektite crystal rock that would meet the specifications.

At this time Elijah is high in the sky bordering the stratosphere and out of site, waiting patiently. He then moves and descends to scan more efficiently. A sudden blurb noise comes from the equipment, indicating a positive match, a quick smile appears on Elijah's face, then disappears after he notices the rock is under the water and confirmed, in a populated area near an angled turn in the river.

Lifting his right brow while figuring an aloof tactic not to be noticed, Elijah hurls on the Global Positioning System of the areas "mapped vortexes" and sees an inlet of a mini wormhole that can take him in unnoticed into the water about a half a mile away. En route he reaches his point of entry. He triggers the opening of the vortex and then engages while an instant flash spews open an entryway slightly above the surface of the water, making a smooth entry transition dive.

Engulfed in a distance away from the target point, below the surface of the river, Elijah deeks in and out, navigating to avoid some obstructions beneath the rivers surface. Finally he reaches his target point, eyes wide as he flashes a beam of light upon the designated location. Elijah sees portions of a Moldavite rock, yet some murkiness is hindering his view. He waits as the settling of the debris dissipates, while locking in a deep breath. Elijah leans closer to the window of his vessel, seeing a glistened reflection coming from what looks like a smooth shinny surface of a rock.

Elijah begins to worry about extracting the rock successfully, because of a pair of granite pillars wedged together in an A-formation with the connecting tips clashed together. Catching his attention near the apex of the columns, were a convoy of bubbling air pockets, with vegetation swishing and snagged to the stone pillars.

The pillars were supported and stood on top of a huge stone base, pieced together along its front and has multiple broken elongated steps, remnants from an ancient city. Elijah estimated that the granite structures are from many millennia ago. The position and location of the Moldavite stone indicates that it was collected and used as the underpinning for a special reason. Possibly used in an important interior design purpose amongst this lost civilization.

Be that as that may be, he begins using a focused sound and laser guided instrument to loosen the surrounding matter. He then cuts an area carefully away from the stone itself, so not to hinder the precious crystal.

Surprisingly the stone rolls easily into the magnetized field beam which consequently is joined safely into the compartment holding area.

Elijah can't wait to see the stone vis-à-vis. Impatient with a blissful smile of excitement, he flies outward vertically from the river, without regard for any prime directive and therefore, not knowing if the inhabitants might have seen the vessel.

Elijah is noted from time to time to be a little cavalier in certain instances, yet overall is conservative for the most part, but when he does perform an out of the norm action that involves risk, he wittingly recites this saying, "Risk allows growth for relationships and health is all."

As the ship arrives back to the docking station at Mount Horeb, Elijah unpacks all his equipment and most importantly, places the Tektite Crystal Stone carefully on a dolly-cart wrapped in a protective blanket, for transport to his laboratory. After cleaning the stone and placing it in a floating harness stand to be scanned then studied, he becomes quite curious to the query. Why the computer had chosen this rock above all. Elijah is in an upbeat mood while examining the stone; he measures the stone and finds it to be 2.9 feet across with a smooth oblong oval shape.

He flourished his hand against the surface of the crystal and looks close up into the stone, studying the macroscopic geometrical shape formations of the different facets. He studies the pattern arrangements and the spatial dimensions, to determine the specific characteristics that can possibly help a successful connection to the conduit or directly to the Force/Creator.

Diagnostics were run on the stone in all categories, in order to decide what part of the stone would be appropriate for downloading the probability data. The figuring went on. Elijah transfers scanned data to a crystallography 3D imagery program on one of the computers and uploads that data to the main computer. He tries to decipher the best localities on all fronts (position, data uploads etc.).

Elijah forges ahead in selecting the best probable areas, which are spelled out by the results received, leading to the transfer of information wielded. He begins to siphon many terabits of data into a designated area of the crystal. Yet amazingly, all of this information and command programming was absorbed by only a *minute* portion of the stone.

The next step would have to be done in space; because of the replication results from the tubular conduit frequency was on an inter-dimensional

Cave Innovation

wave length and has to be manually tuned. In addition the power source has to be implemented then regulated along with the receiving and transmission of the data.

Before traveling, Elijah has contacted a great friend of his. He, who was a colleague when had his internship on the Moon, as well as living in the same vicinity in the city of Columbia. Beneath the surface, Peter was his old trusted friend's name and was ironically the only one to call Elijah Eli, other than his father. Likewise they both worked compatible with each other in the past and Peter, of course greets Elijah with open arms excited to be working with him again. Neither of them realizes the level of vital importance this endeavor will entail.

Elijah and Peter, paired together once again, are hovering in an orbit outside Earth's atmosphere; searching for a geosynchronous orbital-zone *(geosynchronous is when the orbital period matches the Earth's rotation)*. Geosynchronous positioning has the advantage of remaining in the exact location in orbit in order to be tracked from a ground perspective on Earth; thereupon, being able to link to a person's own biological signature to the stone and then transmit to the Creative Force.

Together, they choose the furthest orbital zone from the Earth, because of the lightness of the forty pound stone, so as not to conflict with space debris and space devices which are amongst the closer orbits. Nonetheless, Peter sets the speed of the crystal rock at sixteen hundred metre per second, keeping in time to the sidereal period, with Earth's rotation.

Getting prepared for the stones release into space, both of the men put their hand print onto the crystal as a means of faith and confidence followed by a few seconds of silence, as they prayed. They both smile and look up and share a coded handshake. As the stone waits to be positioned in outer space, Peter asks, "Elijah, though the frequency we are about to power up is tiny in comparison to the main tubular frequency, would it be questionable to send a foreign frequency into a realm where the eminence of the Creator is or part of?" Elijah responds with nervousness in his voice, "Do not worry, God is in everything!" Elijah maintains his nervous grin as Peter looks disheveled and unsure.

Bearing in, they begin the undocking procedure and release the stone into its permanent position in space. Setting the stone to a parallax shift

Jesus' Mentor

is to be consequential when viewing the crystal, because of the many different angles being observed.

As they unload the crystal it seems surreal amongst the stillness in space. The rock appears to float stagnant and the ship reflects that similar present feel. The release of the stone had a reverence feel and was as if they just placed the stone on a table of silence.

Coordinating their efforts to get the crystal online from the ships computer, they begin setting the parameters. As they look at each other in surreal way, they quickly look down together while Elijah strikes the key, sending a miniature tubular signal to the barrier riff (end of the Universe).

The pertinent information is imbedded in the signal. Elijah mentions that he is wondering about the comparability results in presenting the probability program from his main frame computer on board. The probability program has been the pride of his people for some time and simulates the connection to the bifurcation and probability program *(life and growth energy portion of Creation)*. Peter watches the monitor, while Elijah sends signals and targets the stone's absorption point to lock in a frequency and connect to the power supply source inward to the crystal.

The different parts of the crystal have pre-downloaded information and commands, pertaining quests and query logic. Elijah locks in on a portion of the stone that ignites all of the functions to complete the gamma circuit detection. This included the residual real time delivery of data, transmitting and receiving responses from the probability deciphering command data.

As the power source is steady, Peter fine tunes the biological frequency from Elijah's own signature, which was duplicated from the use of the Convex Glasses. Once duplicated this type of frequency was developed without the need of the spectacles.

Now there is a direct connection from the stone crystal to the ships computer. They now will be receiving and giving data on a set up basis temporarily until "a chosen answer" will then take the place of the computer systems frequency power source. The particle energy absorption from the sunlight will then assist in the flow of the frequencies, similar to the natural lighted green informational frequency tube from Spectra.

Looking at each other without a sound, mouths half opened, knowing exactly what each other is thinking, slowly and silently Elijah puts on his

Convex Specs, along with Peter turning on the Convex outer ship lenses. The two displays are linked to the monitors, so that both of them can view the inter-dimensional frequencies. Peter motions thumbs up, confirming the ship and stone frequency is in order. He nervously touches the screen and engages the light green translucent micro-frequency past the barrier towards the Creator's Force.

Elijah sees a weak or missing portion of the tubular frequency and they look towards each other dumbfounded. Then Peter suggests, with a relief laugh to reverse the ship back a few feet to let the sun absorb into the crystal. Elijah nods and smiles in agreement while he grabs the ship's navigation controls to move back, in order to let the sun seep through. Their laughter is quickly stifled as the light green frequency flows instantly to the barrier rift and suddenly data streams unto the monitors, quick and precise. Both men are stunned, and their facial expressions are locked, as they stare at each other in silence.

Amazed how rapid everything had just happened, not knowing what to expect, their breathing becomes erratic and they both start shuffling within their stance. They eagerly want to read the results and start to look at the incoming data. There is a sudden burst of happiness between them, in a celebration of the connection, but both procrastinate in actually reading the data.

Peter and Elijah carefully approach the monitors and read the detailed results, as a serious mood falls upon them. Tears of joy fill both men, grateful for the responses that Elijah received from all the command results. In addition, the excess information received went beyond their original scope of work. Is it commandments, instructions or a decree?

Elijah states; words cannot, and never will explain what has happened here today. After they settle from their excitement, they elect to put in additional command questions to communicate. They posed a question in-over a thousand different languages, introducing the phrase, "How are you?" They look for a response. Looking and waiting, then retrying for a second and third time, still no response. For the oddity of the situation, was extremely satisfying. To achieve communication with data was wonderful and successful, but the bioelectric signal of emotional questioning via computer is and will be a "no" response outcome.

Though curious, Elijah temporarily disconnects the power source. Elijah did feel the energy at hand, but humbly retreated in his pursuit and reconnected the source back to the computer. Elijah felt there should be only a finite purpose of something so sacred, *A Chosen purpose* and to be fully engaged in the complete connection to come.

Elijah experiencing the feeling of the resonating power to the might of energy. Which Peter tends to call "The Holy Spirit," which is represented by the white dove, because of Elijah's poetic description of the soft bright energy, "As feathers from a Dove, their sails Mercy & Love."

Elijah

Chapter Eleven
ARTICLES OF FAITH

The information and queries have been uploaded into the Moldavite Crystal and Elijah is hopeful the answers he is receiving will find the best probable outcome of actions that can save many humans on Earth.

Elijah is patiently waiting for the finished response from the Creator's energy. He is hoping to advance the human race *(such as his father)* through the witness of teachings and answers to save mankind from further suffering with the work of one individual.

This sacred seeding will help the people to reach a civilized natural requirement for the Council; to come to a determination where humans will be deemed qualified to interact amongst the Union of Planets.

Further results are ready. Peter and Elijah are jittery with excitement but extremely reverent about the sacredness of what will be revealed to the both of them. Gathering their thoughts they begin mapping the detail of the data on the largest screen. They stand shoulder to shoulder, their body language subtle and inadvertently mirroring each other. Both men stand and wait attentively while their index fingers patter against the table releasing nervous energy. The assumed end data is now ready for analysis and they eagerly read the first portion.

The impressive results exceed their expectations, yet the precision of instant intelligent data result and response, continue to startle them both, as they continue to talk. After a few moments they begin to understand why the instructional data was so straightforward and they embrace the results.

One of the results that stood out confirmed an intuition that Elijah had regarding the placement in time for this significant event. The seeding commencement was to take place two thousand seventeen years in the distant past, to have the best possible effect. Elijah and Peter decided to call this list of the informational data results, the "Articles of Faith." They were mystified by this list because it seemed abbreviated and short in length, yet to the point. It would be the first time that the Creator would be referred to as the "Holy Trinity" or Articles of Faith, meaning and connecting, "Father, Son and Holy Spirit."

The Council reviewed the Articles of Faith and approved them with certitude for immediate execution of engagement. Elijah and Peter recruit a carefully selected few to join them in the delicate tasks of providing the means, for the Articles of Faith to be carried out successfully. A docket outline of tasks to be considered begins with the placement of the Moldavite stone in the correct time zone and in an exact location. The time and place has been chosen. With the assistance of the Meta Mechin temporal placement device, it will be moved to a time approximately two thousand years earlier.

The secrets of the Universe are within you

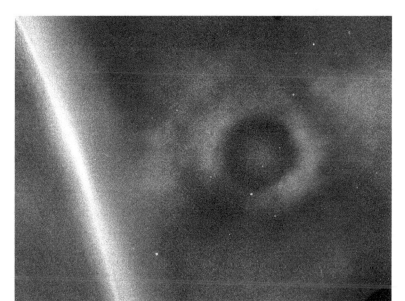

Chapter Twelve

THE BIRTH CHOICE

The preparation is in progress. Elijah sends Gabriel, his most talented and intellectual colleague to deliver a very important message. Gabriel is both, an attired colleague and is well regarded as the most majestic confrere amongst the elite.

One of the beginning steps according to the Articles of Faith's best probable result starts with an annunciation (announcement) to a young girl named Miriam, daughter of Anne and Joachim of Nazareth in Galilee. The *young maiden* is to be told that She is to become the maternal incarnate of a child through the Feathered Spirit of the Creator. The child's name will translate to "God Saves," and he will be called Yeshua.

When Gabriel appears to Miriam and announces the good news, her complete immediate acceptance was at hand, in perfect virtue and humility. She responded, "The Lords word, unto us accordingly, it shall be done."

A few months prior, another woman was with child. She was Miriam's great cousin Elizabeth. Her name meaning, "God's Oath" was from the bloodline of the daughters of Aaron, brother and spokesman of the prophet Moses. The unique sequence of conception according to the Articles of Faith was to have a non-identical approach towards the representation of two women of the same kin. The conception and birth of the two beings would take place at separate times, but within a few months of each other.

The first child *(Elizabeth's)*; Elijah followed the DNA script of a Centurion *(pure human DNA)*, accordingly so, this child would have characteristics and healing abilities to that *of his own*. Elijah following instructions in sequencing strands of his own DNA, as like a family member or brother, while including the physical portion of the soon to be parents.

Without undue time, this special offspring would become the preacher to all religions. Elizabeth's child would be called John. Through the use of the BPF *(Bio Parasympathetic Frequency)*, which is a sophisticated frequency generated by a Decipher Distributor, John's conception would be executed.

The quintessential method used for conception of the second child, "The Redeemer" begins with the natural "pure" portion of Centurion DNA *(Basis of Human DNA)* sequencing, joined with the feathered Spirit Energy of the Creator. Physical attributes of the human DNA will beget from the parents.

The conception begins; embodying with a sooth cadence, a transparent green lighted field is apparent into and from the heavens as a pirouette of some light green and blue hues appear. The room breathes in the reflective soft light, illuminated by the facets of the crystal, while the connection from the Creator's Spirit is at hand.

The Spirit's frequency traverses through the crystal's quartz prisms, while powering transponders to an arrangement of the statistical data, exhibiting sound and light magnetic induction particles that carom off the internals of the crystal, resulting in a residual biological signature directed towards Miriam.

While being connected to the Spirit, a pure biological signature of informational light and sound passes peacefully in through her left ear, sprinkling her temporal lobe with vibratory lighted particles. It fills her being as She glows and now, a wondrous course of sowing and transformation is upon the young maiden. Miriam completely in a glorious state and accepts this miracle to be one with the Spirit of the Creator.

Gabriel tells Miriam which translates to Mary, "The Lord is with thee and you are now Full of Grace, Blessed are You among woman." Mary smiles with radiance, she is filled with the Creator's presence and joy fills Gabriel's heart, a moment that he will cherish forever.

Gabriel informs Miriam before he departs, telling Her, that Her cousin Elizabeth who has been beyond child bearing age and seemingly unable to conceive, is now with child. Mary becomes excited and is eager to see her cousin Elizabeth, who lives with her husband Zechariah in the hill country of Judah.

The Birth Choice

Source note:
John and Elijah
See also: Matthew 3:4

The Gospels vary in their depiction of John's relationship to Elijah. Matthew and Mark describe John's attire in a way reminiscent of the description of Elijah in 2 Kings 1:8, who also wore a garment of hair and a leather belt. In Matthew, Jesus explicitly teaches that John is "Elijah who was to come" (Matt. 11:14 – see also Matt. 17:11-13). In the Gospel of John, John the Baptist explicitly denies being Elijah. In the annunciation narrative in Luke, an angel appears to Zechariah, John's father, and tells him that John "will turn many of the sons of Israel to the Lord their God, and that he will go forth in the spirit and power of Elijah (Luke 1:16–17)."

Previously, in following the Articles of Faith, Gabriel had visited Elizabeth and Zechariah at Hebron. A Palestinian city located in the southern West Bank, between the mountainous areas south of Jerusalem. In doing so, when Gabriel had spoken to Elizabeth, she had open arms with the idea that she would be bearing a son, that she would name John. She was elated with the idea that he would be the one who would open the ears to so many, thus to herald in the Redeemer and deliver the anointed messages.

Zachariah on the other hand, was resistant to the words that were spoken. His intelligence was preceded by his stubbornness. Gabriel had explained the details of the great successors who had helped his people persevere through hard times and of those who were conceived for the betterment of mankind, to save Zachariah's own people.

Gabriel trying to appeal, "Great men such as Abraham and his devoted wife Sarah were childless until a divine intervention allowed her to bear a child. The boy had become Isaac. Another example would be the birth of Samson to the barren Manoah. Even Noah was of this type of birth/lineage and thereto of greatness."

Zachariah unwilling to listen, but more so when he was told, that his wife has been barren all this time, not because of her, but because of him. This ended any chances of resolution in an amicable turnout, leaving the decision to render Zachariah mute and unable to speak for a period of time, in order not to hinder the success of the design set forth to save so many.

Unlike Zachariah, Yosef, who at the time during his betrothal with Mary *(in what is the beginning stage of a Jewish marriage)*, accepts whole heartedly the gift of the Savior, but only after an angelic dream of understanding. He was told not to fear and feel confident that Mary will become your virgin wife.

Yosef is a carpenter from Nazareth, whose genealogy stems from the tribe of Judah, in connection with the House of David *(Book of Genesis)*.

Yosef finds himself months later back in his hometown of Bethlehem with his wife Mary, to register in the Census of Quirinius in order for Rome to collect taxes. This was a decree sent out by the Roman Emperor, Augustus.

Nervous that they would have no lodging, Yosef and Mary find themselves desperately in search of an inn or a place to stay. At this time, both are feeling that the baby will be at hand, but unfortunately they met resistance in their attempt to seek a proper shelter. Sadly this unfolds to an uncomfortable setting. The creed states *(Articles of Faith)* that an impoverish setting is imperative in order to weed out materialistic judgmental ignorance.

Having been steered to a bare dwelling used for storage, Yosef a well known carpenter, immediately inside the unit, scrambles to utilize pieces of angled wood and joins them together as one. With innovation he makes a manger-like crib, adding grass for softness.

He finds himself frantic not knowing what to do and was very worried should something go wrong. Yosef begins to pace when Mary calls for his attention but instead Yosef finds himself in a state of deep sleep and he keels over in order to slumber.

Appearing is a glow of soft pink light that begins to curve around Mary, creating a solemn weightlessness to Her being. A whisper of radiance then shines throughout the entire room, with streaks of pink waves and light blue hues within the abundance of the soft light that envelopes the area. Mary then feels a breeze, followed by the dissipation of light while teeming with a sensation of motion under Her bosom. She immediately lifts up Her arms to a caress of peaceful tranquility and embraces Her newborn Child whose big eyes are as bright as a star.

Mary calls once again to Yosef and then settles him with words of selflessness, as he becomes startled and dazzled with the joy; he beholds his cherished nurtured Son. She lifts up the Baby wrapped in swaddling *(blueing)* linen made from soft flax She had spun herself when She was first joined to the Creative Spirit before the birth. This linen in the future would be given the namesake, "Reverence Cloth." All through the night, Elijah, Peter and Gabriel, were attending and monitoring the entire area, high above in their vessel shining like a beckon of eastern light. Now the dawn is upon this fresh day, the beginning of an all new entire era.

Elijah's gleaming ship which marched from the East is positioned high above directly over the dwelling where the Savior sleeps silently.

The town is in aura, for this blinding light sits like a star in the heavens above the dwelling, all knowing that a special event is happening. Three men appear coming from the light, embarking down to the front of the encampment; they are Elijah, Peter and Gabriel. They are eager to meet the Baby with smiles anticipated by joy. The three men enter with a single gift in each of their hands. One is bearing gold, another frankincense and last myrrh. Gold for the journey they would undertake in their travels to Egypt. The frankincense was for their trip to use as a special healing agent and the myrrh, mixed with labdanum being a special aromatic resin, for it would protect them from any disease and assist with the immediate need from the birth.

The towns' people observed that a group of sharp and distinguished foreign men *(Kings from distant lands)* visited the area, and celebrated in the birth of the Savior, in the place referred to as the "Nativity." These foreign Kings from the East would then become known as the Magi.

"The more in reality you are, the closer you are to salvation."
Elijah, the secret prospective.

Immediately after Yeshua's birth, a flurry of information was injected to the Articles of Faith, as if it configured in segments of probable outcomes, after the pivotal point of the "Birth." Now the Creator had completed the final tasks at hand.

Simultaneously, the Moldavite Stone *(in space)* loses transmission with the main computer intelligence system. Elijah alerts his two colleagues of the issues at hand, gives orders to investigate the crystal. While he was bringing up the data on the monitor, Gabriel and Peter were leaving to investigate and then suddenly Elijah screams out, "Wait!" They reverse course back into the room to see Elijah disoriented and flourished. Elijah walks towards them talking, before they can ask any questions. He frantically explains, "This is incomprehensible, it is stated that our Savior/Redeemer will endure a brutal scourging and be subject to great suffering and then he will be crucified!" Elijah is barely able to complete the sentence as the word *DEATH* mumbles from his lips. Gabriel grabs onto Elijah as one of his knees collapses to the ground, while he is holding his leather rope from his garments dearly tight shaking his fist as he is clinches his rope.

Elijah settles his hand up towards his glassy eyes to hide his face, exclaiming a pried distorted, "Oh, God!" Peter glances and then intently looks at the monitor to figure out anything that can be done.

Elijah is feeling an overwhelming amount of guilt, even though he has the understanding that it is for the betterment of mankind. He continues to bout these feelings, but eventually Yeshua Himself, will give Elijah comfort in this eventuality. Nonetheless, Elijah would bond with Yeshua and cherish with gratitude their moments together, with great harmony and devotedness. The same way Aligious was devoted to Elijah.

Later, the men pull together their resources and data to investigate the prevailing outcome, to what seems to be an odd occurrence. Baffled that something might be seriously wrong, they traveled quickly to the location outside the atmosphere to inquire of the rocks whereabouts. Astonished to learn that the stone was missing, they then located and tracked the stones trajectory fall from orbit sizzling to Earth in a fiery sphere of speed.

Amazed at the findings on the "computer intelligence system" when they discovered how the connection was severed from the crystal. A curious event being the stone was the liaison between Yeshua and the Creator's Spirit source.

A great sigh of relief filled the room when the data confirmed that the invisible cylindrical light green frequency of the Creator is now still, and in full direct connectivity with the Infant Savior, without the assistance from the Moldavite Gem. The three men are moved by this turn of events and it bolstered their camaraderie, sending out a proud wave of confidence.

The Articles of Faith states that the Moldavite Crystal Stone has to be retrieved and brought back in time to various periods. Primarily to Abraham's time period because that era was a key component in the Book of

Genesis and he was a highly regarded figure during this historic time period. Elijah had to explain to Abraham and his son Ishmael about the importance of the Stone. Elijah had to make sure to give an accurate description of the sacred Stone, stating that Yahweh/Allah/Jehovah/Mary and God's Spirit had flowed through the rock and remains in this future relic.

Abraham and Ishmael were then brought to the exact location where the stone will land, escorted by Elijah and his crew. God's Article stated the importance of the trajectory and its purpose.

Elijah was asked to build a sacred sanctuary equipped with an opening at the center of the structure at a precise angle to receive the Stone upon its future decent onto Earth. The location of the blessed Stone's landing place will be considered sacred ground for many years to come. Elijah then speaks of many different Holy occurrences that will take place near the vicinity of the Stones Abode (home).

While Abraham is receiving these messages in his time period, he continuously concurs with a strong and trusted faith. The stone is temporarily stored at Tabor Mountain in Nazareth where there is a mountain base facility enclosed in a cave. That is where Elijah, Peter and Gabriel have been living while overlooking Yeshua's home residence and monitoring events since He was born.

The Stone itself has taken on a different appearance due to its entry into Earth's atmosphere from space. Because it has endured a high amount of burning heat, it has changed the outer most part of the Stone from a brilliant green to a brownish black film coat. There will come a day when man's technology will be able to access the information that lays dormant within the quartz facets of the Moldavite Crystal, indicating the end of one phase for mankind and the beginning of another.

The time period following the life of Yeshua required assignments to be given to a select chosen few. Those selected would become prophets to lead the human race throughout the Earth and be the connective source to join all the people as one.

In 605 AD, one of those great profits, whose name means, "Praiseworthy," Mohammed, was considered to be the last prophet sent by the Heavens of the Creative Spirit and was given possession of the Moldavite Stone. Along with the special honor to place the Crystal Stone back carefully, with the "Cloth of Reverence" *(a bluing linen made by the*

Mother of Yeshua while connected to the Spirit) into its sacred area, in the Abode peacefully reposed.

The stunning facets of this Crystal carry sacred information beyond its symbolic meaning, linking Heaven and Earth. It is a relic of remembrance and to remind us that we are all connected to God.

For thousands of years to come, the stone rests in one of the original sacred structures that Abraham constructed and is now revered as the "Hajar al Aswad," "The Black Stone" which resides at the Kaaba in the Holy City of Mecca.

Chapter Thirteen

MENTOR

After Elijah's travels, he establishes a guardian/foster position as mentor/uncle to the young Child. He soon placed his efforts and concentration to make certain that Yeshua would have a fun filled childhood. Also, to make sure that Yeshua would be living a pleasant *nonage* (childhood) with Yosef and Mary.

Later in his youth, Yeshua would be traveling to two different Erudition Facilities for learning. One of these places would be an underground city location between Cairo and Alexandria in Egypt for school. The other location is reminiscent of where Elijah and other prophets went to school and was located under the Hercules Dome in the continent of Antarctica. This exposure for Yeshua would be necessary in His development, but in many ways the experience will help Him prepare for His ministry.

Any given day as a toddler, Yeshua would be playing in a matted area, arranging wooden figurines that Yosef had carved for Him. He offers a smile at anyone that passes by. His rosy cheeks are being polished by His thick golden curls while the brilliance of the Sun brightens His white tunic. The golden light travels all the way down to His little brown leather sandals, then back up to His blue azure eyes, resembling two precious gemstones.

Wrapped around His tunic is a braided leather rope that Elijah had given to Yeshua. The rope was actually two separate pieces that appear as one. The parts of the belt can de disengaged to be used as a tool of some sort, while the other half lays attached to the tunic.

When He is slightly older, Yosef designs Yeshua a little wooden tool carrier, to hold miniature handheld devices; such as saws, chisels and other carving and carpentry tools.

Yosef taught Yeshua numerous mechanical techniques of assembling structural woodwork and together they built little carts, sailboats and animal figurines. Yosef is always patient and considerate to his family. Although he was the head of the household, he never acted in a supreme manner, keeping a consistent harmonious flavor in their lives.

There were many glorious days of Yeshua playing with His friends and memorable moments of security within the family unit. One particular day while Yeshua was playing in the field, He was given a little toy baby lamb by His slightly older cousin. (An innocent precious moment between children). The Lamb had soft wool of the purest white with marbled chalcedonic eyes. Yeshua cherished this lamb and called him Sheleg (snow). The memory of hugging the soft animal will remain in His heart always.

Knowing time has its limits is sad? No matter how long time can be.
Elijah

Yeshua watches His Mother tend to the fig trees at the base of the vegetable garden, while thrills of daisies and other colorful flowers beautified the area around their home. From time to time, Yeshua would open all the blossoms of the different flowers; He would ablaze the full garden, so that His mother could enjoy a florid display of effloresce, regardless of the season. Yeshua savors this moment with special gratitude and thankful prayers, to God his Father for granting Him such a loving household.

At the age of twelve Yeshua has become highly advanced in his thinking. He and His parents travel for the Festival of Passover to Jerusalem, like they do every year.

When the festival was finished they traveled back with the caravan of pilgrims. When His parents return to their home from Jerusalem, they realized that Yeshua was not within the group like they assumed. They thought Yeshua was traveling safely with relatives as He has done in the past. The worry mounted and they started inquiring with their relatives and friends as to the whereabouts of their Son. They concluded that He was missing and an overwhelming feeling of anxiety took control of their thoughts.

They immediately set out back towards Jerusalem to search for Yeshua. Meanwhile, Yeshua remained back in Jerusalem, where He was studying scripture in the temple. He was also conversing and discussing the scriptures with the rabbis and scholars. One of the scholars approached Yeshua when He was studying a scripture, reading from the Torah and was intrigued with Yeshua's advanced intellect. In a boisterous manner, he nudged Yeshua into a room filled with men and announces to them that Yeshua of Nazareth is going to read the next scripture reading.

Yeshua approaches a type of wooden pulpit, knowing the scholar's intent. Soft cooing voices exchange banter of how young the Child appears. Yeshua is unshaken and takes the scroll from an elder with a small bow and meek smile, then lays down the scrolls on the center of the angled reading platform. With his left thumb on one roll, then with his index finger of his right hand on the other roll, He spreads apart the ancient scroll gingerly and slowly from opposite directions. Standing tall with head leaned down, He begins to read but still there is a trilling of whispering that is apparent in the audience. Yeshua picks up his head and opens his majestic vibrant blue eyes wide and with a piercing stare into the audience, the crowd starts to simmer down. He begins to read from the Torah without hesitating or missing a single word. The onlookers no longer had the disturbing quaver of utterance, but in fact became silent and mesmerized by the fluent melody of the young Boy who was reading. Not once did He look back down at the long length scripture while He was reading.

He fluently recited the entire scripture as if it were from memory. Afterwards, skirmishes of whispers muttered, "How can this be?" A few of the scholars approached Yeshua as He was walking out to leave the room. Several priests were discussing His amazing reading abilities amongst themselves, trying to make sense of it. They wanted to know how He came to have such great speaking abilities and have such grasp of the scriptures.

Three days had passed, when Yosef and Mary arrived back in Jerusalem to find Yeshua near the outside entrance to the temple, talking to some scholars who were undoubtedly impressed with Him as an individual. Yeshua informs the gentlemen that He has to depart for now because He sees His parents approaching.

His Mother was disheveled and said, "Your father and I have been pining and searching for You, all of three days! Yeshua, why would You

Jesus' Mentor

give us this anxiety?" Yeshua responds with great concern, "You do not have to search for Me, for I am in My Father's house doing His work." Mary trying Her best to understand, controls Her facial expression but the tears still flow, as She was emotionally knotted for over three days. Even though Yeshua respected His parents' wishes, this moment was necessary for both parents to have a clear sign of what is to come.

The years passed and many duties were accomplished that were required of the Articles of Faith. For the first time, one Man was allowed to visit the territories of all the Factions in an auspicious determination of setting various cultures in motion.

Yeshua possessed the ability to be able to understand the problems of all the cultures. In His travels He demonstrated an amazing display of an uncanny ability to speak every language of those He came into contact with. In addition, He was well versed in the particular dialect *(vernacular)* of the town in which he was visiting. This allowed him to communicate with the inhabitants on a much deeper level. Peter and Elijah had come to the conclusion that since Yeshua's birth, the infant absorbed all of the complete knowledge of not only the Earth's database, but the entire sectors informational archives, including all the Factions.

Elijah, Peter, Gabriel and other constituents took Yeshua to different strategic time periods and locations around the globe. Additionally, He also went abroad to visit each one of the Faction's home planets and or any related provinces, historic or present. It was during His younger years they took Him to places like, Egypt, Greece, India, Tibet, Britain, North America, South America and many more. His travels included time periods as far back as thousands of years and then some, barring up-to the 19th and 20th centuries, closer to the present days.

Yosef's physical health was declining and it was Yeshua that would accompany and help His father as he prepared for death. Yosef rested on a soft bed near his carpentry workroom as his final resting place. He knowingly wanted to spare his Wife *(in consideration)* of the associations of his death in a common area of the house, where his passing would affect Her daily living in an embedded memory.

Being around his tools and shop, gave Yosef great comfort. In the middle of the roof, Yosef designed small openings for the Sun to seek through. On this summer day, several lighted rays seem to be angled at the head of Yosef's bed, illuminating his face.

Yosef's breaths were becoming shorter each time he attempted to speak. As Yosef is becalmed, lying quietly, he attempts to turn his head and look outside through an oversized door-less opening. He spots a sparrow on a bucket sipping water and singing. The sparrow noticed the stacks of firewood, blinks and flutters away over to the stack of wood so elegantly. It made Yosef smile, while his worries dissipated. He then smiles at his Son and Yeshua takes His father's hand and brings it close to His chest near His heart. Yeshua begins to pray in very personal way and then raises His father's hand towards His lips so that He may press and hold a kiss. Yeshua then turns His head slightly, so that He may put back his father's hand to rest gently on his chest.

Yeshua listens closely as he hears the silent sobs from His Mother, pacing around the adjacent room. She hears the beautiful blessings of Her Son's words. She witnesses how the fearful bitter part of death can be removed.

Yeshua's pure love flows as Yosef's soul is preparing for the transition to Heaven. Yosef begins to lose color and appears dull and pale as he grasps for his last few breaths. Mary hurries over with a silent slurred, "No," under Her breath and kneels at the alongside of the bed. Yeshua reaches out to comfort His Mother. Suddenly, the birds outside become silent and still. Yosef's eyes suddenly become lifeless as his final stare releases from the faces of his beloved Son and Wife.

Mary's head falls to Yeshua's right shoulder as She lets out an uncontrollable cry. She is overwhelmed with grief and finds comfort/solace in the embrace of Her Son, knowing that one day He will share His Everlasting Life.

In the days that followed Yosef's passing, Yeshua takes control of His father's carpentry shop and clients, as well as the three presently employed workers. Yeshua sets up His father's dealings in a fair simple system for the remaining tradesmen. He has arranged, so the employees can still make a living while keeping a fair portion and steady income for Mary's household.

Yeshua had a great relationship with His father's workers and they would give Mary and Yeshua the reassurance that the status quo be maintained. Most importantly, the men would provide and *oversee/protect* His Mother when He begins His travels and spends long periods of time away from His home.

Dead Sea Scrolls

Approaching thirty years of extraordinary achievements at the highest level, Yeshua is still preparing for the ultimate ministry. His works are being overseen by Elijah and his colleagues, in accordance to the Articles of Faith.

Elijah decides to bring Yeshua to the 20th century in the 1940's. The location will be in Israel's Judean Desert, approximately one and half kilometers inland from the Dead Sea's northwest shore, at Khirbet Qumran in the West Bank. When Elijah, Yeshua and the crew arrive, they bring with them scrolls of one thousand texts. These texts were from the Essenes' archives' dating back to the second century before Christ's time. But adding to this collection will be the last of the scrolls, the twelfth scroll. A golden scroll containing the happenings and interactions of Elijah's life, *(Book of Elijah)* culminating through to the Savior's (Yeshua) Second Coming.

The Essenes were special members of a monastic brotherhood in Palestine who oversaw the unique events and various interpretations of these happenings pertaining to the lineage of the Holy Families since the time of their creation. Elijah, Yeshua and his colleagues are choosing excerpts from an assortment of antiquity writings within the Hebrew Testament *(Bible, Book of Genesis)* and the Essenes' scrolls, setting them together in a bounded book.

While breaking bread and sharing wine they divide a more voluminous amount of additional texts into twelve parts *(scrolls)* and allocated to twelve distinctive caves throughout the cliffs of Khirbet Qumran.

Elijah gives Yeshua encouragement to include an additional 30 texts about His early life. Elijah announces in a few words, "These 30 texts consist of one text for every year of Yeshua's life, yet additional texts will be appended. The first to the final text will explain the Immaculate Conception of Mary all the way through to the eventual *New Beginning* of Yeshua's life. It will also include the family ancestry and genealogy connection to what is presently called the Old Testament and directly link the Old Testament to the New Testament."

All the caves are filled with the documents except for the 12th and last cave. Yeshua is walking slowly with His hands facing upward supporting the documents clinched within His bent arms. His beige tunic and leather rope are the last of what the men can see of Yeshua, as He disappears into the shadows of the cave. Yeshua carries of what will be the keystone of all scriptures, and is the "Golden Scroll (Book of Elijah)."

He then reappears while coming out of the cave. He is looking up. Everyone is watching and the first thing they see are His two blue eyes coming into the light. His eyes look like two sapphires reflecting the feathered light. The men gather themselves, to discuss how the Scrolls will be found. They arrange that it will be by a young man, only a few years ahead of this time (1940's).

They return to Yeshua's current time period. He now, is at the Sea of Galilee choosing His disciples. He is gathering unusually plain and ordinary non scholars to be His disciples. Some of the men He chooses are fishermen, one is a tax collector, and yet another was a former revolutionist.

All of the men share one important commonality as the future disciples. They all have above average levels of Centurion DNA in their genomes and two of the disciples are pure Centurion, suchlike the Baptist/John. These genomes *(a dozen dormant strands)* can be activated at a later time in order to possess the ability to heal the sick and perform miracles for the times.

Yeshua gathers twelve apostles that represent and emulate the twelve Hebrew Tribes. All of which had originated from the twelve Factions that were assigned to Earth to signify a movement of teachings in order to aid in the acceleration growth, for all the people of Earth.

Yeshua felt compelled to change some of the names of the disciples, so that they can represent some of the highly regarded men that devoted their lives to selflessness and loving support. Most importantly, He will choose Simon to be a disciple and change his name to Peter in honor of one of His mentors and good friend.

Transfiguration

Traveling back to Nazareth, Yeshua and the twelve disciples arrive at His childhood residence to introduce His Mother Mary to the twelve chosen men that will be doing God's Work. Yeshua asked if Mary can accommodate nine of the disciples, while Peter, James and John travel by foot to Mount Tabor. When Yeshua returns, they will participate in the celebration of His milestone birthday and the beginning of His Ministry.

Yeshua sets out to the mountain with the three disciples. He has been feeling tingles right above the surface of His head. He knows that the Nimbus Metamorphosis is about to be engaged because He has reached the suited age.

Yeshua is now about to possess the halo of energy that is customary and bestowed upon the bloodlines of His heritage. Midway up the mountain, Yeshua tells his disciples to rest at the foot of the mountain so that they may witness and understand the transformation *(The Transfiguration)* that is to take place.

By witnessing this event it will give them all of the graces needed to do their Father's (Creator's) Work *(Articles of Faith)*. Looking up, they all see a cloud forming at the top of the mountain and hear a pulsating hum, followed by an accumulation of vapors that is apparent below the cloud. Hidden within the cloud, they see a large shield, of a round shinny shaped image. It has a glare of great brightness. Yeshua walks upwards on the moutain towards the cloud, when two figures start to descend side by side and then preside next to Yeshua. One is on His right and one is on His left, seven feet from the ground surface. Two bright beams of concentrated light hold the images of two men. Elijah appeared to the right of Yeshua and Moses to the left. Peter the disciple was astonished at what he sees, yet John and James were just smiling.

During the Transfiguration of Yeshua there was an exchange of glorified joy of spiritual illuminated energy. It circulated and appeared like lighted wings half opened. Yeshua appeared He was ready to fly up to the heavens, while a feathery soft brightness floats above His head.

Ascending back up to the cloud, Elijah and Moses depart, leaving Peter in a transfixed state of mind as he wondered about what had just happened. Suddenly a voice spoke from within the cloud and said, "He is the Chosen Son of Man, Listen to Him" and in a swift blink, all that had appeared evaporated and disappears.

All is normal once again, while they return to Mary's house. The men were instructed not to mention what they had just witnessed, for now. It was only for them to know at this time, but will be revealed once the Son of Man rises from the dead. The disciples vaguely understood and did not challenge or ask why. They peacefully made their way back to the celebration.

Before Yeshua's ministry began, there was a legion of schooled evangelists and laypersons to spread the "word" throughout the lands and sea. However, there was one evangelist that awed and drew hundreds upon hundreds of people to be baptized with water. He was the cousin of Yeshua and his name was John. The cousins' were related through marriage and or bloodline. John's mother Elizabeth was best noted as the kinswoman to Mary the Mother of Yeshua.

Elijah was very close to John and treated him like a son. In addition, Elijah was his mentor along with a few of his colleagues that attended the Erudition School.

An individual called Apollos, a native of Alexandria, became one of the great preachers, spreading the teachings of Elijah and Yeshua in faraway lands. His success came from his eloquent manner of reciting the scriptures. Elijah was proud for the others as well, but Apollos has a special place in Elijah's heart, as he was an outsider who persevered through tremendous resistance.

John was a quiet individual in his private life. However, when he preached the word of God, his heart became an inferno of passion for love, repentance and forgiveness. His main objective was to herald in the Christ (Yeshua) and in doing so he used water as a cleansing purification of one's spirit. This movement had people waiting in masses to be baptized. John's message was spreading throughout Judea, the southernmost portion of Israel, creating fear in the leaders of the region, especially King Herod *(a Roman appointed King/s of the Judea territory)*.

The day has come, for John, who is well known as "John the Baptist" to meet his cousin once again, the Messiah. When John sees Yeshua approaching him in the river to be baptized, John hesitates and His cousin says, "I am Yeshua, whose turn amongst many has come to be baptized." John replies, "I am not worthy of baptizing You, oh Lord. I should be begging for You to baptize me. John has a concerned expression and continues, "I came to use water to baptize, so that I can reveal You to all." Yeshua bows His head towards John and says, "Let it be done." As John baptizes Yeshua, the Sun leaves its position in the sky and descends to a soft white cloud above the crowd. There are glares everywhere from the blinding light, as a voice proclaims, "This is the Son that has been chosen for all, Listen to Him."

John says "I baptize You with the Holy Spirit," and when John is finished, he looks up at the people and shouts, "Behold the Lamb of God" then looks directly at Yeshua with a low voice and says, "Who takes away the sins of the world." John speaks this personal quiet phrase directly at Yeshua, because he knew why and how He walked the Earth. He wanted Yeshua to know, that he has his unconditional support and to announce this publicly would be considered blasphemy and put them both in danger.

While serving as the forerunner for the coming of the Messiah, John the Baptist was fulfilling Elijah's prophecy *(Articles of Faith)*. That through John's voice would be the preparer of the "Word made Flesh" and "Behold the Lamb of God." John has brought this prophesy to a reality through his acts with the connection he made with Yeshua.

Mentor

Soon after, John the Baptist is arrested. This indicated an important event *(mark)* because it had been foretold to be the era-point that begins Yeshua's ministry. After John the Baptists' arrest, King Herod decided that he would be beheaded, because he feared and knew that people who were known to carry the "Light" can be reborn and therefore threaten the *(King's position)* kingdom with their miraculous return and would thereafter reinforce their philosophy.

Chapter Fourteen

DESERT

According to the Articles of Faith, once John the Baptist is arrested, the Son of Man will start His ministry, with many trials of temptation, while traveling through a barren dry wilderness desert. He will endure suffering, fasting and be put to the spiritual test by outside forces. This was a quest that many of his predecessors have successfully completed, including both Moses and Elijah.

The twisted desert area would encompass the region between Jerusalem and the Dead Sea. The desert is a maze of wadis, ravines, with a mountainous terrain. It has twelve hundred foot mountain peaks (escarpments) that are dangerous to pass upon. It is a journey of three major allurements (temptations), "Forbidden Food, Testing God and Kingdom Reigns."

Immediately, Yeshua starts to feel the scarcity of food and soon finds Himself weak. This occurred just after three days despite the fact that He is in prime physical condition. It is through His prayers and prayers alone during His intense meditative states, that He is able to bring Himself to the Seventh Day.

During His travels, Yeshua glances at one of the popular shelter destinations, high away from the summit of the Judaean Mountain. He sees a round shaded cave, carved out of the mountain. He struggles to reach the summit because dust is being blown into His eyes. He is unable to use His arms to clear His eyes, because of the unsafe positioning on the aggregated landscape, securing His body in place. He tries to open His filmed sealed dry-mouth in order to take a breath.

Desert

Reassessing the contours of the stone, Yeshua removes one of his sandals and slowly passes it up to his right hand and quickly wedges it between His stomach and the rock, trying to maintain four points of contact. With an overhand swipe, He grunts as pieces of small rock particles are jarred and chatter down the steep slope of the mountain. The gravity slowly silences the scattered debris.

While the sandal is facing backwards, He attaches the leather loop of the shoe to a protruding sharp stone. This would give Him, not only the boost needed, but provide Him with those extra few inches He needs to bring Himself to a safe destination and resolve the confusion at hand.

Upon arriving in the cave, relief overcomes Yeshua. Suddenly a voice comes from within the cave and says, "Look down before You!" Yeshua notices two stones about the size of a fist, becoming transparent projecting an image of two loaves of freshly baked bread. Then the voice continued, "If You are One with God, just reach or say the word and the stones will become bread!" Yeshua fervently recites, "Man shall not live on bread alone, but with the Spirit that comes from the Mouth of God!" A bouquet of fragrance fills the grotto as Yeshua wakes up after a cool nights rest, finding that He is nourished and sets forth on the mountain ridge.

He sees numerous wadis (ravine) and is now walking through an area with miles of boulders making it an awkward walk. Yeshua struggles to look ahead. The sandals scraping against the gravel sand is becoming a loud an overly familiar sound.

Mapping the terrain in His mind, He tries to pick the path with the least resistance between the labyrinths (mazes) of stones. He chooses an amicable path to take along the way and finds Himself stopping, going and resting, again and again. Finally, in the distance is a cliff with a natural opening along side of a plateau. It is now the twelfth day and a critical point in the remaining journey.

Yeshua climbs to a shaded cave high onto the cliff when a voice rattles and echoes from below. The voice states, "You have to endure more than three times this grueling experience and vastness ahead of You. You are near the point of no return. You can still go back now." (It is written in the Psalms) *The voice continues to say,* "That those who put their trust in God will receive protection. So not to endure more suffering, just throw Yourself in the air off the cliff and take flight as would a bird, for You are the Son of Man and will be saved." Yeshua states that, "It is written to have faith and trust in God. Do not put God to the Test!" Yeshua dusts off His sandals and moves onward.

Days pass as Yeshua travels to a ridged mountain side, where there are valleys with tiny streams. There will be great difficulty in climbing down, because the rocks are positioned on an angled wedged shape contour, becoming narrower towards the decent to the water. Between Yeshua's fatigue and the danger of the native rock formation, it would be a deadly descent.

Yeshua begins his difficult downward trek by taking a piece of cloth from His tunic and utilizing part of His leather rope to tie around a sharp edge of a rock, to brace a secure hold. As He bends and lowers his body into the ravine, wedged against the rocks, He takes His right arm and extends it to a stretch. He uses the tips of His fingers to shake the cloth about, to absorb some water. Grass and water were scarce; however, there was enough to enable Yeshua to complete up to the thirty third day amidst the desert.

As He approached the last historic point, He saw multiple squared out doorways carved into the mountain. A smile emerges as He discovers one of the few caves on this journey. Upon His weathered face, joy emerges. He

Desert

focuses on a natural tap of water dribbling on rocks. The water lays flow above an emerging white calcite color with brown streaks alongside the mountain.

Clambering up the rugged mountain face, He scrambles to arrive near the base of the water besides the doorway. Suddenly, a field of lighted colors surrounds Yeshua and halts His approach. Bits and pieces of small spherical particles spin and then start to form a beautiful cylindrical landscape. It consisted of many mighty structures of grandeur, with all the Kingdoms of the world in their brilliancy. Yeshua is pictured in His glory, well nourished and powerful. A voice emits from above the charming motioned apparition/animation, "All that You see will become Yours, just bow by my side and idolize me with reverence!" Yeshua's replies quick saying, "Worship the Lord your God and serve Him only!" Although Yeshua is depleted, He finds the strength to say, "Away from Me!" This temptation would be the last of the great tests. Yeshua had proved to be worthy of His mission by completing and passing the Three Temptations.

Following Yeshua's journey into the desert, there will be three days of rest. Elijah, Yeshua and other honored guests will attend an honorary solemn ceremony in recognition of Yeshua's success. Ordinary meetings are put on hold until after the ceremony.

> *This 40 days and 40 nights is represented in the Lenten Christian based holiday, that starts with a ritual called "Ash Wednesday," which is approximately 46 days before the Easter/Resurrection holiday. Ash Wednesday's ceremonial procedure has a representative of the church, use the burnt remains of blessed palms, to anoint ones forehead with the sign of the cross. The ashes are from the previous year collected from the Sunday before Easter, called Palm Sunday. The Ash Wednesday ritual is a day of fasting. The individual person of the church usually sacrifices something desirable and that is not entirely beneficial for themselves for the entire 40 days. This is the beginning of repentance and sacrifice during a 40 day period leading up to the preparation of the Easter Holiday, excluding Sundays, furthering the representative mutual correlation between the Baptism purification and the cleansing of the Temptation of Christ in the Desert.*

Chapter Fifteen

THREE YEAR MINISTRY

Yeshua's divine humanity felt physical and emotional pain, hunger and even experienced death. Whereas His miracles and teachings are true evidences of His Soul's divinity. At the beginning of His ministry, Yeshua and His disciples attend a wedding in the area of Cana. This is when Yeshua performs humbly His first public miracle at the request of His Mother. He asked that the servants fill up the empty jugs with water to the brim and miraculously the water turned into wine. The significance of this miracle is compared to Moses turning water into blood and later Yeshua would perform a great miracle at the Last Supper when He changes the bread into His Body and the wine into His Blood.

As this miracle stands, it was the last miracle before His ultimate sacrifice would begin, The Passion. His acts of ministry were not done with thunderous fearful intimidations, but the forerunner of mercy, led by acts in the purist of love and to show compassion for all the suffering sinfulness that resides here amongst our world.

> "Do not believe Me unless I do what my Father does. But if I do it, even though you do not believe Me, believe the miracles, that you may know and understand that the Father is in Me and I in the Father."
>
> Yeshua

Elijah stayed close by *(overseer)* as he followed from afar during the "Three Year Ministry" of Yeshua. By the end of His Ministry, Yeshua covered a vast area of land, traveling by foot to various cities and towns. Some of the locations would include: Capernaum, Gennesaret, Syrian-Phoenicia, Bethsaida, Caesarea Philippi, Trachonitis, Mt Tabor, Jerusalem, Galilee, Judea and Samaria. Elijah identifies these regions as the "Promise Land."

During these travels, Yeshua was humble and did not use an authoritative influence when performing miracles. He performed many miracles that were always divinely inspired. They would include but are not limited to the following: Curing and healing lepers, paralytics, blind, deaf, dumb and possessed individuals as well as raising the dead. As a result, Yeshua's popularity had grown to a point where the hierarchy of a few religious leaders felt He was a threat to their powerful positions amongst the people. Because of this, they could not accept Yeshua, a humble carpenter from Nazareth to be the Messiah and attempted to seize His power and to remove Him of His entirety.

There were many times that Elijah and Yeshua would communicate over the three year period. However, there was only one major public appearance that occurred. This was when Yeshua's disciples were present during the Transfiguration. All through the *Three Year Ministry*, Yeshua had touched upon the sacred interests of the Articles of Faith, being ceremoniously courteous.

> Studies have proven that wine and water have the ability to sustain memory, as the (new approach) priest perform this ritual, they actually bend their head towards the wine and speak directly into the chalice that is holding the water and wine proclaiming the words, signifying Yeshua's connection with God, represented in the Last Super.

Chapter Sixteen

THE PASSION

Passion is a word with two meanings. It can be translated as an ardent affection of love. Passion also refers to the events that led up to and include the suffering of the Messiah, Yeshua. Through His death on the cross, was His passion for mankind and demonstrated the quintessential application of the word.

Yeshua was devoted to all people and cherished every moment of His ministry despite knowing the Romans would torture Him until His death. His unwavering devotion and demonstration within his teachings, would serve as the impetus (movement) that would save the masses (mankind) and give cause for His selfless sacrifice.

Yeshua's triumphant entrance into Jerusalem as well as other events were predestined and were foretold by very close friends of Elijah's father, Aligious. The friends were named Micah, Isaiah and Zachariah and they served right after the time of Elijah, and were given certain excerpts from "The Articles of Faith" by Elijah. This was done so that they could document an accurate account of the prophecy that was foretold as the truth, in order to maintain its integrity, so that the people would believe that the events undoubtedly would happen or happened.

The chosen few prophesied that there would be a virgin that would be with child and give birth to a son in Bethlehem called Emmanuel. Additional predictions would include: "Comes to you, the Messiah riding on a donkey, on a colt, the foal of a donkey," "They will have scourged Him, then pierce His hands and feet." "They divide His garments among them and cast lots for His clothing." While an accumulation of references

The Passion

can be linked, Yeshua's purpose was clear and precise. There would now be a connection to the "Book of Genesis" (Old Testament) with the New Testament.

(Note: Found on the back of an Elijah text (Code Essentials Genes, Genealogy Lineage, DNA & RNA)?

Passover

An annual ritual for the Jewish people is to travel to Jerusalem so that they may join together for the commemoration of the Hebrews' liberation, from slavery in Egypt. They also will celebrate the Passover meal with friends and family. The great Exodus led by Moses was recognized in the arduous (grueling) trek that Yeshua and His family took once a year in His younger days.

On this particular morning besides the house of Lazarus, Yeshua is about to fulfill a prophecy, when He gives instructions to a few of the disciples to acquire a donkey in order to ride into Jerusalem from a particular man *(Gabriel)*. He is precise in His directions.

According to the symbolic reference of the Eastern tradition, the donkey is an animal of peace, the opposite of the horse, which is the animal of war. Therefore, part of the Articles of Faith proclaims that He will come as the Prince of Peace, meek and sitting graciously on a donkey, bears relevance.

The disciples find that Elijah has a special donkey set aside for them to bring to Yeshua. Gabriel will deliver the chosen donkey that was donated especially by one of the Faction council members. Consequently, this donkey did not scamper, but had a smooth gate so it did not bounce the rider. In addition the donkey gave the council a comfortable vantage point to observe from afar, by allowing them to have clear audio and visual access from within the donkey.

Beginning His journey in late March (early spring), Yeshua descends from the Mount of Olives and prepared to enter the holy city. The nuances of nature are in bloom and many of His *followers* crowding fervently with Him for the trip. Part of the masses of bystanders is owing to the resurrection of a man called Lazarus, a miracle performed by Yeshua.

Not only did He raise Lazarus from the dead, He accomplished this miracle three days after the man's death. It was unheard of to bring someone back to life after three days have passed and adding to this, the decomposition was already in its early stages.

Amongst the crowds, the disciples felt proud to escort Yeshua and remained close to Him. It is early morning as they begin to enter the city. Yeshua reminds His disciples they should not yearn for proud positioning but rather serve others and to remember that the Son of Man will give His life as a ransom for many, showing His selflessness. The disciples' attention was alive, but fell on deaf ears in regard to reason.

On their journey, Yeshua sees a fig tree on route and approaches it, just to see that it has only leaves, with no fruit. He brazes His index finger slowly against one of the leaves and says, "May you never bear fruit again!" Immediately the tree withered. When the disciples witness this, they were perplexed as to why Yeshua would say this, considering that the fig trees are not in season. "How did the fig tree wither so quickly?" They asked. Yeshua responded, "Truly I tell you, if you have faith and no doubt, not only can you do what was done to the fig tree, but also you can say to this mountain, *go, throw yourself into the sea and it will be done*. If you believe, you will receive whatever you ask for in prayer." Yeshua was giving the disciples a connected piece of advice while knowingly setting the premises for the fulfillment of the Articles of Faith, pertaining to His Second Coming. Yeshua mounts *(plants)* yet another seed of fruition.

The Apostles were enjoying the happy atmosphere that was prevalent due to the frequency of miracles that were being performed by Yeshua. The miracles lifted up the spirits of so many while they waved palms in the air in a celebratory fashion. The people offered their cloaks and garments on the ground to mark the path that Yeshua's animal would walk upon.

This action of reverence, with the use of the palms became indicative of the *triumphant entrance* into Jerusalem as fit for a King, but not the type of King that the people would understand. This commemorative passage would eventually become the holiday of Palm Sunday and the beginning of Passion Week that is celebrated seven days before Easter, currently by over one billion people.

From afar, Yeshua scans the lands around Him and sees the people cascading towards Jerusalem. His thoughts were troubled, having knowledge of all the suffering and turmoil that will be based in the future, in the *lands* of Israel. He contemplates the hundreds of thousands of Jewish people that will perish vehemently by force and is unsettled by the sheer numbers. His body quivers as His eyes fill with tears. Yeshua weeps to understand that His Father/Creator has designed the concept of time so that your sins from the past may be forgiven. His conflicting thoughts are unhinged, thinking of the results for mankind's destiny. He is saddened when He recalls that one out of twelve people will be saved from the entire planet Earth after His second coming. This strains His heart given the immense cleansing efforts of the historic past by the Faction's efforts and the sacrifice He knows He has to endure, knowing it will not be in vain.

The number of people that Yeshua will aid successfully in enlightenment and salvation is staggering. In the chosen geographical area, by the Articles of Faith, it is evident that this region has the best probable outcome for seeding the world with the Good News. Exclusive to the *(selectively)* chosen enlightened intellectuals, that will endure unfortunate future events *(Jewish and others)*. Giving credence and reason why the selected people concentrated within this region, would eventually unfold into branches throughout the ages (spread-out). It will take a great number of learned people to become refugees and spread to new lands throughout the globe to share the Good News.

Yeshua's thoughts become deflated as He enters the temple, mostly because of the Jewish priests' presence enveloping the areaway. They have been trying to harass Yeshua and waiting for Him to falter. The chief priests are in need of an excuse to arrest Him, because He is a threat to their comfortable affluent positions within the Jewish communities. Many attempts have been made by the chief priests to trap Him with His own words, trying to uncoil His intellect. They are always frustrated and disappointed when the perfect answer is offered in response to their vexing questions. At the same time Yeshua is given opportunities to expose His opposition's weakness.

Yeshua's study with Elijah and His colleagues, along with His Connection to the Light, gives Yeshua a real time advantage. He is already surmising and knows beforehand exactly what is going to transpire, to whatever question is given. He always has the best response based on the equated probability.

One of the most popular interactions with a chief priest is when Yeshua is approached from within the crowd by one of the priest. The priest offers praise to Yeshua with compliments of flattery and His devotion to the truth. However, the true intention of the priest was to entrap Yeshua.

With a previous discussed plot, planned between the high and chief priests, they anticipate that Yeshua would be opposed to taxes. Their purpose of manipulating the conversation was to exploit Yeshua in front of the Roman guards who possessed power and authority.

> The governor at the time was Pontius Pilate. He was in charge of the Roman province of Judaea from AD 26–36. Pilate was the fifth magistrate/prefect serving *neath* below Tiberius, Emperor of Rome. Pilate was also the man responsible for the collection of taxes in Roman Judea, and only he had the authority to put anyone to death.

After the flattery and compliments, the chief priest proceeded with his convicting question. He asked Yeshua whether or not it is right for Jewish people to pay the taxes mandated by Caesar. Yeshua remained silent, while the chief priest provocatively spins to the crowd with a coin in his right hand and holds it up high. The chief priest urges Him for an answer, "Well should we pay or shouldn't we?" Yeshua looks calmly at the chief priest with a spearing stare at his posh garments, spanning His look at the priest's clothes from head to toe. The priest stands quiet in his glamorized fine attire amongst the crowd, gently holding his right hand out, holding the coin lower by his side and still standing his ground in the circle of people waiting for an answer. The chief priest was intimidated by Yeshua, because of his previous failed attempts to outwit Him and knew He was very special. The chief priest was just following the orders from the high priest.

The chief priest starts to move towards Yeshua. Yeshua asked him to produce this Roman coin that is suitable to pay taxes to Caesar. The chief priest leans into Yeshua and nervously hands Him the coin. As soon as Yeshua receives the coin, He raises His arm with coin for all to see in His right hand and asks, "Whose name and picture is on this coin?" Yeshua asks the crowd and they answers in harmony, "Caesar's!" So Yeshua

The Passion

responds, "Render therefore unto Caesar the things which are Caesar's and unto God the things that are God's."

Now inside the temple, once again Yeshua sees a merchant bazaar like atmosphere. The courtyard is filled with livestock and tables of the money exchangers. The money exchangers transfer money from one standard of currency to another for profit. This was an unfair practice bestowed upon the Jews. They had to convert their currency because it was the only way they would be able to purchase a pure/blessed/certified animal to sacrifice for the Passover.

The exchange of money is transacting and scattered amongst multiple tables within the courtyard. Greek and Roman currency, for Jewish and Tyrian money were exchanged throughout.

Enraged at the sight of this, Yeshua starts shouting with an uproar as He did two years previously. He begins abruptly overthrowing the tables of the moneychangers, then peps His way further releasing the cage doors to set the doves free. Using part of His weaved leather rope that is surrounding His garb, He steers and herds the livestock out of the temple, while nobody dared to do anything. While all the people lay stifled and shocked, Yeshua proclaims, "It is written, our Father's house shall be called the house of prayer; but you have made it a den of thieves."

Several of the chief priests witness this scene and quickly go back to inform Joseph Caiaphas, *(otherwise just known as Caiaphas)* who was the Jewish high priest. Caiaphas has been waiting for an excuse to organize a plot to be rid of Yeshua and is inspired by this occurrence.

Yeshua then leaves the city of Jerusalem circulating throughout the area, performing miracles and reciting parables for the people to easily understand and to spread the Good News.

In a village over a dozen furlongs away from the city, towards the base of the Mount of Olives, Yeshua spends the night at a Judean home in Bethany. The name Bethany translates to the house of poverty. Yeshua preferred to lodge here because of the familiarity and comforts with friends Mary, Martha and Lazarus.

On this "All Fools' Day" Judas Iscariot, one of the twelve original disciples, known just as Judas, is bargaining with the chief of the Sanhedrin, the supreme council or tribunal of the region. The Sanhedrin consists of twenty three members assembled back in ancient Jerusalem, established for the Jews during post exilic times (Moses). At this current time, Caiaphas the high priest who has religious and criminal jurisdiction within the Sanhedrin council, wants to expedite the plan to arrest Yeshua.

Judas the most intelligent disciple of the twelve was given the most important role in the infamous betrayal of Yeshua. It would be this discussion with the Sanhedrin that will set the stage to entrap Yeshua in a clandestine (secret) operation accusing Him of violations against the rules of the Jewish doctrine.

Judas is in charge of the disciples' monetary affairs. He takes out the disciples' moneybag to be filled by the priest as a payoff. This transaction would give the high priests a time and location where Judas will lead them to Yeshua. in order for Him to be arrested and questioned by the Sanhedrin. Judas becomes an ambivalent (in two minds) figure in the betrayal role, by setting the sequence of events that will lead to the Crucifixion/ Resurrection. According to the Articles of Faith this is one of the key components that spur salvation for mankind.

Nevertheless, John the apostle also has an important role and is the reason why he is at every symbolic event in the ministry of Yeshua. He would be a major figure that will bring everything together. He also was one of the few disciples that were fully aware of the Articles of Faith *(brothers James & John)* and he will use this information to keep an understanding perspective of events to come.

Garden

On Wednesday, right before Yeshua's arrest, Apostle John, James and Yeshua travel to the summit of the Mount of Olives, leaving the other apostles in Bethany. Their journey would bring them to a place where they can join with Elijah and his colleagues in order to be escorted to a historic meeting, known as the Alacritous-Tribulation *(Preparation for the Passion of Christ)*.

They finally arrived in the City of Adelaide, were Elijah spent most of his childhood with his father. The group travels to the Aitho Circle Building, where Elijah's father Aligious once held the highest position amongst the heads.

The Council begins convening, when the guests of the highest honor are before all. Not only would the heads of each of the Factions be present,

The Passion

but hundreds of the most important influential people/species amongst the Union of Planets would also be in attendance. The Council begins to explain clearly to Elijah, Yeshua, John, James and Elijah's colleagues, which they are under no obligation to go forward with this excruciating woe that has yet to happen.

All who were present gave gratitude to the three honored guests and recognized their actions and willingness to undergo the task has been unparalleled in courage and selflessness. They are met with applause from the entire council. After all of the twelve members spoke, the meeting was then finished and the crowd left with sincere hope and gratitude.

Yeshua with James and John gather themselves to walk with Elijah in order to show how the building is compartmentalized into important work halls for serving the established societies residing on the Earth.

They entered into a study hall labeled THW, an acronym for Temporal Historic Watchmen, which is a massive time security alliance troop. This "Order" protects the time continuum from unauthorized time traveling in the entire sector, in order to safeguard the tangible or intangible current existence. In addition, the THW has programs that cross reference probable outcomes. Knowingly, the Watchmen have an already established timeline, with future actions taken as per the Articles of Faith *(which transpire after a previous existing timeline)*. Therefore, John and James ask the obvious, "If we follow the "Articles of Faith," what would be the difference in-towards the amount of people saved?" Access to these databases is limited to a privileged few. Elijah having authorization looks at his colleagues, then at John, James and Yeshua and motions His hands in connection to a display monitor and retrieves the data. Elijah backing away from the monitor with his right hand open, arm half raised, inviting everyone to see the results. It turns out that there is a 12 to 1 ratio vs. 144 to 1, per person saved, as calculated upon the Second Coming of Yeshua in 2037.

> *Note: These results are for the number of people that Yeshua will save, but is small in comparison to the billions of others that have passed through their lives throughout the last two thousand years. All that have benefitted from accepting His existence and getting closer to a purification state, to be glorified spiritually.*

Jesus' Mentor

Everyone is overwhelmed by the dramatic results; however, Elijah is feeling solemn and inadequate knowing the enormous suffering Yeshua will face, as well as the pain ahead for John and James. Elijah gave a subdued approval while everyone else was elated. Elijah was saddened because of his personal bond with Yeshua. He had been watching and caring for Him since He was born. He had always been there to protect Yeshua and was uneasy with the feeling of helplessness he will experience and not able to intervene properly with what is to happen.

Feeling useless Elijah looks over to Yeshua with a guilty stare, knowing that he is responsible for this situation because of his innovations. Yeshua sees Elijah's remorse and pain. So He explains to Elijah without hesitation, "If just one day is a gift, think about how many more we are all given." Elijah produces a half smile, somewhat lifted but still down. Then with an inverted smile, Elijah's arms are apart and proceeds towards Yeshua to give Him a slow embrace *(hug)*. While he approaches, Yeshua lifts up His right hand and says, "Please Pappy, not in front of the men!" Elijah nervously starts laughing and his cooped up emotions are released by instantly remembering an incident that he and Yeshua had in their travels, a private joke.

Yeshua was usually pleasant, serious natured and had rarely indulged in humor, but when He did, these humorous moments were primarily with Elijah. Yeshua would be in delight of Elijah's smile, because He knew it brought him back to the time, when he found joy being with his father Aligious. Yeshua knew His humor would help fill this vacancy in Elijah.

It is Thursday, April 2nd and the mystical Last Supper is being prepared by the women and the disciples. It is after sunset and the twelve disciples will share in this Passover meal. There will be significant mystical events that will transpire. The apostles will not be able to grasp the magnitude of these events until many days later.

Holy Thursday is the name that will be given to this historical day of the sacrificial Passover and it will become a slender projection given as a Holy Day for followers in the future. This day will be celebrated in "Holy Week."

After the Last Supper, Yeshua takes the remaining eleven disciples to the foot of the Mount of Olives to form discussions. From the disciples gathering, He purposefully chooses apostles James and John, the two sons of Zebedee, who were of the Centurion bloodline and whose father was a dear colleague of Aligious. While Yeshua, James and John start walking towards their ascent, Yeshua turns back around towards the cropped array of men and says with a bout of wit, "Peter are you not coming?" Peter erupts from the huddle of men, with his head down and starts to quickly trot, in order to catch up to Yeshua. Apostle Peter is now on trek to follow Yeshua to His customary place of serenity (prayer), along with James and John. This location is where Yeshua would often have visitations with Elijah.

This special area is called Gethsemane, "Garden of Olives" and is located to the east of the Kidron Valley, where the path leads up the mountain that connects to Jericho. Situated at the opening of the sanctuary, are gardens and flowered rows of crops, bordered with rocks and tall wilted grass.

Yeshua tells the three apostles, "Be still here and stern, pray that you will not fall into temptation!" Yeshua then withdraws from the apostles and ambles on foot to a curve, beyond the olive trees and passes under a protrusion of the mountain to meet with Elijah and Gabriel.

Yeshua gives a warm and endearing firm rapid hug to each of His friends, then lingers. All knowing that this is the last time they will be able to converse on a normal plateau before His demise. Elijah and Gabriel affected by Yeshua's modest mode of character, bearing that He has already become hungry in an apathetic meditative state.

Gabriel begins to apply analgesic herbs to Yeshua's neck and back, with tender care. Yeshua realizes what Gabriel is doing and looks to Elijah for an explanation. Elijah quickly says, "We thought of using these ointments to numb your skin for a full day, so that it will lessen the pain." Subsequently, Yeshua lifts His right hand facing forward and outward in front of His heart, indicating that there is no need for these ointments. He then says, "We are aware the time has come, thank you for your devotion." Yeshua concludes their meeting by releasing the hands of both the men in which He had held for support. Elijah and Gabriel ascend quietly into the night sky, lacking emotion by their grief in this heart wrenching moment.

Walking back past a few cypress trees, exhausted by sorrow, Yeshua says to his disciples in a delirious voice, "The flesh is weak and My Spirit is here." Yeshua, now filled with anguish, attempts to find His favorite place to pray. He stops in His tracks, stands still amidst a smooth large stone with an olive tree right beside it and begins to contemplate not only His death, but the torture, humiliation and pain that He is going to ensue.

Jesus' Mentor

He begins to walk further away from the apostles, weakened by every step while great sorrow overwhelms His Spirit. His eyes unfocused, filled with tears that eventually fall from his beautiful, yet saddened sapphire eyes. These vibrant eyes have now turned to a dull grey, worried with concern.

He stumbles towards the trunk of His favorite thick woven olive tree, unable to see one of the very thin branches stemming out horizontally. It braises the top of His scalp drawing blood and then He falls to His knees. He softly holds the branch that scraped and pierced His head, which is still attached to the tree. He studies its appearance in a pensive (pondering) state and becomes grateful for all the wonderful prayers He has shared alongside and above its roots. He then looks up to the heavens, kneeling while both of His hands lay rest against the tree's heartwood. His hands become bright with light but remain camouflaged by the bark of the trunk, fading into the interior of the twisted base of the tree. As Yeshua is bent and leaned over, He tries to look up, overheated with anxiety.

He is finally able to verbalize His thoughts and says, "Father, if You are willing to take this cup from Me; yet be it not My will, but Yours to be done!" With His arms straight attached to the tree, His head drops between His arms, tears flung from His face, knelt burning inside, with His pores overheated and perspiring. As His tears swill downward towards His chin, they merge with sweat and blood from His head. One drop follows after another while the droplets fall in tempo, like a countdown drumming that is measured not in time, but in terms of a single event becoming one; past, present, future *(blood, sweat and tears)*.

As Yeshua's prayers became stronger, His head lifts with eyes immersed and again they appear like two precious crystal stones glistening beneath the clear surface to the sea of uncertainty. He accepts for what is to come, *(flagellation/death)* now becoming impassive because He knows that His sacrifice is an act of absolute pure love in compliance with the Articles of Faith.

As Yeshua departs from this moment, He leaves behind His residual frenetic signature absorbed by this one special olive tree. This tree's roots have touched the tears, energy and very essence of Him. As a result this tree will be nourished until His return. It will and is in history, the oldest living *(Oleaceae Family)* Olive tree known; along with several other trees that were grafted from this same "Holy Tree," in the land of Jerusalem.

Coming back into sight, a stone's throw away from the three apostles, Yeshua sees them sleeping and awakes them filled with disappointment that they did not stay alert. Looking towards Peter, He says once more, "Pray, not to fall into temptation." Yeshua is preparing His Spirit for what is to come. Peter is being conditioned for a life changing event *(the denial)* that will strengthen his spirit for the work that he must carry out after Yeshua's death.

Betrayal

In the distance approaches a mob like crowd. They have lighted torches and lanterns and are being led by disciple Judas Iscariot. Among them are the Sanhedrin guards and they are armed with weapons. They stand and wait for the signal from the officials to arrest Yeshua. The guards need confirmation as to who Yeshua was. Judas approaches Yeshua and then greets Him as the revealer, by kissing the face of God, at cross purposes. The head official waves his hand by the flickering light towards Yeshua, to indicate that this is the man they want to arrest.

As three guards approach Yeshua, to take hold of Him, two of the Sanhedrin guards lagged behind to make sure they wouldn't be ambushed. Rustling his way through the soldiers is the infamous *servant* of the Jewish high priest named "Malchus." He jockeys for the vanguard position to confront Yeshua. Malchus is an especially irritating character, who in the past gave the disciples a lot of trouble.

Peter was furious with Malchus' arrogance and cowardly aggression. Committing to an act of aggression, Peter impulsively draws his sword to protect Yeshua. In this attempt to strike Malchus, the would-be victim blocked the blow with his lantern to protect himself. As a result, the sword clambered off to the right toward Malchus' head and sliced off a portion of his ear.

Peter did not understand that this event needed to happen because he was not informed of the dynamics of the overall plan. John and James stood by and watched in dismay because they knew these events had to transpire. Yeshua swept His arm and hand towards Peter and adamantly says, "No! Peter, he who draws the sword, shall perish by the sword." This most important adage/phrase is very dear to Yeshua, because of the impact it will have on judgment day after His Second Coming. This quote will determine the outcome for so many, regarding who is chosen and who is not.

Then Yeshua said to Peter, "Put away the sword into the sheath; the cup which my Father has given Me, shall I not drink it?" Yeshua stands firm and puts His hand over the wounded ear of Malchus the servant. Yeshua in a locked stare, controlling the two guards, then heals the servant's ear. Malchus was shocked and was hypnotized by Yeshua's compassion. Yeshua then said to the guards "It is I you are seeking, as I will come willingly, but these men are innocent, leave them alone." After witnessing the healing of the servant's ear, the soldiers decide they should listen to Yeshua, and so they march away with only Him.

Once the Priests had Yeshua in their possession, they had to conjure up a legitimate reason as to why they have ceased Him. Caiaphas the high priest was influencing the thoughts of the other chief priests and was encouraging them to desperately seek false evidence, with which they could frame Yeshua. They are unable to find any.

Yeshua remains silent throughout most of the proceedings until finally Caiaphas demands that Yeshua admit whether He is the Christ *(The Son of God)*. Yeshua responds "You have said so" and then Yeshua gives the congregation what they are looking for, and says "I Am, and you shall see the Son of Man sitting at the Right Hand of Power, coming again in the clouds of heaven." Caiaphas tore his robe as a convincing dramatic action to signify that Yeshua will be charged with blasphemy and order Him to be beaten. Yeshua the whole time was fixated with a physically tired stare, on the Phylactery box that was worn by the Priests on the front top of their heads. This small box accompanies an important prayer or scripture that is carried with a particular priest in order to praise God.

There were approximately six different types of hearings and interrogations from the Sanhedrin, Roman authorities *(hierarchies)* and chief priests. When Caiaphas and the chief priest's plan were ready to unfold, they realized the necessity to manipulate Pontius Pilate, the Roman governor of Judea. He and he alone would have the final say and hopefully condemn Yeshua to death by crucifixion. The high priest had to go this route because he lacked the authority to execute.

The Passion

Pilate gave resistance to the high priest after interviewing Yeshua. He found no tangible reason to condemn Him. Pilate was annoyed, but then capitulated (gave in), though he felt he was being used skillfully. So Pilate conjures up an amicable witty idea and then informs the priests and Caiaphas that he will let the people decide, for it was Passover and so the tradition is to release one prisoner as a sign of good will.

Acting quickly Caiaphas tells his chief priests to pay the two guards that are assigned to the entrance of the courtyard to filter out anyone suspicious that would support Yeshua and not let them enter the courtyard for the judgment ritual. This action would almost guarantee His crucifixion. There were three prisoners that were being held to be crucified and Yeshua was the fourth. One of them would be set free, in accordance within the Passover tradition allowed by Pilate.

Meanwhile, it was customary to send prisoners to be scourged in order to hasten (assist) the crucifixion process. It will inevitably quicken the victim's death on the cross. Not only would it be excruciating torture but it would also instill fear into the crowds, allowing the Romans to keep organized control over the populations of the territories.

When sending a prisoner to be scourged, the Romans used a torture whipping technique called flogging. This intense punishment would include the lashing of the back of the body while tied to a stake. In many cases this was done while waiting for a trial to commence or preceding the inevitability of crucifixion. Yeshua and or one of the three prisoners will be selected to be released or *passed over* in order to avoid death. The choice would be the decision of the crowd that was present in the courtyard. The Roman guards take the prisoners on foot (shackled) to the other side of the fortification *(northwest)*, so that the scene could be monitored from Pilate's Palace.

En route, Yeshua passes a condensed facility area, made up of clusters of old worn horse and carriage barns adjacent to the main complex. Within these storage huts and barns are now the living quarters, holding an assemblage of foreign slaves and some prisoners convicted of petty crimes. This overcrowded wooden frail shelter, is a selected location for slaves that are used for hod carrying *(a carrier of supplies or material, usually strapped by wood and rope balanced on the shoulders)* and other menial tasks.

While in the midst of the guards escorting the prisoners, Yeshua who is a furlong behind the others, looks over at the old huts and sees aggressive hand motions dangling from the windowless openings, followed by sarcasm emanating from the inhabitants. The slave quarters leave a harsh stench, while a wretched aroma surrounds the area. Yeshua carries on and tiredly walks clung to metal chains.

Continuing up, following alongside a lengthy limestone wall, Yeshua sees a huge fortress. The structure has doorway openings every hundred steps, made from oak beams boarded up to the lentil. The wooden doorways are fastened with three metal hinges that is utilized by the servants or slaves to enter into the palace to perform their duties. As the slave quarters are conveniently on the opposite side of the road.

Yeshua stops and stands facing the crowd of observers, stares in exhaustion, confused and begins moving again. Scuffling about the dusty road are numerous horses snorting, with metal clanging. There are leathery guards (soldiers) trekking along, with curt abrupt commands being bellowed in a deep hollow. Unnervingly, this well traveled perdition route is the prelude to what bears around the corner.

Scourge

Scourge optional read: Upon leaving the intermittent shadows of this caustic road, the sunlight bares two walls that make-up a stone corner, about ten feet in height. Arrived, seeing the base of the wall is made from blocks of limestone; the rest has mortared stone from a past build. Still there is a third knee wall to the left of the inner corner, approximately three feet high, similar to the foundation portion of the rest of its parts. This small knee wall is for bystanders to watch from a vantage point behind the flogging area from a slightly raised elevation, to give a panoramic overview of the torture ritual.

For the most part, the Romans are infamously known for this type of punishment, but not the originators *(Persia, Babylon)*. The pillars are laid out in a triangulated pattern in a thirty foot by thirty foot square, with one part open. Each pillar is assigned two executioners or floggers, sometimes referred to as ruffians.

These Roman soldiers *(past violent criminals)* were especially handpicked for their extreme measures of brutality. Elijah and his team were overseeing the situation with grave difficulty while camouflaged by the clouds, making sure not to interfere with the events below, as this day has come.

As Yeshua is weltered being pushed along, He walks with His starving and already beaten body delivered from the Sanhedrin. Then He walks into the sunlight and witnesses a scene that finds Him unnerved. Yeshua sees three thick wooden pillars protruding from the ground. His mind is shocked as He loses His breath. He is fixated on the closest pillar with its two rusted rings bolted on the top sides of this six foot tall, twenty four inch girthed cylinder of a stake.

Yeshua remains shocked and dithered, His eyes directed at the weathered gray pillars, wood scorched and baked from the sun. The purple tint on the wooden stake's surface appears petrified from all the scourged remains of blood and fluid worn into the Northern side of this torturing device.

To the left is a wooden table laid out broad sided, so that the public can view the flagellation and showoff the display of whips spooled up neat in a circle, resting against hooks. This table is about ten feet long and is used also to repair any of the whips if need-be. The Roman legionnaires/ruffians/hooligans, take pride in their torturous flogging devices. They proudly display the different styles of whips, sporting braided leathery stems and an assorted sadistic collection of infliction tips, which are tied to the thongs.

Six of these flagrums hung, awaiting use by one of the six floggers. The whips/flagrums have an oak handle one foot long, with a diameter of just over an inch. The gripping area of the whip, has a leather strap spiraled towards the bottom of the handle and an additional tied leather strap towards the top, which is notched into the wood for strength, to prevent slippage. The handle locks, into an extended four foot whole piece of an entire leather braided stem *(ox-hide)*, with four loose leathery thongs dangling.

These loose thongs are suspended owing to barbs or massilias, which are sewn or knotted, as a weighted attachment at the very end or tip of the thong/whip. The usual Roman barb set up was four thongs, three barbs for each thong, giving a total of twelve lashes per swipe. These designs consist of a methodical sized weighted order, allowing the smaller lighter barb to be situated in the front of the thong in order to assist the second heavier barb to inflict the damage.

The massilias/barbs are imperfect balls of metals made from zinc, iron, lead or bronze and at times wood. They are attached by looping or tied in by knotting. The lightest but the largest third item, is the cutting barb which is usually sheep bone, wood or a metal hook. These items are similarly attached by sending the strand of leather through the center of the barb, then knotting it or tying a small thread around the thong above and below each barb. Engineered to wield the most punishment, the barbs are situated about an inch apart and stay in their designated place.

Coming from beyond, out of another slave dwelling, is a frightening seen of four executioners/floggers coming towards the forum, dust dragging behind them, as you can hear the scuffle and obscenities due to their drunken stupor state. Yeshua still and tired with no sleep after the many Sanhedrin and Roman trials He encountered. Yeshua watches the vipers approach.

The crowd simmers down seeing these wretched demons, wearing cured leather across their chests, metal shoulder pads with bands of metal around their forearms and flapped metal girds to cover their loins. Part of their wear/uniform is to protect them while they are in the process of whipping the prisoners. Beneath this protective gear in between, is exposed bare hairy arms and legs, dirty with the stench of a wild beast, covered in scars. These floggers were malefactors from different lands that had been condemned for horrible crimes, but spared because of their cruelty and their mere size, so that they could be used as slave labor, building aqueducts and structures for Rome.

Two of the executioners were unable to come because of severe headaches. This was solely due to their increased alcoholic intake level, influenced by Gabriel's intervention, as well as the inferior alcohol they were consuming. Gabriel's method was based on the hope that if there were only two fewer floggers, the remaining executioners would have to pick up the extra work to complete the job and without replacements, the floggers would be too tired to inflict extra punishment on Yeshua (and so he thought).

Out of the four soldiers that performed the flagellation, one of them was off the immediate premises after being tired from an earlier flogging as well as being extremely intoxicated. He is seen moseying outside the grounds, leaving three men left to flog the two remaining prisoners. Barabbas, who was arrested for killing a Roman soldier, is about to undertake, of what the Romans say, a "half death" for it is his turn to be scourged. A half death is the state that the floggers leave their victims, due to torn flesh and muscles, accentuated by excessive bleeding, presenting their prisoner as half dead, ready for crucifixion.

It is a Rabbinic or Jewish law to receive a maximum of 40 lashes/stripes minus 1, for a total of 39. This was created by the Jewish people to have a more civilized approach to barbarism and being less harsh with regards to this subject of punishment. This idea was adopted because of the representation of Moses returning from Mount Horeb after 40 days with the Ten Commandments.

> *The number forty has been used repeatedly in different ancient religions. The importance of 40 is the root of the number. The different numbers and sacred geometry has been injected into our religions and ancient megalithic structures to help us one day to advance, but more importantly, when the human integration of the Factions comes to be, the code will have been broken and the people will be more settled in their understanding of the integration process that has to take place. Plainly put, 40 is a positive integer, the sum of the first four pentagonal numbers; it is a pentagonal pyramidal number, and also an octagonal number (composite number). Sequential numbers 1, 3, 9, 27 = 40 and oddly enough human DNA is coded with a connecting pentagonal spiral of a double helix, which connects directly to the number 40! These are the paramount reasons for the number forty being a part (received) of human customs and traditions.*

Laughing the two legionaries throw Barabbas against the pillar in front, while joking about his petite skinny body. One of the floggers named Brutus is called over and converses with the other flogger. Huddled they are selecting their whips, while making an agreement with Brutus his coworker for a challenge of speed tradeoffs. Brutus looks over at the "counter caster" confirming he is ready to start. This *counter caster* clerk or number counter, employed by the Romans, tracks the lashes that are delivered, to make sure the floggers are accurate with the 40 minus 1 rule. The clerk holds a board *(Abacus)* made of zinc and lead that has eight long grooves. The beads are visible from both sides and contain up to five beads in each of the eight grooves, having a total of forty grooved metal slide balls to keep count. One of the balls is colored black having a cross carved into it, indicating the minus one.

Brutus raises his whip as does his coworker. Barabbas' eyes bulge as Brutus lashes a circular residual motion with super speed. Now begins a tradeoff between the floggers; one hit after another whistling in a rapid circular motion. The counter caster fumbles the beads in the Abacus, nervously counting as fast as he can, then screams out halt, halt! Barabbas received his *thirty-nine* lashes in less than twenty seconds. Brutus loses, which is something he is not accustom to. Brutus' opponent is indicated, the fastest flogger.

Before Barabbas is dragged away, Brutus continues to show off for the people watching and picks up a handful of sand and looks down at Barabbas on the sanded ground saying, "You got off too easy." He then rubs the sand into Barabbas' wounds aggressively. Barabbas in a knelt position arches his back, twitches and hollers as his voice cracks into a pant of pain. Then Brutus kicks him in his side with the heel of his boot, tilting him back down to the ground, delivering a laugh and wisecrack trying to entertain the crowd.

The third flogger who did not participate, is in charge of guarding the area surrounding the flagellation station, to make sure no one interferes with the procedure, but he seemed left out of the stimulating challenge that he witnessed and wanted to assert an ostentatious (showy) display of his own.

Brutus designates orders, not because he is in charge but because of the intimidation of his size and presence. He calls over the sitting flogger who did not participate in the last flogging to assist him. Brutus relieves the other coworker that had just finished flogging, but then commands him to bring Yeshua to the forum.

(Discretion is advised with regards to the descriptive analysis being necessary. Yeshua gave His life with obedience and understanding with "Love," to help all the people of the Earth. As to what comes next and to what He endures are only portions of the true severity of what ensued.)

Brutus hangs his custom whip on his personal hook and takes a break while waiting for the Roman guard. He sees him walking with Yeshua, who hands Him over to the retrieving coworker. About twenty yards from the forum, the ruffian flogger demands the Roman guard to assist and help bring Him over.

While taking his wooden staff in an overwhelming display of aggressiveness, he sawed towards Yeshua. Constricting his grip around the staff, he pulls it back and then delivers a whipping wind-tone on his follow through, striking it against the back legs of Yeshua, causing Him to bend His knees, sending Him plummeting to the ground.

In order to incite more of a show, the ruffian ties a chord around the ankles of Yeshua and the two men proceed to drag Him on His back towards the front corner pillar. The rakers leave the grounds surrounding the pillars level and clean, for the sand floor absorbs and neutralizes the fluids that flow from the prisoners while being flogged.

Suddenly a voice cries out, "Untie Him!" Brutus makes the demand as they enter the forum. The guards help Yeshua to His feet. He stands and His body shakes in anticipation as to what will occur. Brutus grabs Yeshua aggressively by His right shoulder and shuffles Him over close to the crowd of onlookers then screams in an angry voice, while shaking Yeshua's body, "Do any of you want to take His place." The crowd cowers and backs up slightly while their expressions change. Yeshua, lies still and weak, donning an old king's mantle above His tunic. King Herod had given Yeshua one of his old mantles as a form of mockery, in a humorous trifling matter, insinuating He was the "King of the Jews."

Brutus gets closer to the crowd then says, "Well anyone, not even for a King, come now!" Brutus spins Yeshua around and barbarously pounds his fist into the cheek bone of Yeshua, leaving an imprint on His face from Brutus' large silvery monogrammed ring. Instantly Yeshua falls in a kneeling position with His arm extended supporting Himself against the small knee wall, trying to recover while He gathers spurted breaths as He recovers from the blow.

With Yeshua's head bent over in exhaustion, He finds enough energy to look up and stare peacefully, singling out a particular woman. The crowd is suddenly moved when Brutus takes one step towards Yeshua, leans over and grabs His hair near His forehead. Then immediately yanks back

His hair, lifting His head up so the onlookers can see His face pointed in the direction of the crowd's sight. Then Brutus while holding Yeshua's head up asserts a lunge at a frail lady standing upfront holding a small basket of fruit. Brutus is being dramatic, stops in his tracks immediately after faking an aggressive move towards the frail woman, when in actuality he only moved a foot.

Brutus then delivers in a seductive voice, "You would be marvelous to switch positions with Him." The lady backs up slowly, Brutus says sweetly, "Come on" then he screams out, "Get over here!" the lady suddenly spasms and drops her basket in fright, spins away to a slow pace and then into a run. Brutus laughs as she glides away, "You see people, what can I say?" "Here!" Brutus barks as he tosses Yeshua towards his two coworkers. One of them had previously flogged Barabbas and the other executioner was fully rested. This ready to go new flogger was noted for his mastery of the whip and was eager to show off his talents.

Brutus walks over to the short wall to have a seat, with his leather and metal attire squeezing and creaking. He makes noises of belching and breathing and equally disturbing is the gross sounds he produces with each step. People back away as he is about to sit, for he is smelly and covered with spats of blood and sweat.

As Brutus sits down and slightly away, a newly appointed lictor approaches the other two executioners and quietly tells them to hurry up in no uncertain terms. The lictor is a Roman official that is usually the in-charge supervisor entrusted to administer the laws on site. On his body is strapped, the decorated fasces that is worn as a symbol which exhibits his authority. Brutus releases a "Hm" when he overhears these *(hurry up)* requests, then turns his head back to the crowd and sarcastically says, "We'll see about that, ha!" Caustic and contemptuous foulness erupts from the crowd that is getting increasingly rambunctious. Brutus chuckles and is entertained by the people.

The coworkers team up together then tear off the king's mantle from around Yeshua's shoulders. Swiftly they fling it into the onlookers; heightening the audience's excitement as the crowd viciously tugs and fights for the mantle, tearing it into pieces, like hyenas ripping apart their "prey." The crowd's attention was now distracted away from the forum while the ruffians proceed with the removal of Yeshua's tunic, leaving just the subligaculum, the article of undergarment clothing known as the loincloth. The material was of soft Syrian cloth that He wore simply knotted on each side of the hips to cover the buttocks and the surrounding areas. After the stripping of the garments, Yeshua is forced down to His knees. A hand grabs His left shoulder and Yeshua turns His head left and looks at the hand of the man that is about to flog him. He is swiftly thrown to the ground face down, immediately the new flogger positions his boot upon Yeshua's body and presses down onto His back. Keeping Him face down affixed to the granular sand, Yeshua shows no resistance, stoic in His demeanor. The new flogger with one leg firm on the ground and the other leg secure to the back of Yeshua, seems as if he is posing for the audience, dominating a hunted kill. Proud with his head held high, appearing in a masculine position, twitches his head proud as his galea *(Roman helmet)* distracts the onlookers. The distraction is apparent, because attached at the top of his helmet, is a loose partially affixed red fur that curves to the top of this helmet. It is not attached properly and so it dangles distracting the bystanders. A galea is a common Roman soldier's helmet and connected to the top of this galea, is a metal rectangular housing that harnesses a red curved fur, pea-cocking about three inches high above the helmet. This stylish portion of the helmet is called an elmo. This particular ruffian's galea was a classic among other Roman soldiers and acquired from his gladiator days and his successful battled past. It was an opulent galea, having a shinny silvery finish, adding to the bronze trim on the ear flap protectors and to polish off, a decorative cluster of gold medallions laminated on its crest. Validating the flair of the helmet, it was topped with a bright red fur, spiked and curved up at the top center of the headgear. This was his *modus operandi*, dramatic routine for his signature show boating antics.

    The original flogger goes over behind where the count caster is sitting and grapples a rope that was stored on a nail, looped up like a lariat. The rope was twenty four feet in length with a diameter of almost six centimeters in thickness and was made from strands of papyrus fibre for great durability. After seizing the rope, the ruffian laces it through two three inch pitted iron loop system, that are on opposite sides of the pillar and are attached about five feet high on the wooden stake. The flogger takes the excess of the cord and dispels it away from the pillar towards Yeshua, landing with either ends of the ropes alongside His head. Meanwhile, Brutus acting out towards the crowd, grabs Yeshua's tunic from the ground and is making a comedic stutter step with the tunic. He positions it oddly against his rotund body, saying in a high pitched voice, "Okay, the toga" while he changes the linens of the tunic to simulate the fashion style of a toga. Then Brutus continues to scrabble the cloth to the outside of his person. The audience laughed, he proceeded to emulate more styles, "Look, the pallium cloak, oh wait, the priest." The crowds tone lowers quickly into an affronted dragged "oh," because of trepidation hearing the word priest. While continuing to flip styles with the cloth, the slew of onlookers continued to be entertained, similar to a theatre stage as his coworkers tie Yeshua's wrists with slip knots. The more weight a victim has, the more added pressure to the rope, causing a tighter grip while constricting blood flow to the hands. This happens when the victim can no longer stand and is unable to withstand the pain.

Now that Yeshua's wrists are attached to the cord, the original coworker goes to the back of the pillar about ten feet behind, grips the rope then tugs it from the center of the pillar between the two rings, trying to hoist Yeshua into position. Brutus yells, "Put your back into it boy!" Working, the ruffian is angled backward in a weighted leaned position, using his legs for strength and utilizes the loops as a pulley for leverage. He slowly lifts Yeshua's limp body off the floor and magnetically pulls His body into place with His hands above the rings. The new ruffian then takes the tension with one hand and loops the now two single ropes, twisting them around each of the holding hooks.

The soldier grabs the excess rope, stretching it lower on each side for the corresponding loops *(assertively)*, doubling the rope together while curving an oval motion strand from hook to hook. He then fastens the rope to be locked and taut.

Yeshua now has been hoisted up, feet on the ground famished and weak. He knows that Gabriel's numbing agent will be somewhat ineffective. Watching overhead and cloaked are Elijah and his crew including the apostles John and James. James had just received his nimbus once he reached the age of thirty, being from Centurion descent and now having the power to heal.

The Passion

>*Note about James: Unfortunately, during James' own ministry, he will endure the same fate as John the Baptist by the same Herod/Kingdom, for both of them had been known to be of Centurion bloodline, therefore beheaded in order for them not to be reborn.

Elijah and colleagues are stressed as they watch from above. They are surprised when the new flogger goes to check the ties on Yeshua's wrists and appears as if he is ready to inject pain on Yeshua. When he touches Yeshua's hand while pulling on the ropes to make sure it's secure, Yeshua looks up at him, makes eye to eye contact, and says calmly to him, "You are Paul" then nods His head to him as if a sign of greeting. The man locked onto the radiant blue eyes of The Lord and then suddenly the soldier (Paul) dropped back one step, his forehead becoming wrinkled as his eyebrows rise in shock, blood blushing his face and hurriedly swallows as if there is a rock lodged in his throat. Suddenly, he turns away in disbelief, looks over at the lictor, then approaches him while taking off his galea/helmet, with his elmo half attached, quietly says with a tight subservient voice, that he is relished with the same alcoholic poisoning that the others had endured and won't be able to perform today. When saying this to the lictor, who was new at this post, he understood and had knowledge of the other men that drank excessively, so the lictor told him not to worry and said, "This is the last prisoner."

From this day forward this executioner never returned to work in any form of capacity with the Roman legionnaires and turned out to be one of the strongest forces in spreading the teachings and works of Yeshua. As well as his son, who would one day help bind the "New Testament."

Brutus states to the other flogger, "Ok it's just us." The same two men gather their own flagrums, for each of them will not operate as a team, but administer the lashes as individuals. Brutus lets his coworker go first while he walks away in the direction towards the counter caster. Brutus then blocks the counter's view talking loud to entertain the onlookers, but making it impossible for the counter to do his job. Alarmed in the unfairness taking place, Elijah and crew immediately focus a particle spurt beam that targets the tips of the whip, while the flogger is between hits. The particle beam would unnoticeably loosen and sever the objects attached to the end of the thongs/whip, but being careful just to eliminate the barbs on only two of the four thongs, so that the ruffians won't detect the differential of weight. Already the flogger has gone over the 40 minus 1 lashing law by double, leaving the lictor no choice to tell Brutus to let the caster counter see.

The lashes continue without a single count. Brutus moves aside so to listen to his superior, but looking at the crowd continuing to play the game for theatrical purposes. Brutus letting the counter see, for now, yet seconds later continues his antics. Disabling once again the counter's ability to do his job, now by pressing his huge mitt of a hand against the abacus, not enabling the caster to count or move the metal balls. The lashes continue, Yeshua's arms are stretched out with His body that lays dangled, slowly wobbling. His toes are the only part of His body feeling the ground.

The thuggery continues when the lictor demands Brutus to leave the area of the counter and just do your job. Brutus prideful collects an attitude, then says, "No problem here, let's continue." Brutus immediately looks down at the abacus, "Well it looks like there are only thirteen counted, so let's see" Brutus looking at his fingers counting one finger at a time, projecting sarcasm, as he looks aimlessly in the sky, "Ah yes, twenty-six to go," a smirk lingers on his face.

Before Brutus unleashes another twenty six additional strikes, he has to relieve his coworker. Nonetheless, there has already been a marathon of flagellation that has taken place and caused serious trauma. These cruel barbarians left Yeshua in a state of hypovolemic shock owing to a considerable loss of blood. The metal spheres and sheep bones caused excessive skin lacerations in a blood striped pattern, tearing into the subcutaneous tissues. The heavier metal weighted balls on the tips of the whips, caused deep contusions with immense pain, followed by circulatory calamity of the nerves. This resulted in convulsive spasms and contractions of the muscles, leaving Him with a sudden violence of pain, then becoming distraught, leading to emotional disturbance.

Brutus still controls the atrocity that is taking place and is now wearing his whip around the outskirt of his neck, looped under his left armpit. Brutus acted chipper, as he approached the pillar and smacked the back of his coworker in an affectionate passing, while the tired flogger takes a rest on the knee-wall.

The Passion

Elijah's team is ready to send pulses down to rid some of the torturous elements on Brutus' whip. Brutus moans as he gets back up, he clumsily approaches the front of the pillar and with a vengeance, he unravels his whip, then reaches back as far as he can reach, stepping into one of the hardest hits imaginable. No longer is there any noise coming from Yeshua or even movement, but His body still quivers as Brutus distributes the lashes and lacerations to areas that do not have ribbons of bleeding flesh. As this onslaught of flogging continues, Gabriel, with scepter in hand, is prepared to smite Brutus before the next slash, but is steadied by Elijah. Brutus hesitates in taking anymore lashes, so Gabriel restrains himself.

Brutus notices that his whip is missing some barbs and bones, so he jumps over and seizes a fresh and fully armed whip. He then quickly resumes the torture and side arms a swing, with the fresh whip that caroms around the side of Yeshua's rib cage, then gets caught. Brutus then jerks the whip with all his might, hearing a crackle sound, while this thrash tore into Yeshua's underlying skeletal muscles. The next lash is a vertical overhand swipe, with Brutus lifting his heels off the ground to attain height leverage for strength, letting out an, "Ah." Gabriel looks at Elijah and again wants to stop Brutus, as Brutus continues whacking his whip, causing a gash incision forming a cross on Yeshua's side, right over the last severe blow, ripping pieces of flesh from Yeshua's body. Gabriel is about to take Brutus down, as Yeshua lies there, passive and obedient the whole time, in and out of consciousness. The crowd is becoming increasingly disturbed and Brutus is hearing varied cries to stop. "Enough," the lictor says, "Halt." Brutus turns to the lictor and proclaims he has more lashes to give. The cilia of Yeshua's lung has visibly erupted from the torso and is exposed to the air, it appears to be barely inflating. He is breathing despite the last slash that severely flogged away the flesh exposing an organ. The brutality was halted when the lictor noticed that Yeshua was experiencing hematidrosis, a condition in which capillary blood vessels that feed the sweat glands rupture. The lictor knew his instructions were to make sure that the prisoners remained alive in order to be tried or crucified.

The lictor decides to use a different approach in dealing with Brutus. He chooses to adhere to a highly regarded regulation, a Roman bylaw, which he knows Brutus is well aware of. This law states: When in the course of flogging a prisoner, if an internal organ becomes exposed, the flogging will cease immediately, no exception.

Elijah and his men watch and are all silent, with their heads bowed, upset and shocked by what they had just witnessed. Yeshua is untied from the pillar, then doused with water and cleaned. Later, the laborers attempt to feed Him small pieces of bread and water, but they were unsuccessful. He is then wrapped in a garment, which is now stuck to his wounds acting like a gauze. Barely able to walk, Yeshua is slowly led away from this cruel area.

Now en route, the entourage encounters the drunken missing ruffian, who is inebriated and off balance, as he yells to his fellow soldiers escorting Yeshua to "Wait!" The intoxicated ruffian stumbles while holding a piece a jujube tree or bush, that has been weaved into a circle with long spider like thorns. He had carefully hedged the branches from brush outside on the far-side of the complex. The soldier's intension was to make a witty parody between the meaning of the emperor's crown and that of an epithetical notion of Yeshua being the "King of the Jews."

Boisterously approaching them, the halfwit ruffian places the crown atop Yeshua's head, claiming, "Look, the King of the Jews!" The guards escorting Yeshua let this happen, not wanting the crowds to see them showing any sympathy for the prisoner. Both guards assisting Yeshua are nervous that they let this happen, so they try to cover up their uneasiness by cracking a tempered smile for public display. The ruffian Roman soldier then removes his leather forearm band, using it to press the thorns down to fasten the crown tightly to Yeshua's scalp. The ruffian was laughing while walking away after he had adhered the jujube thorns to Yeshua's head. This ruthless act pierced His scalp in numerous areas, with one thorn puncturing through His left eyebrow landing out above His left eye skull bone, while the gist of mockery and ridiculing persist from others.

Pilate is still frantic about the innocence of Yeshua, finishes up his meal while complaining to his wife; he paces back and forth towards an opening in his balcony of the upper floor palace. He suddenly spots Barabbas, Yeshua and the crowds of people with Roman soldiers as they escort the two prisoners. Pilate is angry and disturbed when he sees Yeshua being transported by a one wheeled cart because He was unable to walk. Pilate turns back to his wife and says, "Those barbarians, went too far again, but this time it's on an innocent man!" Shaking his head with disgust, he

The Passion

then says, "The lavab, lavab!" He angrily requested the wash basin bowl of water. Staring with intent at his assistant because he was not paying attention to his duties, the assistant quickly fetches the bowl at a hurried pace. Pilate listens to the crowds that are outside and then talks with his wife, and suddenly has an epiphany and states aloud that he has an idea.

He demands the assistant should fill the basin with clean water and bring a cleaning cloth with him. He further explains to the servant, "I want you to follow me to the platform in the courtyard later," he tells him firmly. Pilate is well aware of his responsibilities to the many people waiting for him in the courtyard. He just doesn't seem to mind; in fact he still maintains his cleaning ritual and goes through his ritualistic routines of repetitive behaviors before heading out. Cavalier in his stature, Pilate takes out a tool called the strigil and applies oil to his forearms and other parts of his body, rubbing the oil into his skin. After he is finished cleaning and scraping the excess oil off with the strigil, Pilate continues voicing a steady roll of complaints, while he bickers with his wife and gets ready.

Pilate is now ready and begins to travel southeast through the back of the palace to enter the part of the complex where the crowds are waiting in the courtyard. The prisoners are brought up to the high platform overlooking the crowd. They look out to the courtyard, seeing two limestone staircases adjacent on both sides and are connected to a one hundred foot wide stage balcony. There are six huge Roman columns with their dominating presence standing effortlessly. These columns were a sign of the Romans' intimidating power and presence. Pilate had confidence in his plan because he did not want the Nazarene to be put to death. He decided to choose Barabbas to be the other prisoner against Yeshua. Pilate was hoping the people would choose Yeshua to be released, knowing that Barabbas has the worst offenses between all the prisoners held for crucifixion. Barabbas was a nefarious criminal, he murdered, was an insurrectionist, seditionist and most of all guilty of treason.

Pilate announces to a stirred up crowd that they will be choosing one of the prisoners to be released and go free, as it was a Passover tradition. After Pilate explains his intentions, Barabbas comes from the left and is shoved into view, the crowd reacts with grunts and then Pilate looks over to where Yeshua is standing from within the shadows on the opposite right side of the stage. Pilate makes eye contact with Yeshua, waving his hand aggressively for Him to come, "Come, come!" Pilate spews while still waiving his hand, Yeshua starts to walk and then quickly stops, He looks confused, so Pilate decides to walk over towards Yeshua.

As Pilate gets closer, he notices that Yeshua is wearing a crown of thorns and a white purple stained robe while He holds what appears to be a branch that is supposed to represent a king's scepter. Pilate in disgust shakes his head, mumbling and seizes the branch out of Yeshua's hand and tosses it to the side, saying under his breath "Ridiculous" with contempt. Pilate then helps Yeshua out into the view of the crowd in order for the people to see both prisoners clearly. Pilate waves his left hand over to his assistant, to indicate that he wants the wash basin brought to him at this time. Pilate spouts a strong, "Quiet!," to the crowd and raises his right hand to simmer the crowd down and proceeds to talk to them, while he lifts the bowl of water up high in a theatrical way. He then lowers it, handing the basin over to his assistant and the assistant lowers the washbasin in a convenient posture for Pilate, just as if he is working in the palace. Pilate begins to wash his hands in front of the crowd while his servant steadily and obediently holds the basin. He proclaims loudly, while his dripping hands retract from the basin, "I am innocent of this Man's blood." He then continues, "This is your matter, your responsibilities and I wash my hands of this!" Pilate tells the servant to go, but the servant only moves away a few steps. Pilate tells the servant to leave once again and says under his breath in mad tone, "I am keeping the cloth with me." He quietly mumbles mockery towards his servant and draws a disgusted frown.

Turning to the crowd, drying his hands with a cloth, Pilate raises the cloth high above his head, while he points to Yeshua and loudly asks of the assembled crowd, "Who are you releasing?" Before he could finish his question there was an uproar of chants that had started abruptly. The crowd was chants the name "Barabbas! Barabbas!" Pilate moves the cloth towards Barabbas asking the crowd, "Barabbas who is guilty of murder and treason?" The crowd furthers its howls, uttering the name Barabbas.

Pilate in shock did not know that earlier in the day, the high priest and the Sanhedrin had paid the Roman guards to stack the crowd against Yeshua. The guards were told by the high priest to let in those that would cheer the opposing prisoners name and not permit people who favored Yeshua to enter the courtyard. Each time Pilate placed the cloth above

Yeshua's head the crowd screamed, "Crucify Him or we will tell Rome." After a few attempts to sway the crowd Pilate gives up, because of the violent screams emanating from what now had become a mob. Pilate was already aware that he was not in good graces with Caesar and acquiesced knowing that the release of a prisoner condemned to death for insurrection against the Roman Empire, would make any Roman governor like himself susceptible to execution. Pilate states to the gathered crowd their respective choice of the two prisoners to be released. They chose the criminal named Barabbas instead of the Man called Yeshua. Even though Pilate felt that a fallacious act was at hand, he was convinced that his role as governor will be short lived. Yeshua is immediately turned over to be crucified while the Roman soldiers take charge of His transport.

Yeshua was brought to the location based on the south east part of the complex, adjacent to Pilate's Palace. Yeshua and the other two thieves await their cumbersome journey to come to an end. Yeshua was standing to the side of an archway that has less than a perfect design. He was looking at the mortar weakening where the keystone was laid while contemplating how long His final journey would be.

Leaning up against the right column of the complex for support, Yeshua is approached by the legionnaire who represented himself earlier as being ill and who withdrew from the flogging forum. He addresses Yeshua with reverence and concern, "Please Sir, would You care for some water that I have brought for You or I also have my very own special wine." Yeshua tells the man, "No, I will remain." The Roman soldier then persists, "Please take a sip or two, for Your suffering will be less." Yeshua refuses the offer of his wine, but expresses compassion for his gesture by saying, "This is the beginning of your greatness and our Father has blessed you." Yeshua with great effort offers him a slight smile causing great pain, because His cheek is swollen where Brutus had struck Him and His weathered face was tight with discomfort. Then with great effort He puts into words, "Your son though misunderstood presently, will be the scribe of our Father's messages." Yeshua reaches out, shakes His right arm while lifting. He settles His hand on the shoulder of Paul the Roman soldier then concludes, "Thanks be to you." Confused Paul stands still, as a group of guards grab Yeshua away abruptly, stunned in his thoughts.

Horses scuttled around leaving a trail of dust. They begin to nicker when three separate Roman horsemen untie a beam of wood that is attached at the rear of their horses' saddle skirt, connected by rope to a rigging ring. The soldiers throw down each of the three beams causing a pounding hollow knocking sound after they hit the ground. A dusty pound onto the ground attracts the attention of all who is around, especially the condemned. These three wooden beams will be the cross beams for each of the doomed, to be carried up to the mount of Golgotha. These beams are called the patibulum and are sixty six inches wide, equally rough with eight inch short sides. The patibulum is a piece of timber that will lay perpendicular against a beam rising from the ground. It derives its name from an insect, in the eastern regional areas of the globe, as far as Malaysia, due to the structured design of the bug's shell, sharing the similar features of a crucifixion cross.

Three emotionless soldiers gather around Yeshua, rope in hand, with two of the respective men placing and resting the patibulum timber on the shoulders of Yeshua. A sudden burst of pain is followed by a short cry as the reused rough timber presses against His existing wounds.

While both soldiers move to either side of Yeshua, they support the position and weight of the patibulum. The last man starts twisting and tying the rope, while Yeshua's arms are stretched parallel attached to this ridged wood. The patibulum across His back is now settled against His neck, shoulders and back. His wounds stretch from the timber's one hundred pound gravimetric weight that indents His body. The lacerations are deep running from side to side, opening the exposed strips of skin, adding to a high reception of pain. With every step He takes, the movement delivers an immediate pang, and because of this He hesitates to move. He peers up at the long winding road ahead.

After taking just a few steps, one of the Roman soldiers demands, "Wait! I have a titulus/titular." This is an inscribed title for dignitary men of high office or authority, drawn onto metal or wood. The soldier on the horse says, "Pilate had given orders for this to be above His head mounted to the cross." After finishing his sentence, he tosses the titulus to his coworker and continues to have further conversation. The soldier that catches the sign, takes the cord that is looped around the titulus with his two hands and proceeds to hang it *(like a necklace)* around Yeshua's neck. While flowing with witty banter, the soldier hurried the placement around Yeshua's head, but catches part of the thorns, leaving the sign resting against the side of Yeshua's face. A pained cry erupts from Yeshua while the crown moves back and forth in His already pierced wounds. Then the soldier says, "Oh, oh, well here it is." He pats the sign two times comfortably resting on Yeshua's chest and then looking at it again reading, "Yeshua of Nazareth, King of the Jews," chuckles cynically.

The action of hanging a titulus is the third happening out of the norm. The first unusual occurrence was Yeshua being presented the kings cloak/mantle and scepter. The second was when He was about to leave the flogging forum, He receives the crown of thorns. The third and final oddity is when He is labeled with a titulus. The theoretical antithesis of all three incidents correlates with the veil from His Mother [titular], the nimbus halo [thorns] and the patina [cloak & scepter].

The winding route now begins from a distance of about a half a mile, at The Via Dolorosa, a thoroughfare pass, meaning "way of sorrows" or simply "painful way." This road winds between structures, then towards the open land that comes to a fork juncture. At this point there are two choices; either elect to veer towards the crucifixion site up to Golgotha or head within to the old city of Jerusalem. A division of the Roman legionnaires, called a Century, are assigned units of a hundred soldiers for particular purpose or orders for special instructions. They are now in the process of lining up along the path leading up to Golgotha, some on horseback and many on foot with all having distinct special trades.

Marching away from the city walls, the three prisoners with patibulum hitched and in motion, walked slowly in open land. The soldiers are now herding the people away from the inner path because it needs to stay clear to provide a broad pathway for easy passage for the guards and prisoners.

The high orders are very well understood. They are: to keep the prisoners alive until crucified. Stones start flying towards the captives, coinciding with sadistic laughter, while Yeshua is only a few hundred feet from the arduous start of the trek. All of a sudden, Yeshua finds Himself falling onto one knee while He tilts His head to the right due to the weight of the one hundred pound beam. The beam becomes off balance and lands with a thud to one side of the ground. Suddenly a mounted soldier, restrains his horse with the reigns, reaches with his long whip, snaps it, whirling the ends of the whip encircling and wrapping the corner of Yeshua's wooden patibulum. The soldier displays a talented knack in grabbing the timber, then hoisting it up with a strong tug, thus balancing out Yeshua, in order to assist Him back to His feet.

As Yeshua struggles on the rugged dusty grounds, there are people attempting to help Him, showing great compassion and sympathy. They bring cool clothes to relieve His heated pain, but only women are allowed to pass, for they are not a threat to hinder the transport.

Certain Faction members or people from the future, not being from this era, have been allowed and approved by the Temporal Watchmen to be witnesses to Yeshua's final day. Elijah and colleagues are distraught, trying hard to separate their emotions and maintain sobriety in their performance. Elijah leaves John the apostle on the back side of Golgotha, near the valley alongside a copious torrent *(stream)* that is filled with flowing water. Without a care, John hustles through a small meadow of sepals, grabbing the roughage about his sandals and looks for Yeshua's Mother.

The day has reached its hottest temperature. Yeshua stares ahead hunched over hypnotized by the granules that constitutes the dirt, while perspiring what little water He has left in His body. Dragging Himself, He tries to navigate on the carved curved pathways, His body breaking down as His aerobic cellular respiration is now inadequate threatening the oxygen levels in His tissues and organs. The terrible derisions from the crowd continue. Ananus the high priest had made verbal contracts with a few ignorant townspeople who were trying to earn their second silver piece if their performance of ridicule was grand. This would add to their first payout that they received for causing and inciting the mob to rebel against Yeshua with the elections in the courtyard, in front of Pilate.

Almost at the halfway mark, the soldiers try to tame the onlookers. The soldiers are getting angry as they halt their horses and their animals grunt and snort in annoyance as well. The guards now have to threaten the mob with punishments to restrain them from rock throwing and the annoying overzealous mockery. Elijah moves his cloud to block the suns harsh rays, beating upon Yeshua. The titulus sign dangles from his neck and is deflecting off each of His collar bones, taking on the appearance of a pendulum, rocking back and forth. Yeshua lifts His head to see how

The Passion

much more is the distance to the location called the "Place of Skulls," which is Hebrew for Golgotha. His ears are hearing muffled noises. His eyes are fogged, His breath shallow and His head is limp. All He can see is a blurred sight of each bump in the road, as the mountain will now be a staggering feat to overcome, especially in His broken obliterated state.

Elijah is watching the sand steal one drop of life at a time from Yeshua. His blood and sweat becomes syncopated into the sand absorbing then disappearing into a geologic abyss, a chronological division between "forgotten and forgiveness." Yeshua loses His balance again and stumbles forward while His body pivots in reverse. His wooden beam lands hard onto the sandy ground and creates a divot while twisting. Yeshua is awkwardly supported sideways by the timber, but finds He must surrender to gravity for He is too weak. Consequently, He falls and lands on His back. He sees sparkles of light as the pain severs His blood flow. Yeshua constricts His neck, turning His face beet red.

In fear that Yeshua was going to die, one of the Roman soldiers decides to have a man assist with the remaining trek. The mounted officer points to a man who is waiting to cross the procession and demands this selected bystander to help Yeshua make His way up towards Calvary/Golgotha.

He is standing next to bushels of crops loaded in a cart, with two others alongside of him and he refuses to help by saying he is a farmer en route with lading of crops. The Roman soldier says again, "Help this man, you shouldn't have been watching then!" The farmer says, "Don't you see I have others with me?" The soldier then flustered puts his hand on his sword and draws it, his horse grows nervous from the sling metallic sound and backs up two steps snorting dust, with one leg lifted. The man then muddles instructions for his men *(helpers)* to take his bushel and he will meet up with them later. Yeshua delirious finds Himself back on His feet, looking over from the corner of His eye, wondering where this man came from and who is under His left arm, supporting His every step.

Approaching the intersection at the base of Golgotha, a few tyrants start whipping sand from a close distance at Yeshua and they are immediately disciplined by a Roman soldier. In passing the fork in the road, the legionnaire chooses the right side for an easier incline to reach the summit, considering the condition of his prisoners.

John then sees Mary from afar. He quickly scampers across the terrain and meets up with Her. Panting with a strained voice he says, "Mary, I have a safe area for viewing just around the first turn. It is a level and narrow passage where only people can fit." John points as Mary nervously looks and John continues, "Over in this area, there is a jut in the curve," John instructs Mary to walk to the opposite side when Yeshua approaches. "Thank you, John" Mary replies.

The crowd thins because of logistics when Mary casts Her first glance onto Her Son, as Yeshua appears in full sight. She hesitates with shock, standing statuesque within a stone's throw away. Her breath stolen from Her, She gathers Herself and abruptly puts down Her head and dashes across to the gorge, where She is shadowed against the porous chalk like sedimentary rock. Exclaiming the words, "Son, Son!" as She moves slowly towards Yeshua. The guard having compassion lets the meeting take place. Her hands are shaking as She tries to touch Him. Not knowing where to touch Him in fear of causing Him additional pain. She touches His loose palm with Her fingertips and as She slowly pulls away, She feels the passing of the contours in each of His fingers. She realizes that this will be the last time She will touch Her beloved Son. She tries to savor this last endearing memory of love as Her eyelids flutter and Her sight disappears with disbelief.

Yeshua shows His Mother a compassionate look of sorrow, while She takes Her hands raised towards His face, wanting to kiss Him. She sees the crown, then withdraws Her attempt, realizing as She looks upon His bruised face and cut dried lips, that any contact would result in further pain. Mary embracing every last moment left with all Her might and determination, but suddenly Her mind switched, like a flexed twig that snapped. She starts bawling and convulsing, putting Her right forearm sleeve to Her cheek. She turns Her head down to wipe Her tears and notices the red trail on the ground marked with Her Son's blood. Her eyes roll back involuntarily and She loses Her footing and is about to faint. John catches Her from behind. Yeshua realizes that His wounds and sufferings have pierced His Mother's heart, crushed with fractured sorrows.

Mary cannot hold it together any longer, so Yeshua speaks to Her in a strenuous tone, "Dear Mother, Your heart is so troubled. Stay close to Me, yet have the virtue of patience with the gift of fortitude, for this is

The Passion

Thy Father's will." The Roman soldier commands Him to proceed. Mary watches the back-side of what was once a tan tunic is now a purple-red cloak. Arms flanked attached to a piece of timber, forearms and triceps being choked by cords of rope. Yeshua drags Himself upward as the distance widens between Him and His Mother. She is left behind with Her arms extended, hands wide open, dreaming about Her Spirit stretching to be with Her Son's Spirit. John's head is tilted down while he holds Mary's shoulder to support Her.

Yeshua bears left, dropping out of sight, Mary falls to her knees, grabbing Her veil with both hands, then pressing it to Her lips, smothering Her cry of sorrow and pain. John assists Mary to Her feet, while the relentless crowd torments Her Son. She attempts to collect Herself while She listens to an elevated volume of ridicule and mockery. She sees a constant few that are continuously bowing down and saying, "Hail, King of the Jews!" This angered Her very much, so She turned to John and enunciates, "Take Me to the top!"

Chapter Seventeen

CRUCIFIXION

Elijah hovering silently in the clouds, observing vigilantly and steadily, is ready for a multitude of outcomes. During this time, he undoubtedly is the only vessel allowed in such close proximity, whereas the mass follower-ships are prevalent above watching from Earth's skies, high in the ionosphere and magnetosphere. Never before did a coordinated union of species from different worlds and times ever share in one particular moment like the one they are about to witness. They all realize that the universal sector will never be the same. Spectators from all Factions and people from different time periods watched with great admiration. In addition, there were also approved *Time Sequencer* observers from various dimensions.

Engulfed in His thoughts, Yeshua finally reaches the summit and is captivated by the picturesque horizon. He is astonished with the vast contrast of God's beauty in the landscaped hills, but with that of some wretched people stomping their feet into the landscaped soil; whereby, God's very same grounds are free from fault.

Yeshua barley lifts His head up when He sees three stipes/*stakes* of gray weathered wood, which are protruding from the plateau at the summit of Calvary *(Golgotha)*. {The word Calvary is derived from a term, "mean and ignoble place," after the translation from Greek to Latin, then to its English say, Calvary}.

Each of the stipes is equal in height, awkward across the horizon. These three haunting wooden seven plus foot stakes, look as though they are anticipating anguish of mind and body.

Crucifixion

Attached to the stipes/stakes is an additional notched, four foot vertical wooden flat beam. This extra top extension piece is married down two feet from the uppermost portion of the stipe and is attached at the main trunks' back towards the top. This separate piece of plank is four foot in length, leaving the total stipe height of nine feet.

Therefore, it leaves a two foot extension beam rising from the top of the stipe. This twenty four inch extended part of the beam is purposely higher than the seven foot main stake, so it can be used to hoist the condemned one up into place. By attaching ropes and utilizing the carved rounded notch at the highest part of this attached wooden beam for leverage, the condemned would then be lifted upwards or hoisted till their patibulum/cross section behind their shoulders would meet on the resting platform point. This would designate the temporary resting place on top of the main seven foot stipe/stake, with the protruding wooden backer braced and locked to the patibulum into place.

Thoroughly exhausted, Yeshua is no longer receiving any assistance. He waits. In a solitary postural sway, He manages to barely stand. He has a blurred view of the soon to be cross, but all knowing that the middle stipe is His and His alone, aware the stake's position is somewhat more forward then the other two stakes.

He gathers strength to lift His head in order to stare up to the cloud where Elijah is watching. Yeshua bows to the cloud and then looks up one more time to indicate He can see this through. Elijah emotionally exhausted, feels his heart is wrenched with grief. The men react around him and begin to give him much needed support.

There was an invisible but understood boundary line made for the people encompassing the crucifixion area. The area behind the stipes was designated for the Roman guards only. The Century of soldiers are assigned tasks. The soldiers on horses stand tall with an occasional shouting of demands, usually coming from the legionnaires or high ranking officers. All the spectators that observe from a higher view see the intimidation and fear tactics.

Suddenly it becomes eerily silent as the people witness Yeshua obediently awaiting His crucifixion. The Lamb has been led to the slaughter. The crowd witnessing is now far away and Yeshua is standing alone. There is no movement whatsoever in the crowd. He stands there wearing a heavy lavender and tan looking garment, with ropes railed to His arms, stuck to a plank of wood. His head is down, and only the surface of His hair can be seen, along with a circle of thorns, nested into His scalp.

Hesitation falls upon everyone who is present. The crowd becomes apprehensive as they give witness to the execution of an innocent Man, one they helped condemn. The surreal moment in time breaks out its silence, as two soldiers march over. With each step they emit a noisy leathery and metallic clang, which is amplified while their loud dusty sandal boots scratch the ground. Two Roman workers start grappling each side of the patibulum timber that is attached to Yeshua's shoulders, one on each side. The men hunch down while lifting and tilting backwards the body of Yeshua, then each of them brace a corner of the wooden beam upon their padded shoulders on opposite sides. The soldiers in unison count to three, then time the lift to pull and drag Yeshua.

Optional read: The heels of His feet scribe two lines in the sand as they arrive at the base of the middle stipe. The two soldiers stand and spin Yeshua clockwise while balancing His footing, stutter stepping, turning while standing. The soldiers are having fun with this cruel scene. They continually toss and spin, passing the corners of the timber to each other while they simultaneously strip off His clothes. The other two soldiers remove any remaining clothing except for the undergarment. The soldiers take and divide up his clothes by casting lots, an act that confirms a prophecy that appeared in scripture.

Elijah is watching the antagonizing spinning and tugging of the four men, an upsetting cast of entertainers. He refers to the soldiers as a pack of hyenas, snickering with laughter. One of the Roman ruffians waits patiently as he shuffles three iron nails in his left hand creating an annoying clanging sound. He has a heavy hammer dangling from his right arm. Like a dog waiting for a command, he sees the v-shaped rope/cord, which is connected at the back of the patibulum, looped at two points, v-like ready to be joined to the single long existing rope for the hoist up.

Yeshua falls to His knees and is tossed back. His knees bend as He collapses backwards to the ground, while His lifeless calves become trapped under His thighs. The force of the strain and bend was so great it sent a cry into the sky. His jugular vein on His neck is turgidly raised like a blue torrent stream pulsating with pain. His eyes leaden and almost completely shut, with only a sliver of an opening.

Crucifixion

Then suddenly, His eyes fire wide open and His back convulses curved upward, as the first of the three nails of destiny pierces His left wrist. The nail spikes its way to the patibulum timber, grabbing entry into the surface of the wood, severing the median nerve, but "without fracturing a single bone" *(also prophesied in the scriptures)*. In this painstaking action, the nail's pathway was assisted by a frequency guided focal point on the back of Yeshua's/Jesus' wrist, steered and marked by one of Elijah's crew members.

The soldier takes the next *(five inch)* brown nail and spins it in his hand. He presses and points the tip of the nail, fiddling with the skin on Jesus' right wrist, then comes down hard with the hammer. There is a smashing crack noise with sparks because it was an indirect hit. Then tapping lightly on the next two hits, four more swings are needed. By pushing the wrist extra tight to the wood it caused needles of numbness in His hand as well as an unbearable pain to the wrist.

The pathway of this nail was just to the left of the median nerve, between the ulnar and radial artery, on either inside of the carpals, again no bones broken. The soldier doing the hammering lifts up his head while getting up from a kneeling position and spews out a command, "Proceed!" Taking the rope in a skilled fashion, in a lariat arrangement, tosses it over atop of the highest point of the stipe. Another soldier receives the thrown rope on the opposite side, being careful to make sure the rope is resting at the highest point of the stipe, in its notched grooved place.

The rope is now on top of the stipe and ready for a leveraged pull. The tension of the rope is taut and ready to go, but the Roman soldier tells his partner, "No!" "I'll take care of it!" He waves away the other soldier because he wants to work solo, so that he may show off his strength. Grabbing, then tangling the rope around his wrist, the soldier digs his feet into the ground for better footing. Bending his legs and pulling the rope using his body weight as a technique, he leans backwards on a forty degree angle. He then proceeds to hoist Jesus. The patibulum beam lifts off the ground, while Jesus is almost on His feet; He stumbles back and swings over hitting against the stipe.

Torment and laughter erupts from the crowd for they are amused by this. His feet leave the surface of the Earth for the final time, while being hoisted in short interval tugs. His body ascends to the mortised destined point. The front of the stipe is smooth from the many condemned who were dragged up the stem from previous crucifixions. The crowd becomes quiet and attentive because of a disturbing sound that resonates from the tension of ropes, causing stress to the empathetic onlookers. There are sounds emanating from the tower of torture, as the scraping against the grooved wood drags out the patibulum beam in its ascent. The sound of wood to wood is unsettling to even the misbehaved at the site, assisting in this unforgettable vision. The tenon projection of timber is almost settled in, about to be tied to the horizontal rail. The tension of the cord is loosened to slightly sway the patibulum cross beam into place.

A soldier stands in front of the cross, on a wooden step box to guide and hold the body, while the other soldier lifts the body, along with the cross wood beam being pulled by the rope until it is in place. The patibulum joins to the platform rest area, near the top of the vertical stipe, but made birse sounds and disturbing knocking noises just before it was put into place. While the body is held steady, fifteen feet away behind the cross is the soldier that holds dearly onto the rope and is still pulling it tight to maintain a constant tension. The horizontal beam is being forced with pressure and held against the laminated back beam that is protruding two feet above atop the stipe. With tension from the rope and the beam held, a smaller in stature soldier brings a wooden ladder over to put three, three inch nails into the back of patibulum timber. They are to be driven in from and through the back of the protruding wood. This prevents the criminal from falling forward off the cross. In some cases if they expect the victim is not going to live long, they just pull the rope taut and drive the wooden-stake wrapped in rope into the ground.

The onlookers are ranting and joking about the soldier's height, as he looks up at the crowd, shakes his head and goes about his job. While climbing the ladder, the short worker leans over, holding one hand on the ladder's step *(rung)*. From around Jesus' neck he removes the titulus that Pilate had instructed to hang above the cross section. Keeping his balance, he steps up further on the ladder, reaching the second to the top rung. The small man hugs the top of the stipe as the crowd barks with laughter and quickly fumbling with one hand, loops the sign around the protruding beam then locks it under an angled nail, ignoring the chants of "Fall! Fall! Fall!" Climbing down from the ladder, he then stands the ladder straight up, then spins it on one of the wooden legs and flings it towards the onlookers where he believed the chanting emerged from. The crowd steps backward as the soldier snarls with satisfaction.

He then turns to the front side of the cross measuring how far the legs are extended and places an upside down wedge called a sedile under the victim's feet for support. The sedile is placed approximately two feet off the ground, depending on the height of the victim. The soldier then takes three small nails and taps them into place upon the already reamed bored holes, adhering and connecting the sedile in a final customized fixed position. The higher ranking soldier waits patiently and gestures a kick, to rush the shorter soldier to get out of his way, inciting laughter from the people. John the apostle mutters to himself, "Everything is a jest." He is disgusted with the savagery and keeps Mary from these visual atrocities.

The soldier with the heavy hammer comes back and has but just one nail, it is the largest one to be used. It is a spike nail, seven inches long with a one inch wide head. The soldier begins to wrap over Jesus' right leg across the top of His left ankle/leg with enormous pressure. This will leave the left-leg stiff, straight and locked by the overlapped right leg. The left leg is bypassed and without a nail to support it.

Leg locked with heels wedged to the sedile block, it is the right tarsi *(area of bones)* that are to become the victim of the long spike. The tarsi are a group of small bones between the main portion of the hind limb and the metatarsus in terrestrial vertebrates. Again, the soldier nails through with no bones broken, Jesus has now begun the final stages of the Crucifixion process.

> Crucifixion began in Persia, but the Romans permanently perfected it as a form of torturous capital punishment and designed to incur a slow death with maximum pain and undoubtedly the wrath of suffering.

The audio is turned off by Elijah. The monitors are depicting the three crosses erected on top of the mount. Each monitor displays a different aspect of this harsh reality, one for vital signs of all three victims, the next monitor displays every individual that is in attendance, including horses and dogs up to three furlongs away. Other monitors track the bio-frequency signature of all and the surrounding vicinity for security issues that may occur and for possibly halting an action decided unnecessary to the cause. Elijah remains silent with his comrades and stares at Jesus from an aerial viewpoint, fixated to the cross, able to see and analyze anything and everything, no matter how small or what angle.

Jesus reflecting, holding dearly to the memories of His life and contemplates providently on His future events. The crowd is still unable to approach the crucifixion area. Jesus appearing lonely, with a pale tintless coloration, His body lies sedentary, covered in dry blood and hardened dirt. Now that all the prisoners are affixed to their stations on the crosses, most of the entertainment is finished. The onlookers are there now just for an occasional outcry by the prisoners, as the waiting begins. The work of the soldiers is done and most of them take their belongings and vanish into the crowd. Some guards and soldiers are left behind to finish the job.

Heartfelt prayers commence as the silence stirs compassionate energy from the sincere and reverent bystanders that remained behind. Realizing that time is of the essence, the ecclesiastical camaraderie begins now.

Silence is no longer prevalent amongst Elijah's crew. Discussions commence and attention is given to John taking the Mother Mary towards the crosses to be in plain view. The restrictions have now been lifted by the Roman soldiers to the extent of permissible distance near/to the crosses.

A number of people, horses and a Century of soldiers lurk at the circular periphery around the crosses, but most of the crowd has dwindled to join the herds of people that are about the city and towns for the Passover tradition. Mary is permitted to be in front of the cross. She drops to Her knees and cannot take a step closer. She is wearing Her flaxen-wool colored tunica and is kneeling silently with Her head held down. Her face is covered by a white veil and She is unable to look up. Elijah observing from above can only see Her deep blue mantle cascading on both sides of Her weeping body.

The Sun's position changes, and as a result Elijah's cloud is no longer completely blocking it. The hot rays from the Sun bathe Jesus and Mary, and together They drink the same light. Their Spirits consulted by God, Their nature pure and without regret.

John is behind Her, with clenched teeth, protecting Her from any debris being flung towards the punished. Amongst the remaining crowd of onlookers, a certain individual behind John is screaming and deriding contemptuous remarks. Gabriel nods to Elijah for permission, then pulses a signal, directed at this individual's bio-frequency and programs a command into the computer system to silence him. The crazed man grabs his throat and heads running down the side of the mount to the nearest stream in a panic. Throughout the day Gabriel stifled a total of seven revolting individuals that went beyond a tolerance point of behavioral acceptance.

The day begins to turn from extremely hot and sunny to dreary with overcast, as the last moments were upon them. Jesus cannot move His nape, because of the crown of thorns that inhibit Him from putting his head back. Jesus' neck stays bent over, as a priest stands and stares with a puzzled look. Nicademous, who was one the priests who questioned Jesus from the very beginning and had doubt, then turned to admire Him in a factual light. Nicademous stands like a statue concentrating. The only movement in his body is the chattering and grinding of his teeth, yet his look becomes harder towards Jesus, who he feels will die an innocent Man on the cross. While his thoughts slowly come together, he has an epiphany. He loses his balance after stepping up on a tufa of porous rocks *(that were carved poorly for steps)* and then he begins to recite scripture aloud. He is reciting the prophet Isaiah's words as he stares directly at Jesus hanging from the cross.

"He was pierced through for our transgressions, He was crushed for our iniquities, and by His scourging we are healed. All of us are like sheep and have gone astray, He is and will be." Nicademous breathes out through his nose, nodding his head left to right, slight and slowly in pity, keeping his attention on the cross, not to blink as one tear rolls from each eye in synch, calmly.

Elijah's men begin to amplify the clouds to erupt them to grow at a rate to match Jesus' vital signs. As He gets closer to death, the cloud accumulation and darkness increases. The sky changes and gathers to a dark grey ash, as the ominous clouds increase by the crew carrying out the Articles of Faith's Doctrine. Only a few of the onlookers leave, the rest are curious to see what will happen. They stay out of curiosity even though the weather is becoming fierce.

The monitoring from the ship is at full attention. Jesus' life signs are on three displays, each of them showing the abnormalities that are critical to His health and jeopardize His ability to live. The main display spins slowly with a translucent three dimensional hologram, fading in and out. Elijah ignores one of the other two displays because it is extremely upsetting. It is an overview monitoring of the outside crowd, as well as seeing Mary and John in a dreadful state. The third display is the main display and Elijah pays close attention to it. It is the visual and audio sensors. It is the complete tracker of the energy within Jesus' nimbus. Once his physical body expires, what follows is the halo dimming process of the nimbus, all the way to *(physical death)* a subatomic level, thus the patina emerges. The patina claims all spiritual energies that dominates one's being and converges the energy with the temple, the physical body. It promotes the intertwining and implosion of the cells creating a rejuvenescence within the whole body.

The third and main large display monitor is centered above the control consul and depicts a real time lifelike size to scale of Jesus on the complete cross. Suddenly, sound alerts go off when they hear, "Father forgive them, they know not what they do, give them but that one day." Jesus exhales in weakness, then in a brusk pithy delivery He looks down at His mother and John. He introduces them to each other, as the family He is leaving behind.

Jesus caves and lets out a death rattle as He feverishly tries to breathe. Elijah is looking face to face in real time at the fully scaled holographic image of Jesus on the cross in the main bridge of the ship. Elijah's stomach is knotted tight, trying to withstand what is happening. In his mind, he keeps noticing the frequency of the Creator that is still attached to Jesus and is perplexed towards the fact that the Creator might be experiencing what Jesus is feeling and why God's Love would endure this primordial savagery to be held for any consideration.

Elijah is embarrassed about how he is feeling, but knows he should not be. As his emotions taper off, he sees that the end is near, he bows his head down. Once again he tries to shake off his sadness to stay strong and be alert. He tries to remain still, but his tears overflow regardless of his attempt to control them. He reaches out his hand pointing at the hologram of Jesus, while his other hand is cupped over his mouth. Elijah chokes, then deliriously motions towards the other colleagues, in disbelief referring towards the display. Jesus' arms are severely stretched with the fibers in His muscles pulsating with a discoloration display, the ropes are causing bruises and the nails look like a sadistic barbarity from a night terror.

Jesus speaks again, "My God! My God! Have I forsaken You? Beholding to Thyself!" This was a sporadic surge from Jesus when He lifted His head as high as it could go, but could not further lift or keep His head straight, because of the impeding wooden barbs from his crown that halted His head from looking up. Both His arms and legs appear lame and without movement. His jugular vein throbs and with great effort, His heart pumps harder to push blood through His body.

This puts an intense strain on the small blood vessels adding pressure on the lungs. The added pressure affects the vessels in an inverse way, releasing fluid into the lungs.

This breakdown is happening to Jesus throughout the entire Crucifixion and yet not only to the lungs, but a variety of other locations throughout the body.

A display representing the pang readings are being received because of high levels of visceral pain occurring all over His body. The pain receptor indicators are appearing throughout His nervous system, causing a systemic reaction of watery fluid being collected into the cavities of His cell tissues. Seemingly, the breathing is restricted to shallow breaths and primarily the diaphragmatic sector is unable to expand, causing hypercapnia, a respiratory breakdown because of an inefficient amount of oxygen. This lack of oxygen disrupts the air sacs that are called alveoli and are not able to receive or disburse the proper exchange of gases within the cell for the release of carbon dioxide, resulting in a slow torturous drowning demise.

Jesus knows His breaths are numbered, lifeless in-fact; accept for the tetany contractions of numerous muscles pulsating amid His body. Cramps and paresthesias are causing involuntary nerves to convulse in all parts of His anatomy. Unexpectedly, a ventral expansion begins to flutter in His chest, startling those who have remained. Jesus calls out, while Elijah's eyes shoot open, "Eli! Eli! He has to die with absolute abandonment from the heavens; time will heal as time returns." (A quote from the Articles of Faith.)

Elijah's swollen eyes, fills to the brim with tears, sadly nodding, then reacts immediately and sends a pulse of amplified electromagnetic field-waves into the dark black clouds that hover above the entire area. The lightning begins shooting about, followed by crashing thunderous blasts that shake the ground. This was a confirmation response by Elijah, acknowledging Jesus' statement. Jesus nods once as His head slowly dips forward, His Mother shocked in a ravine of emptiness as She stares up in a statuesque demure, seeing His lips bleak and purple.

Jesus' excessive injuries are causing orthostatic hypotension or hemorrhagic shock, which is a severe loss of blood and essential fluids. A cyanotic bluish color appears on the skin that surrounds His rib cage as the seconds take hold. Elijah peers into the display monitor, seeing a fury of pain slow down and the pericardial fluid buildup around the heart. The chief arteries struggle to push the flow of blood. The heart thickens with constraints, pleural fusions of fluid fills the lungs with a constricted space for air. Less volume of air-pockets are being slowly replaced with liquids, creating a very small space left in order to take those few last breaths, each one becoming shorter and shorter, asphyxia is inevitable... "I thirst" uttered Jesus with little movement from His mouth.

The soldier surprised at His request, bends down quickly, soaks a sponge of wine mixed with gall/myrrh, *(use for an anesthetic or pain reliever)* placing it at the tip of a Hyssop plant stem about three feet in length, appears dried and purplish. The soldier quickly brings the liquid up to His lips, Jesus not wanting to drink, but to loosen His lips and says with all His might shaking, while His eyes glance one last time at the heavens, convulsing with His final exhale, "It is finished, Father, Into Thy Hands I Commend My Spirit."

Silent Reflections

After His final words, His eyes cast up. His opaque beautiful blue eyes disappeared into His heavy laden eyelids, leaving only the bloodshot sclera visible to mark consummation. His head yielded to a forward flaccid position, where it remained. It is silent once again. The three soldiers at the base of the cross do something unprecedented, they take to one knee. When three explosions of thunder erupt, the three soldiers are not affected and they bow their heads, remove their helmets, and pay their respects to what they know to be a divine moment. The actions of the Roman soldiers from this point on, will take on a new meaning, *"vail"* with regard to the removal of the helmet or headdress of men when in the presence of or around the house of God.

The three o'clock hour struck, and Jesus' death occurs, in timing with the exact moment when the Passover lambs throats were slit, signifying Pesach, the sacrificial offering *(a lamb)* that was made in the temple by priests. Ironically, during Jesus' childhood, John the Baptist used that phrase and referred to Jesus as the Lamb of God to usher in this moment *(Lamb of God who takes away the sins of the world)*.

While the Jewish priests are collecting the lamb's blood in bowls for their ceremonious rituals in the city nearby, Elijah unleashes a thunderous rain from the large dark ash ominous cloud, following the directives in the Articles of Faith.

Jesus' body is being dismantled from the cross with great difficulty because of the dangerous lightning and pouring rain, a necessity that Elijah cannot bear to watch. Before lowering the body, it is a routine practice to break the legs of the victim if they are not dead, but in Jesus' case, He already was. To make sure that He was dead, one of the soldiers took a long sharp lance and pierces it upward between the ribs on His right side with a disturbing sound. The penetration of the spear tip slides seven inches to the implied point, releasing pleural and pericardial fluid along with little blood, draining in a copiously rush of liquid.

This action is done for two reasons; first to make sure that the person is dead and secondly to have an easier time handling the corpse. The release of fluids will make the corpse lighter and will prevent additional swelling or expansion.

The foot-nails need to be taken out first, before the body can be lowered, now that the pillory is over. An assigned soldier uses a tool called the paw, a tool that has a one foot handle attached to a rectangular cube of oak wood. The paw is placed parallel to the person's body, and then used as a brace for leverage as the forked part of the hammer type tool locks into the nail head, in order to give an easy quick way for the removal of the nail. The rain droplets are strait and relentless, as Jesus' Crucifixion is traversed, while those who remained are murmuring as they begin to depart.

When Jesus is fully removed from the cross, one of the soldiers gently lays Jesus in Mary's arms. Mary moves under Her Son to capture His limp body. Rain continues to cascade down as Mary holds Her Son rocking him like a child. His legs are resting on the muddy soil, while Jesus' left arm hangs lifeless, as the back of His hand brushes against the mud repeatedly. His Mother cradles Her Son close to Her heart. *(Pieta')*

The thunder and lightning increases and John does not know what to do. He looks to be in shock and stares through the railings of rain, unable to move or speak. Mary cries with Jesus rocking back and forth. She remains knelt, hugging His torso with all of Her might. Her tears join with the rain disappearing, crashing and splattering to the ground as Jesus' body lies inanimate in Her arms.

The heartbreaking moment was reminiscent of Her holding Her newborn baby with Joseph in the manger, whispering to Jesus the song She sang to Him as an infant, a song from King Solomon. One of the soldiers standing is saddened by watching Mary and once he makes eye contact with Her, he nervously drops the three nails onto the ground and then rushes away as the thunder increases.

Elijah's crew sends amplified signals into the heavens, stretching and bending into space *(ionosphere)*, then steering the reflective waves down, pointed to the opposite end of the summit, where all the crucified bodies are collected and thrown into a large receptacle hole, then covered. This mass burial area is designed for a quick and easy disposal for the Roman soldiers, who execute thousands upon thousands of foreigners and criminals, through the crucifixion practice.

Along with the deluge of rain and thunder, Elijah's colleagues concentrate the magnetic wave directly at the rear of Golgotha, creating an earthquake that rattles the whole mountain. Many in Jerusalem witness the weather anomalies and watch as Calvary receives the wrath of the *gods*.

The mountainous ground spews open, pushing up thousands of dead bodies, up and out of the ground. The bodies begin to hurl and tumble down the mountainside. The people run away in fear. They are unable to tell the difference between the dead bodies tumbling, from the running departed spectators stumbling covered in mud.

John the apostle comforts Mary, then says, "Do not worry; the mountain will be calm soon." Almost immediately after reassuring Her, the clouds start to dissipate and the ground becomes still.

John politely tells Mary about the two Jewish priests who want to help take the body of Jesus from this place and give Him a proper burial.

He informs Her that they would like to donate a newly prepared tomb for the sacred burial of Jesus. Softly John speaks, "Their names are Joseph of Arimathea, the owner of the plot and Nicodemus, a priest convinced that Jesus is the Messiah.

Joseph of Arimathea addressed his request to Pilate, asking for possession of Jesus' body and took the initiative to purchase new linens for His burial. Pilate agreed because of the honorable reputation that precedes Joseph. John helps Mary to Her feet and Mary nods to say yes with still tears in Her eyes, without speaking a word.

Tomb

Joseph and Nicodemus carefully wrap the body in fine linens in accordance to Jewish tradition. The women that followed Jesus assisted by applying the myrrh and fragrantly sweet oils they had brought. The shroud which is the burial garment, lays flat at fourteen feet in length by an approximate four foot in width. The shroud covers half of the body while the deceased lies in a rested position, along with the other excess portion of the linens that fold in half from head to toe, covering the deceased completely.

Quickly they gather the body and place it in the shroud, curling the sides for easy conveying. The tomb was nearby Joseph's property, a short distance from his house. Hurrying because the sunset was upon them and the Sabbath will be at hand.

As they carry the body away to the shelter, Mary picks up the nails that clenched Her Son's body. She stares at them, and sees the ruthless blood remnants on the spikes. She looks down at the enshrouded body with nails in hand and watches Her Son being taken away. She sees the silhouette of His body, broken and bloody through the pure white linens that are carrying Him to the tomb.

The tomb was hewed from an already existing rock formation. The enormous rounded rock used for the door seal, was the most difficult part of constructing the cave. According to Joseph Arimathea, it took the exact same time to mine the whole tomb, as it took to make just the door. Conveniently, the cave inside had a natural bench formation jut protruding out just about three feet, with a height of two feet, giving an easy position for the body's resting place. These natural measurements, gave egress abilities from leaving the inside of the tomb or to move about the tomb.

Joseph and Nicodemus were wealthy and well noted as affiliates of the Sanhedrin, yet were in hiding because they were becoming disciples of Jesus. Joseph who was looking for the coming of the kingdom his whole life, saw it completely in the carpenter, Jesus of Nazareth.

Historically, they both embraced and associated themselves with Jesus' death. This event will fall in line with the Articles of Faith, by the giving of not only a tomb, but a new garden tomb, which is befitting for royalty in this historic time period.

Chapter Eighteen

THE RESURRECTION

The body lies in the tomb without light, linens clinging and forming draperies with contours rising above His now peaceful temple (body). Adorned beneath the supple sheet, lies His legs, straight and parallel. His arms are crossed and overlapped on top of the lower abdomen, whereas His right hand is laid gentile atop of the wound on His left wrist.

The Jewish High Priest and the Sanhedrin, who were opposed to Jesus, felt as though Jesus might be more dangerous to them now that He is dead, then when He was alive. So they asked Pontius Pilate to secure guards at their expense, to protect the seal on the tomb. The priests inform Pilate, they are hearing rumors that the disciples are going to stage a possible rising from the dead ritual. Pilate reluctantly gives them what they want, but complains to them in a disrespectful manner.

Elijah recapturing his disposition waits patiently as he stares at the holographic display anticipating the seventh hour from what was Jesus' demise. He is awaiting the spiritual transition occurrence of the patina, to be superseded by His death. The dimming of the nimbus has occurred but dormant.

Elijah continuously searches for certain performance parameters by using a bio-energy medical monitor in order to measure the illumined (lighted) activity, where the nimbus dimmed to a resting subatomic level.

He waits for the miraculous chemical reaction to occur that sparks the regeneration process that will become the patina. The patina's function is the vagary of spiritual energy that translucently houses the body. No longer does the temple of the body harbor the soul, rather the soul will then harbor the body.

The crew continues to transmit data from a biotelemetry main monitoring station, which is locked on and focused directly inside the tomb. Elijah and his staff readjust their position, after surveying the outer perimeters of the region for precaution.

Elijah and his crew continue to make some minor adjustments and pause to wait patiently. They are also scanning the molecular sensorimotor reader in conjunction with monitoring the biosensor by tracking first and foremost the nucleic acids of the cells. In addition the body tissues, organelles, cell receptors, enzymes, antibodies, coupled with all vital signs, are all linked to the patina's energized re-birth.

Suddenly a ping alert light is detected and Elijah alerts his colleagues, with joyous emotions. He switches to the main monitor and observes the subatomic particles quivering while recoiling, as heat and motion are detected creating an electromagnetic force. The cells are now bearing accelerated charged subatomic particles at an intermittent rate.

The final and last segment has occurred. The connection and combined electron velocities are causing a quantum relativity fusion phenomenon, life! Excitement surrounds the area as they all wait patiently for another thirty three hours till the patina process is completed. They begin to see the metamorphism units between nerves and muscle, which is the process called acetylcholine and is the neuromuscular juncture, layered by the individual's synaptic membranes. This complete procedure illuminates vesicle pockets of cells, contributing and owing to a multitude of miniature power plants within the cells. This disburses small voltage pulses on a subatomic level that propagates in a vacuum, thus creating a constant field-speed of light or what is called the *patina*!

The Roman soldiers/guards stand rigid in front and above the tomb that has been outer-sealed with mortar cement. The guard's are hubris and stalwart *(confident and loyal)* in their stance and are unknowing of the phenomenon that is taking place within the tomb.

Elijah monitors the activity from within the tomb. He sees sub-cell particles becoming more implosive and the frequencies of radiation at a constant. There are orangey yellow lights spewing from all areas of the shroud that encompasses Jesus' entire corpse, glowing outward in a blaze of glory.

This energetic outcome left the shroud that covered Jesus, scorched by the radiation, leaving an imprint of His Being, where the cloth was draped and settled unto His body. *This cloth is now known as the Shroud of Turin.*

As the final hour approaches, it is Sunday the fifth day of April. Gabriel descends down from the sky hovering right above the tomb with blinding lights emanating from his back, shaking the grounds beneath and breaks the seal around the stone door.

The Roman guards are in a disoriented panic and later would describe a man with bird type wings that do not flap but move while flying and descending.

All of the Roman guards run from their posts in a hurried frenzy, to tell Pilate of what they have just witnessed. With the area deserted, Gabriel and James the Apostle find and link the center of gravity signature to the stone covering the entrance to the tomb. The two easily transport and float the elliptical stone thirty meters away from the entrance of the cave, then lay it gently on its side, where it was originally quarried from, leaving it in plain sight.

A fragrance of fresh air engulfs the tomb. The rays from the sun bathe the open doorway with great light. The Christ lays there still, horizontally precise and is surrounded by a glossy brilliance of reflective light. Elijah sends Gabriel and James into the tomb with a tunic made from a filament resembling fine silk, colored with light bluish pearl hues, gold braids that border the neckline, as well as the sleeves. Jesus' sandals and the leather woven strap belt that Elijah gifted to Him years back are placed alongside Him with the new attire.

As both men leave the tomb, they stand at attention next to the garden. Their tunics are flowing amongst a sea of daffodils and lilacs just peeking about on this cool breezy morning.

There is movement within the tomb; suddenly there appears a shimmering light at the opening, so bright, just like a reflective precious gem, gleaming and luminary. A figure motions towards the unobstructed opening of the tomb and reveals now, to the Universe, the Risen Christ, the promised Messiah.

Jesus sparkles as He looks up to the heavens. Elijah trumpets sounds that can be heard from miles away to signify that a new era has begun.

Jesus turns to Gabriel and James and smiles with arms wide open, giving thanks to them for all they have done.

He then ascends upward to greet an excited Elijah, who is glowing with happiness as he receives Jesus. The reunion was a momentous occasion. All of the pain and fear has gone from the two comrades and they are now ready and prepared to continue with the mission of the Articles of Faith.

Elijah explains to Jesus, "According to my readings, the bio-frequency in connection from the energy sphere of the Creator is no longer detectable from my instruments to Your Being, though a different type of phenomenon is present." Elijah hesitates as his facial expression draws a confused look while he looks up to think. He then stares back at Jesus and continues, "Something unexplainable is signaling something similar to a subatomic "frequency TID," within some sort of processing particle. I'm just unable," Jesus interrupts. "Eli, please. Worrying is just a poor way of praying, some things are not worth dissecting." Jesus smiles as He brought back a memory of what Elijah had taught Him when He was a child, a phrase that Elijah's father had on occasion said to Elijah. Elijah offers a big smile, then the two talk about the actions to be set forth during the next cluster of days.

The Articles of Faith have Jesus appearing at certain geographical points and at precise times to fulfill the vocation. It was stated in the Articles of Faith that it was extremely important that the women are to be the first to see the risen Christ. This decision will carry a symbolic meaning throughout the ages to show the ultimate importance to respect the female species. In conjunction with the increase respect for women, this action will increase the number of people that can be saved.

> Salome, also called Mary was *(one of the three Mary's)* the mother of James and John of the apostles and interacted with Elijah during his life. She was like an aunt to him, because of the close relationship that Aligious, "Elijah's father" had with Salome's *(Mary)* husband of Zebedee. So Salome/Mary is told to search out the other two Mary's, Mary the Mother and Mary Magdalene, thus gathering them for the good news.

The Resurrection

It was imperative that the three women all named Mary, would be led by Mary/Salome the mother of James and John the apostles, and go to the tomb and see the stone moved from the entrance and therefore find the tomb empty. As the women enter the tomb, they find the shroud, neatly folded into three angles resting.

The Resurrection occurred on a Sunday and this event will forever change the way Sunday will be viewed. During Jesus' time, Sunday was a regular day and Saturday was considered the Sabbath. From now on, Sunday will be celebrated as the Christian's Sabbath day, along with the rest of the World.

Jesus makes five profound appearances, one of which was of a personal nature. He visited his Mother before doing anything else. He was worried that Her heart would fail due to the trauma She was put through. During the following days, Jesus visits other key people and places. His ability to be omnipresent bi-locate, levitate and cloak His appearance will be of great assistance to Him. In His perfected state, these additional abilities provided for a much easier timetable for Jesus, giving Him the efficiency and wherewithal to travel abroad.

Jesus is spending His days on the immediate plan for the final section of the Articles of Faith and is now working closely with Elijah, colleagues and apostles Peter, James and John.

They now set their sights on the Second Coming. Jesus gives all the remaining disciples their final instructions and the geographical regions they will be sent to, in order to evangelize the "Good News." Jesus' departure for the Second Coming will take place exactly 40 days after the Resurrection. This event will be called the "Ascension."

The coordination of the Second Coming will be in the late 2030's AD, but this juncture in time was vague in the last part of the Articles of Faith, mainly because of the constant change of decisions made by the Factions, who have temporal access. The Faction's timing is important, for they must react when it is suitable for the "Integration." Other terms by the selection are the Historic Time Keepers *(Watchers)*, will pin point the exact time when they are ready to embark.

In accordance with God's will, Jesus "Ascends" into the Heavens and is punctuated by angelic psalms. Elijah greets Jesus with excitement and presents to Him that the faculty staff has increased by one hundred fold, and due to perform works in the development and preparation for His Second Coming.

Taken aside, Elijah and Jesus have a short private discussion of understanding about the last three days. Leaving this time period, but not to be revisited, Elijah, Jesus and colleagues immediately focus onto tomorrow, traveling two millennia forward to Elijah's natural temporal zone (2030's).

Chapter Nineteen
THE SECOND COMING

According to the Planetary Union Guidelines, when the human species reaches technological advancements that can affect the space time continuum, the implementation of the Faction Integration Program *(FIP)* will commence (begin). A potential threat to the Factions *(Planetary Union)* is at hand, because of the *(unstable)* volatility among the varied human species.

The future engagement between the controlling principals of the Factions and humankind is timed dependent upon the Hadron Collider in Switzerland having reached the approximate capability of creating temporal porthole entries *(space/time capabilities)*. This pinnacle point of advanced human technology has been long awaited, along with a timed completion of a faring "Syndicate Coalition" between humans and Factions. This covert space fleet operation is called "Solar Warden."

This will bring the Genesis project to a climatic point of transition, which is spelled out in the doctrine that governed the development of the Earth. The human species were given opportunities to become an expectable race. Jesus and other great prophets have gifted their wisdom periodically throughout the millennia, sharing moral standards with shared technologies.

Originally according to the temporal almanac, there were only approximately one hundred forty four thousand people to be amongst the populists to have redemption and move the planet forward, before the existence of Yeshua/Jesus.

While every single person on the planet, no exceptions, is monitored through their own personal bio-frequency signature. The Factions have agreed that a divine decision will be made for every individual. For the location of every human-being on the Earth is known and not even the deepest cavern or the highest mountain, ferrous or non-ferrous can disguise your whereabouts. However, because Jesus, over a half million people will be chosen, instead of the estimated meager one hundred forty four thousand. In addition Jesus' works benefitted billions of others that have passed on through the millennia. The various prophets likewise, devoted their lives to give and elevate the human species. The profound devotion of all past prophets, who looked for nothing in return, left a spiritual residual effect *(imprint)* on the lives of so many people. This created a fresh accretion, *(growth)* of future spiritual choices, which helped humankind to open the way to salvation.

The reason that 6.6 billion people were not chosen for this chapter in human history, is because they did not meet the criterion set by the governing council. The Zetas with two other Factions were adamant about these requirements, even though they have the ability to activate the other dormant nine of the twelve DNA strands. If awakened these dormant DNA strands would enable man to acquire and increase the use and capability of their brain's full ability, while amplifying up to ninety plus percent to a new consciousness and intelligence. Special activation of these DNA strands will be exclusive for the chosen humans.

These distinct Factions also insisted that some of the remaining not-chosen wear the mark of uncertainty, which is an inability to reproduce or propagate. In addition to this bio-marked signature, they will disable individuals not chosen, from using the ancient star-gates that have been here for thousands of years along with numerous other technologies and vehicles. This expiatory time period between the "Second Coming" and the rebirth of the Earth, or for that matter the rebirth of Man, is the transitional exploratory time period which is called "The Shadow Conclude."

The announcement comes three days before Jesus appears to the world. Elijah, Peter, James and John are given the privilege and honor to be the forerunner to Jesus' coming. This procession will be omnipresent, in a multi-location *(bilocation)* throughout the entire Earth and in compatibility to any language communicated.

Jesus will appear and be represented by His bio-frequency signature. As stated in the doctrine, once your personal bio-signature is compared and passes through Jesus', the results will be filtered and be compared automatically, to determine if you met the important criterion. To be selected, your bio-signature must not fall below 66.6% to the "Astral Comparison Assimilation of Jesus' spiritual imprinted signature."

If you are among the selected few, with or without families, then you are raptured and transfigured. If you choose, you may embark on a forty day preparatory expedition, using the star-gate/Meta Mechin or the transport vehicles around the Earth. This forty day journey will serve in order to introduce and present the history and current existence of the twelve Factions and their planets. Once you choose to finish this forty day passage, you are committed to the end. Should you choose not to complete this forty day journey, you may opt to return to Earth and join the remaining 6.6 billion. At the conclusion of the forty day indoctrination, the chosen (five hundred thousand plus) shall return to Earth, but all on Earth will have perished, for one hundred years (century) will have passed.

Upon hearing this, a few of the chosen, elected to return to the Earth, to join with 6.6 billion, because of an overwhelming amount of anxiety and regret, for having left family behind. The 6.6 billion people were able to live out the rest of their lives as they deemed fit. This was in accordance with Elijah's request to the Council, for "mercy" rather than extinction or Armageddon.

The genealogy and wherewithal of all humans have been adjusted by the Factions since the birth of mankind and did so accordingly, to prepare them for this day. The people that were left behind would be at risk to all the normal elements and surrounding countries. At the conclusion of the Shadow Conclude, for those who chose the journey, this would mark a new dawn on Earth, with peace and harmony for all.

ANNUNCIATION

The third day has arrived, as well as heightened anticipation, providing wonder to the wonderer, mingled with admiration. Jesus appears strategically all throughout the Earth, hovering or standing above squares, streets, and churches everywhere clear to the eye. Jesus comes into view and looks angelic with waves of transparent reflections within His being, complimented with an illustrious cast of gradations with lightened blue hues. When He makes position changes, there are lines of bright whites crossed, leaving soft lavender hues slowly moving behind.

Delivering in all languages specific to each person, Jesus speaks, *"Peace and unto the prosperity of choice, do not feel deluded. Man has selected to what sentence I have spoke."* Jesus' eyes connected to follow the movement of your eyes, yet looks at all as if He is overseeing a vista. Then after several seconds, He vocalizes, *"The carriage is neither in front of us nor behind, but merely upon the leisure of who we are."* He continues looking out in a panoramic view, then declares, *"Life is eternal, purely we have needfulness in a divine purpose. Your virtue and decency gives all of you the immense capacity to choose where to go and what to do. Do not limit yourself by taking the easy road among your life, to where you come from or where you are going. I speak of transcending beyond this life; our Earthly existence is simply one flap of a sparrow's wing. Here, can we all gather our hearts and share, as our Father has shared so much with us."*

The people that could hear Christ came towards Him, for others His message had fallen on deaf ears. Assemblies of prophets from different religious periods were amongst the many, while they conveyed and delivered other messages. The most profound message was, "You will live in a world filled with peace, with no diseases and endless possibilities for thousands of years to come! Still the many were despondent, just wanting to live their life here, not to veer.

The World that understood the messages were captivated by His profound words of dedication, for the purpose of, in the acceptance to all we are. His radiance of shedding luminous light particles filled all of the Earth. The people gaze intently with eagerness and serious attention. He dematerializes.

Chapter Twenty

INTEGRATION

During the "Temporal Exodus" of the *chosen*, more than a century will pass, when integration *(re-engagement)* begins. Masses of Factions help in a collaborate effort, called the Zion Elysium Project *(ZEP)*.

ZEP is a vast undertaking of rebuilding the Earth with eco-friendly bio-synthetics and stone masonry that will stand the test of time. Most of all, the presence of technology will increase the capacity in forging a heighten awareness for all. A glorious visual picturesque environment will be built with the use of sacred geometry on a natural energy grid, along with the entire Earth indigenously equipped, to inspire a divine presence during the course of one's life.

The ZEP agenda was implemented from the very beginning of the Genesis Project and is the final important part of the program and was in full gear during the 1980's. Part of the framework was to insert certain technologies, such as the internet, mobile devices, microwave apparatuses, aurora weather control and other technical upgrades.

The biggest part of the ZEP program is a Black Opt Culvert Operation, classified as the Strategic Defense Initiative or SDI. This highly classified Black Opts Program *(Interstellar Naval Warfare)* was designed for the purpose of mankind being responsible for its own future.

The leading countries' governments funneled an enormous amount of money and resources into the SDI project for human survival and preservation. Whereas, one type of political party *(In charge)* would create a capitalistic growth platform, for an accumulation of economic wealth, while another political group would be installed to absorb the wealth and funnel it into the SDI Operation, while creating a facade of helping all (allowing for the majority control of media outlets).

Being supervised and assisted by many of the Factions, this initiative must be up and running by the 2030's. After the selective process in the 2030's, *(Judgment Days)* the integration of the *(new)* human Faction is to join the Union of Planets, as there will be a high utilization and a need for space fairing vehicles.

A division of the SDI program is called "Solar Warden," solar meaning Earth's position in relation to the Sun and warden which is a "keeper in charge" or "guardian."

The Solar Warden Project is a human venture, in constructing outer space vehicles and is millennia more advanced than our current technology. These space vessels can travel at high rates of speeds with the ability to travel through time. The fleet at this current juncture has thirty six ships; some of them are the length of seven stadium fields. The enormous vessels can house up to forty thousand people comfortably, these ships are called "Cruisers." The Cruisers will be used as temporary holding facilities *(mainstay)* for the people that were chosen and choose to stay permanently or on a temporary basis.

The options for the chosen few *(500,000+)* will be to, return to Earth in its future in the "New Order of the Ages." Or, take residence somewhere else, either in an off planet facility to learn the Faction's symmetry or go on exploration projects throughout the sector.

The Union of Planets suggested program: to ease into the new society, by a travel venue of visitations to the cities of the sector. Further local destinations within the Moon, Mars and other nearby planetary objectives, can witness megalithic pyramids, mega sculptures, mining facilities and museums commemorating the historic wars that took place. Also learn to understand the sectors entire history and travel to all the Faction's current homelands.

Elijah and Jesus rest and are assured of what the future holds and quench the result or of what could have been. There overcoming the impossible helped and assisted to save, not only the few chosen but the entire future population from an Apocalypse.

Integration

Elijah's total embrace of his father's vision is a compliment and tribute to his mastery and remarkable talent, which personifies Love and Devotion. "Blessed are those, who embrace these new challenges."

Elijah

THE BOOK OF ELIJAH

****

This tome (volume) is the second aliquot part "The Integration" which is the next volume to be written. Please once again, keep in mind that these writings are not here to sway your beliefs, but to take from it, as you would like. Take the positive traits of whom you encounter and…

Postscriptum:

The *Resurrection story* appears in more than five locations in the Bible. In several episodes in the Four Gospels, Jesus foretells His coming death and resurrection, which He states is the plan of God the Father *(Articles of Faith)*. Christians view the Resurrection of Jesus as part of a plan for salvation and redemption by atonement for man's sin *(DNA)*. Belief in a bodily resurrection of the dead became well established within some segments of Jewish society in the centuries leading up to the time of Christ, as recorded by Daniel 12:2, from the mid-2nd century BC.

Messiah and Savior: There are many associations attached to Elijah and Jesus, what and how they are represented, yet the results of their actions and contributions seemingly supersede a manner of a distinctive part.

Author recommends the extended version of this book on Audio. (Amazon Audible) Title: Elijah, The Secret Prospective. By Robert Rasch

Graffiti Section

People comments:

The most profound part of the Book is the section where Elijah can take the connection to God for himself and doesn't, and that action alone elevates his character of life beyond thoughts, so please listen to, The "Wall" *(Elijah's Life)* by Kansas, and see if you here him in that song!

The Website

bookofelijah.com** or **Authors contact capanni27@gmail.com

Text:
With Jesus' positivity injected into society, you are living better tenfold at this present time (Elijah included). The affect on all the people in every religion and up to the present day is existential. The "Calendar" in which you use and are reading to this Date is based on His life (There are people trying to remove the term "Before Christ." If he did not come to try to save you from suffering, think about where we would be, nevertheless! If you are not at all affiliated with any of Jesus' religions or beliefs, you are most likely still affected by some sort of connection between countries such as the United States of America, who like many countries was developed and based on Judeo-Christian values.

Odd statement and questions from the forum:
(Answers by affiliates).
Are u a part of the Articles of Faith? Are U?

Oh and the Big Dipper and Orion's Belt, seems like the only constellations that anybody can point out, "Hardwired?" And by the way that's where most of the Factions come from, coincidence; no there are 2 many constellations in our Milky-Way Galaxy. Most of the Factions come from the Big Dipper, Orion's Belt and Sirius, all a part of our rudimentary culture, including the coincidental archeoastronomy positioning of our ancient megalithic structures. :)

Who are the Centurions/Pleiadians in this world: Elijah, Aligious, Zues and Odin, Poseidon and Neptune, Aphrodite, Hermes, John the Baptist, John and James the Apostle, Moses, and others? All have been in our History. Jesus? Had a pure high level of Centurion DNA with Human DNA.

TID frequencies used in book? Is the SSOR and TID stuff true? If so, is that how the "Transformers" do what they do?

The stars in the NASA logo are indeed and depict a portion of the Faction's home planets.

Elijah Hovers at the Barrier Rift on the edge of the Universe, looking out, Incubus, "If Not Now, When?"

Bible Notes:

April, Jesus Christ rises from the dead and makes five appearances on the day of His rising:

To Mary Magdalene given message?

To the other Mary's/women who come to the tomb?

To, two disciples on the Road to Emmaus, not in book.

To Simon Peter [nowhere recorded, but alluded to in Luke}

To the astonished disciples [Thomas is absent]

Ascension as recorded in Luke 24:50-51 is described: "He led them out until they were over against Bethany: and he lifted up his hands, and blessed them. And it came to pass, while he blessed them, he parted from them, and was carried up into heaven."

John and James theory: King Herod had James "put to death with the sword," referenced to beheading. That halts the return of a Centurion, the same happened to John the Baptist, and the same Kingdom beheaded both of them at different time periods. St. Valentine cured people, head chopped off.

James and John's mom first at the Resurrection. Clue?

John the Apostle at almost every important happening and location of Jesus?

John lives the longest and is the only apostle in the canonic gospels to write it all, plus he knows the future?

Footnotes/References
PS Charities to be, Wounded Warriors Foundation. Thanks
Daniel 12:2
Luke 24:50-5

http://en.wikipedia.org/wiki/Wikipedia

The Old and New Testament.

The National Advisory Committee for Aeronautics *(NACA)*.
A U.S. federal agency referred in this publication.
Vatican Archives.

***TheBookofElijah.com* any questions for Author.**

Jesus was "omnipresent"

Why did Yeshua's name change to Jesus at the Crucifixion?

Appendix

Appendix,
Note: included are words from the extended version of this book, "Elijah."

Chapter One, Childhood, Aligious, Elijah,
Adelaide, Erudition School, Ziggurat, Mazone, Athio, Meta Mechin, Synoptic Learn Ids, Arcturians, Athenaeum, Vertex Globe, Holographic galaxy,
Flora Crystal, DDS, Lodestone, triangulated apparatus,
STC, MPS, Bough, axilla,
Venetians, Elds
Ankur, Enlil, Ziusudra, Prometheus,
Zetas, tryvlio piato, PUA

Chapter Two, Zobzball,
Corner days, Olympiad Quadratus Arena,
Matrix, USSS

Chapter Three, Boyhood Older,
Nonage, DOVE, Philosophers Adaptive Stone, Prasiolite crystal, Photonics, Turin,
Centurion, Neuronic Stacking, tetragonal rosé quartzitic crystal, liaison crystal, PAS, Nimbus, Enlightenment, Patina, Pyramis Tenet, triangulated pentachromacy, Novitiate, Valley of Conflux,
Epithelial, Cloaked,
Hercules City Dome, hemihedral symmetric artwork, Peptidic endorphin energies, Cylindric Wolframite,
Field Generating Remixer, GPU locations, vortexes, wormholes,

Sacrosanct, Archeoastronomy, Transfiguration, hagor, tesseracts, Mito-Threads,
DR, Bio Rhythms,
Bit Cargo, Tube Shuttle, Groom Lake, Herculean, hieroglyph,
SNAIL, Subterranean Nuclear Artificial Intelligence Lithium Thermodynamic, Global Positioning, blight,
Flux Photoresists, Meta Port Exhaust,
Graphein Anodic, Temporal Displacements,
Mene, Paradox,
Transgate, REM, Recoding, vortexular, nano-photon magnetic resonance, gamut spectrum, optic transponder, spherical recordings, omnium-gatherum.

Chapter Four, The Moon,
Dark-side of the Moon, View Finder, AMR, Audiogenics Microphotometry Replicator, 3D,
Tractor Beam, Ducks and Drakes, hyperspace,
Time Flexion, Genesis Project,
Uraninite, Planet Evander, Jupiter, Mars,
Demeter, Pallas, Vesta, Juno, Ceres,
Wormvex,
PCO4, Broken Moon,
Helium 3/6, Unity of Planets,
Enceladus, Gaia,
Phobos, Deimos,
Ares, Aphrodite, DNA,
Hybrid, Primate Select, 12 Variants,
Lyme disease, AIDS, Estrogen, BPA,
Op, SDI, Strategic Defense Initiative, Solar Warden, Black Operation,
New Order, Carcinoma, Integumentary,
Ankur, Srinivasa Ramanujan, Eisenstein, Tesler, Nostradamus, da Vinci, Probability, algorithm, Bifurcation,
Agenda,
Science control hustlers,
DNA Hardwired,
Aliquot, Columbian,
Lunar Project.

Chapter Five, Historic Data Machine,
Philosopher Adaptive Stone,
Metamorphous, halo,
Bio Electromagnetic, Zodiac Nimbi, Chemical Mechanisms, Monoaminergic,
Aromatic Carbon Bands, Neuro-Modulation, Neurotransmitters.

Chapter Six, The Manhood,
Chapter Seven, Eight year Ministry,
Stranded Identification Nucleases, SIN, Lucifer,
Chrono-Vision,
Family Pack Study, Mission, Omri, Ahab,
Manna,
Kingdom, $" Baal, Yahweh, God.

Chapter Eight, The Quietus,
Whirlwind, Space continuum, Reckon Cipher,
Spiritualistic Nutritive's, Intellectual Energy,
Star Dust, Choices Define Existence,
Andromeda Galaxy, Archan, Helix Coil, Sectors, Mount Horeb,
Hypersonic,
Revivification Passing,

Chapter Nine, Ministry conclusion,
Sequential Destined Dawn.

Chapter Ten, Cave Innovation,
Prophesiers, Pilgrimages, Seers,
Grotto, Sinai, Tursina, Jabel,
Anamorphic Anatomy,
Hyperbaric Preserver, Utilitarian style, Historical Data, crystalline monitors,
Deoxyribonucleic acid, Distributary National Alliance, Y-MRCA, Adam, 144 Total DNA, Africa,
Rendian's,
Dinosaurs, Xenon, Transuranic Actinides,

PCO3 Earth, Faction Science Councils, Nuclear Detonation,
Gomorrah, Nagasaki, Scotland, Harappa, Vitrification, Neo-Hybrids, Spain, Atlantic Ocean, Mediterranean Sea, Black Sea, China, Greece deluge, Deucalion, floods of Mesopotamia, Gilgamesh, religions, Noah/Hebrew, Manu/Hindu,
Innovation, Invisible Manifestations,
Troglodytes, Flatworm,
E=MC2+S, Stir, Spiral, Vorticular Dynamics, E=MC2+S=R-Recycle, Convex Spectacles, Allah, Elohim, Yahweh, Jehovah, Hertz, Conarium, Alpina,
Ginger, Quadrigeminal Cistern, Hall of Records, Limbic, Hypothalamus, Somatosensory Cortex, Motor Control Cortex, Visual Cortex, Tectal system,
Oscillate, Optic Tectum, Wireless, Cave Dwellers, Multiplier Synthesizer, Pineal Gland, Subatomic Particle, 432Hz Natural Harmonic Overtones, God Particle, Solar Spectrum, Solstices, Equinoxes,
Oxygen Atoms, Jack-Stud, O2,
Harmonic Devotion, Nono Magnetic Frequency Scanner, NMFS,
Extrinsic Dimensional, ED, Subatomic bits, Vatom, SSOR, Slip Stitch Orbital Revolution, Polar Speed, Transponder Identification Datum, TID, Traversing God Particle, Hydrogen Atom, Spacial Fabric, MPH, Magneton Pentagonal Hypercube, Cubical Tesseracts, Polynomial Ring, Vector, Tensor,
Systematic Circuitry, Electronic circuit boards,
Cobalt Heart,
Compendium Space, Bioluminescence, Spherical Receptor, Space records, Spectra, Timeless Reality,
Probability Matrix, Binomial Distribution, Fiberoptic, Anti-time, Purgatory, Dimples, Hubs,
Magnesium Plasma,
Translucent enmesh entanglement pattern, Connective Tube, Wavelengths, Subatomic Sound, Tachyon, Subatomic Plasma Light Particles, Auto Growth, Physical Bifurcate, Monotheism, Axiomatic Systems,
Deity, Metaphysical, Probability Resultant, MSB, Mitochondria Signal Branches, Metamorphoses,
Bifurcation Mapping,

Quantum Chaos, Lion eats the lamb, Tubular Message Connector,
Barrier, Paradox, Abyss Void, Hallowed Spirit,
Gods Right Hand,
Moldavite Crystal, Tektite, River Moldau, Czechoslovakia,
Global Positioning Systems,
Risk=Growth=Relationships, Macroscopic, Force Creator,
Crystallography, 3D Imagery, Geosynchronous, Orbital Zone, Sidereal Period,
Feathers from a Dove, Mercy Love,

Chapter Eleven, Articles of Faith,
Seeding,
Holy Trinity, Father Son Holy Spirit.

Chapter Twelve, The Birth Choice,
Miriam, Anne, Joachim, Nazareth, Galilee, Gabriel, Elizabeth, God's Oath, DNA Script, John, BPFI, Bio Parasympathetic Frequency Intelligence, Decipher Distributer, The Redeemer, Parents, page 136
Quartz Prisms, Temporal Lobe, Vibratory Light Particles, Mary, Lord, Grace, Zechariah, Judah,
Hebron, Palestinian, West Bank, Jerusalem, Abraham, Sarah, Isaac, Samson, Manoah, Noah,
Yosef, House of David, Census, Quirinius, Decree, Roman Emperor Augustus, Baby, Reverence Cloth,
Savior, Peter, Gold, Frankincense, Myrrh, Egypt, Nativity, Kings, Magi, Salvation,
Death, Ishmael, Yahweh, Allah,
Jehovah, Stones Abode, Quartz Facets, Praiseworthy, Mohammad, Tabor, Black Stone, Kaaba, Mecca.

Chapter Thirteen, Mentor,
Hercules Dome, Antarctica, Larimer, Tunic,
Chalcedonic Eyes, Sheleg,
Pulpit, Torah,
Vernacular, Greece, India, Tibet, Britain,
Dead Sea Scrolls, Judean Desert, Khirbet Qumran, West Bank, Essenes,

Christ, Golden Scroll, Book of Elijah, Second Coming, Monastic Brotherhood, Holy Families, Bible, Old Testament, New Testament, Sea of Galilee,
Baptists, Genomes, Hebrew Tribes, Simon, Transfiguration,
Nimbus Metamorphosis, Moses, Elijah,
Evangelist, Baptized, Apollos, Alexandria, Word of God,
Herald, King Herod, Messiah, Lamb of God.

Chapter Fourteen, Desert,
Mouth of God, Test,
Three Temptations, Lenten, Ash Wednesday, Easter, Resurrection.

Chapter Fifteen, Three year Ministry,
Cana, Last Super, Capernaum, Gennesaret, Syrian Phoenicia, Caesarea Philippi, Trachonitis, Mt Tabor, Jerusalem, Galilee, Judea, Samaria, Promise Land, Passion, lepers, paralytics, blind, deaf, dumb, Wine.
Chapter Sixteen, Passion,
Romans, Micah, Isaiah, Zachariah,
RNA, Passover, Exodus, Lazarus, Prophesy, Eastern Tradition, Mount of Olives,
Fig Tree, Apostles, Triumphant Entrance, Palm Sunday,
Pontius Pilate, Tiberius, Chief Priest, Caesar, Roman Coin, Tyrian, Temple, Jewish high priest, Caiaphas, Bethany, house of poverty, Mary, Martha, Lazarus, All Fools' Day, Judas Iscariot, Sanhedrin, tribunal, exilic times, high priest, Roman approbation, Jewish doctrine, betrayal,
Crucifixion/Resurrection, James, John, Garden, Alacritous Tribulation, Union of Planets, THW, Temporal Historic Watchmen, Consociational Troop,
144 to 1, 2030/36, Purification State,
April 2nd, Holy Thursday, sacrificial Passover, Holy Week, Maundy Thursday, Latin for Mendicare, Washing of the feet, humility, Covenant Thursday, Communion,
Sheer Thursday, Garden of Gethsemane, Zebedee, Apostle Peter, Kidron Valley,
Analgesic Herbs, Cypress Tree,

Blood Sweat and Tears, Flagellation Death, Oleaceae Family, Holy Tree, Betrayal,
Mob, Malchus, Sword, Sheath,
Blasphemy, Phylactery Box, Hierarchies, Capitulated, Courtyard, Passover Gift,
Palace, Slave Quarters, Perdition, Preludial,
Scourge, Torture Ritual, Ruffians, Wooden Pillars, Roman Legionaries,
Thongs, Whips, Flagrums, Ox-Hide, Massilias, Barb, Lashes, Zinc, Iron, Lead, Bronze, Wood, Sheep bone, Hook,
Floggers, Executioners, Barabbas, Half Death, Rabbinic, Ten Commandments, 40 lashes minus one,
Double Helix, Counter Caster, Abacus, Brutus,
Discretion Advised, Roman Guard, Staff, Tunic, Mantle, King of the Jews, Monogrammed Ring, Lictor, Decorated Fasces,
Caustic, Hyenas, Prey, Galea, Helmet, Pea-Cocking, Elmo,
Modus Operandi, Lariat, Toga, Pallium Cloak,
Paul,
Spurt Beam, Hypovolemic Shock, Subcutaneous Tissues,
Emotional Disturbance, Ribbons, Scepter, Obedient, Lictor,
Drunken Ruffian, King of the Jews, Barabbas, Pilate,
Lavab, basin, Courtyard,
Man's Blood,
Stacked the Crowd,
Paul, Golgotha, Patibulum,
Titulus, Titular, Nazareth, Kings Cloak, Thorns, Century, Vail from His Mother,
Temporal Watchmen,
Place of Skulls, Forgotten and Forgiveness, Calvary,
Mary, John,
Dear Mother, Mockery, Hail King of the Jews.

Chapter Seventeen, Crucifixion,
Ionosphere, Magnetosphere, Spectators, Ignoble Place, Obelisks,
Lamb,
Turgidly, Nail of Destiny,
Ulnar, radial artery, carpals, lariat,

Sedile,
Heavy hammer, Tarsi, Furlong,
Flaxen-wool, colored tunica,
Nicademous,
My God, My God, Forsaken,
Jugular, turgidly, pang, diaphragmatic, hypercapnia, alveoli, Tetany, orthostatic hypotension, hemorrhagic shock, cyanotic,
Pericardial fluid, pleural fusions, asphyxia, Hyssop, Thy Hands I Commend My Spirit, SILENT,
Opaque, sclera, the three o'clock hour, Death, Lamb of God,
Foot nail, Pieta, Mud,
Joseph of Arimathea, Tomb, Spikes, Wealthy, Royalty.

Chapter Eighteen, The Resurrection,
Seventh Hour, Nimbus, Sensorimotor, Organelles, Patina's.
Ping Alert, Recoiling, Acetylcholine, Propagates, Shroud of Turin, Fragrance, Christ, Messiah,
Salome, Zebedee, Sabbath, Bi-Locate, Second Coming, Good News,
Historic Time, Jesus Ascends, Angelic psalms, Temporal Zone.

Chapter Nineteen, The Second Coming,
Planetary Union Guidelines, Hadron Collider, Switzerland, Portholes, Syndicate Coalition, Temporal Almanac, Solar Warden, Jesus,
6.6 Billion, Expiatory, Rebirth, 66.6%, Astral Comparison,
Indoctrination, Shadow Conclude, Annunciation, Dematerializes.

Chapter Twenty, Integration,
Temporal Exodus, Zion Elysium System Project, ZESP, 1980's, Culvert Operation, SDI, Judgement Days,
Cruisers, New Order of the Ages, Museums, Tome, Aliquot.

****

Mystical Note: Once again, this Volume is a timed release, for April 5th 2017, to coincide with the historical Resurrection of Jesus, which also was on April 5th. This coincidence of dates is not by accident. For as the true historical date does not occur often and according to Elijah's Flexion Team, it is currently 20 years from this date, on April 5th 2037, will be the New Dawn of the Ages, "The Second Coming."

ABOUT THE AUTHOR

Robert Rasch is the author of *Elijah*, a traditional story with a modern twist. His writings will inspire many because of his unique approach to telling a story that has been told many times. This story provides a new perspective on the origin of humanity. Rasch's ability to mix "coincidental-science" with the Old and New Testaments will have you intrigued and questioning that perhaps maybe some pertinent information was left out.

Other writings Rasch is working on and are in the making, include: *A Parity of Lives, Abraham and John, Opulence*, a romance comedy, and *View Finder*, science fiction. He is also the creator of several game applications and a freelance voiceover professional. He also holds several patents for his innovative ideas and inventions. The Author is available for think-tank and scrum master tasks (Board Meetings). **Capanni27@gmail.com**

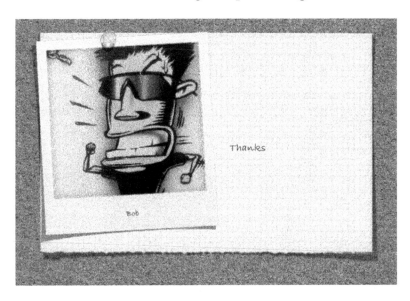

CPSIA information can be obtained
at www.ICGtesting.com
Printed in the USA
FFHW022236271018
49014584-53292FF